UNHOLY ALLIANCES

Kevin Land Patrick
River Walk Publishers

Published in the United States by River Walk Publishers
Electronic Format ISBN: 978-0-9968045-1-6
Paperback Format ISBN: 9780996804509
ISBN-10: 0996804501
Library of Congress Control Number: 2015915750
Kevin Land Patrick, Basalt, CO

ABOUT THE AUTHOR

Kevin Patrick is the founder and president of WATERLAW-Patrick Miller Noto, a law firm that practices exclusively in the field of water law, water rights, and water planning (www.waterlaw.com). He is an accomplished water attorney who has represented many of nation's most prominent companies, people, and water providers. He has appeared in state and federal appellate courts, including the US Supreme Court, and has written and spoken on water and infrastructure issues throughout the United States, Europe, and South America. He is also a PADI divemaster and avid traveler. He lives with his wife and son outside Aspen, Colorado. This is his second novel, following *Threatened Waters*.

He can be contacted by visiting www.kevinlandpatrick.com.

Profit is sweet, even if it comes from deception.
Sophocles

Russia does not want confrontation of any kind. And we will not take part in any kind of "holy alliance."
Vladimir Putin

There is no avoiding war; it can only be postponed to the advantage of others.
Niccolo Machiavelli

ACKNOWLEDGMENTS

My first novel, *Threatened Waters*, was my first foray into fiction writing. It was a labor of love and a bit difficult for me. This novel seemed to flow easily, and I can honestly say it was fun to write. I suspect my interest in espionage and thrillers was spurred by my father, who was in counterintelligence when I was a kid growing up. My family was a typical post–World War II baby boomer family that really didn't know exactly what Dad was doing, which made it all the more intriguing to me. My mom kept my sister and me on an even keel no matter what country or state we were living in. I owe the most to my beautiful and great wife, Andrea, and my incredible son, who somewhere in the last year surpassed me in height.

I want to thank my sister, Claudia, who helped in the early version proofing. Having a high school English teacher as a sister came in very handy. I also had a number of people whom I would call "readers" who read early drafts and provided input. Claudia, Ramsey, Ray, Robert...thank you.

Kevin Land Patrick

PREFACE

When I was in law school performing research at the National Energy Law and Policy Institute, I could see the fragility of energy markets and the importance of water. Nearly forty years working in the water industry and dealing with water and energy infrastructure on a day-to-day basis has made me somewhat knowledgeable of the value and vulnerability of each resource. I have taken steps to omit critical information and locations as well as add a bit of misinformation to ensure this book is never used as a template for wrongdoing.

Manipulation and charisma are two sides of the same face. Great men as well as evil men have succeeded by the use of both. Knowing whether the appeal of a person, belief, or skill constitutes truth and good is what separates the accomplices from the virtuous.

Kevin Land Patrick

CHAPTER 1

NAPOLI, ITALY

He watched the crew throwing lines on the dark pier. The sleek Ferretti-Pershing yacht was nearly thirty-five meters in length; its true asset beyond its looks was its massive triple drive props, which were powered by over twenty-six hundred horsepower. The steel-gray Italian yacht was as fast as it was luxurious. Zach could never hope to stay up with it if it made a run for the open sea. His small boat was fast, but not that fast, and the lack of a deep-V hull meant he would bounce mercilessly in the open sea. Zach prayed the yacht was not going beyond Capri.

Capri's lights were visible thirty kilometers to the southwest. It was just past midnight, and a sliver of a moon cast faint silver shadows on the black, windswept sea as the large yacht motored past the jetty, slicing into three-foot seas. Zack followed a hundred meters behind. Lights emblazoned the name of the yacht in gold inlay on its stern: *Gulf Vision*.

He made a call. "Elle, Zach Greer; I'm glad I caught you. I'm following Ratani. His yacht's headed out of Napoli. Hecox is on board, and I think Foltz. If he is headed out of the area, I'll lose him. I need satellite coverage." He hoped the agency's satellites were in a position to quickly find and track the yacht.

"I'll make the call. I'll see what I can do and get back," Elle said.

Zach watched as the yacht came up on plane, throwing water ten meters in the air behind it as its massive props bit into the sea. The faint lights of Sorrento and Capri were visible in front of the yacht. At least it wasn't headed out to sea, Zach thought. As soon as Zach made it past the jetty, he switched off his boat's running lights and brought his boat up on plane. He followed the white-churned wake and far-off stern light of the yacht. Even in the yacht's wake, his boat slammed on each swell as it strained to keep pace with the performance yacht. Spray drenched him, salt water stinging his eyes. The boat and his spine jarred with each wave.

He strained to see through the spray when his eyes saw the white gel coat of the dash crack and explode. For a moment it didn't register. The dash shouldn't come apart from the pounding of the waves. Then he knew. The windshield shattered and sparks flew from shells striking the aluminum windshield supports. He turned hard to port to see a red burst of automatic-weapon fire erupting from what looked like a zodiac in the dark waves. Then another zodiac moved in from starboard. They had him boxed in, and they were much faster.

The engine compartment burst into flames, only to be extinguished in a flash of vapor from the Halon fire-suppression system. The boat surged bow down off plane and plowed to a stop in the waves, its propulsion gone. Both zodiacs opened up coming in from starboard. With only a handgun, Zach knew the outcome was certain. He rolled over the port side into the dark water. He could hear a fusillade of rounds striking the boat. Both zodiacs approached from starboard, firing into the boat from less than twenty meters.

Zach fought to stay afloat as his shoes, jacket, and pants dragged him beneath the surface. He took a deep breath, submerged, and struggled to shed the jacket, which enveloped him like a shroud, dragging him deeper. He fought one arm free and surfaced for air. The boat was wallowing in the seas, dangerously close to striking his head. He shed the coat but hung onto it. He went under, sinking while unlacing his running shoes. He cursed himself for wearing laced shoes. Out of the shoes, he fought back to the surface with the coat and shoes in hand.

Tying the shoes around the coat, he forced them down, below him. This would only work if they disappeared; all trace of him needed to disappear. Still hearing rounds striking the boat, he took several deep breaths and swam as hard as he could beneath the surface ahead of the bow and away from the sinking boat—out into blackness. His eyes stung straining to see in the dark salt water.

His lungs burned for air. He surfaced, trying to come up without a splash. He could hear the zodiacs continuing to fire on the boat. He submerged again, trying to put distance between the bow of the crippled boat and him, away from light, surfacing for breath each time with as little disturbance as he could.

When he was forty or fifty meters from the boat, he stopped and looked back. The boat was sinking, nearly submerged. Both zodiacs were visible from the fires on the sinking boat. One of the zodiacs trained a light on the boat and the water surrounding it. They were looking for him. Twice the light swung toward him, and twice he submerged in time. He watched the boat sink below the waves and with it all light.

The zodiacs circled several times slowly, then raced off. His adrenaline began to dissipate. He began to feel the cold water on his skin and accept the blackness of the sea surrounding him. With virtually no moon, everything was black. He was alive, but by his guess, miles offshore. He fought the darkness around and beneath him and the fear it brought.

He started swimming for the lights of Napoli. The jetty he left would be the closest land. He tried to stop his thoughts; he knew that night brought predators and the discharge from urban centers concentrated sharks. He tried to comfort himself with the knowledge that even though the Mediterranean had its share of the four feared sharks - tigers, bulls, great whites, and oceanic white tips - their concentration was far less here than nearly any other sea. He pushed the fear of sharks from his mind, feeling confident that he would succumb to hypothermia and drown first.

CHAPTER 2

TYRRHENIAN SEA

Gulf Vision sliced through the seas at thirty-five knots. The polished teak floors were in contrast to the ivory Italian-leather furniture arranged on rich Tibetan rugs. A glass bar with three stools was occupied by two middle-aged men surrounded by four women in their twenties in skintight party dresses that clung to their flawless bodies like wet skin. The speed and movement of the boat was imperceptible as soft music played.

The electric sliding stern door opened, and the quiet was at once interrupted by the near-deafening sound of the engines and of the boat cutting through the night sea. A tall, thin man of fifty entered; his eyes and accent revealed his Middle Eastern descent. The door glided and sealed behind him, returning the silence. Both men at the bar looked into the man's eyes for guidance.

The man spoke in a low, accented tone. "I hope everything is satisfactory, gentlemen. I apologize for my absence, but there were things that needed my attention."

A Moorish-looking man appeared to take the man's jacket and lay leather slippers in front of him, which he stepped into. The man sat on one of the white leather sofas across from the bar, where he was brought a cup of tea.

"Is everything all right, Amir?" the taller man at the bar asked in an English accent. "I saw concern in the crew's faces."

"Yes, of course. It was nothing; a festering thorn has been removed. We'll talk in the morning of this and our next steps. But for now, we have a short ride to Capri. Enjoy your night...and company," the man on the sofa said, rising, taking a sip of his tea, and walking alone out of the salon to the master suite below.

"Mille grazie, Senore Ratani. You certainly know fine Italian hospitality," the squat man said in a thick Milanese accent.

"Ladies, let me pour some more Crystal. It seems that you have but two to entertain this evening," the Englishman remarked, standing up from his seat and pulling one of the two open bottles of Crystal champagne from an ice bucket.

A tall, blond, green-eyed Italian woman, with legs that soared above his waist, walked to the Englishman and pressed herself against his chest. The feel of her firm breasts against him caused his pulse to quicken. She smelled faintly of vanilla—the smell of a call girl. "What's your name? Is this your boat?" she asked.

"William. No, I don't own the boat. Its owner just went to bed. I, ah, finance such pleasures. And you, what is your name?"

"Isabella. The other girls are Hungarian. My family traces itself to Etruscan blood. The true Italians." She sauntered across the room toward the stern window. She was well over six feet in her stiletto heels. A banded tattoo encircled her left ankle. She stopped as if to pose, forcing her chest forward, accentuating what nature had not given her. "Come with me; I want to see the stars."

William walked toward her as if a trance, while the shorter Italian man smiled, knowing he was now the object of three Eastern European consorts, their combined age nearly matching his.

CHAPTER 3

LONDON

The analyst was uncomfortable this close to her. Elle Hardwick's six-foot, striking figure was even more intimidating this close. As his boss, she was stunning to look at, smart and more demanding than any boss he had ever worked for. The talk was that she was being groomed for the London station chief slot. Elle pulled her short, black hair behind her neck with one hand, resting the other hand on the back of his chair as she stared over his shoulder at the screen displaying the satellite imagery. She switched on her headset connecting her to Langley. "Shaw, are you seeing this?"

"Yes, we have it on screen. I suppose the first picture is Ratani's vessel in the harbor. The second feed looks like a small vessel on fire. Right? When was this taken?" Shaw asked. For twenty years, he had run field assets for the CIA. The weight of placing men and women in danger never grew easier. He'd agreed to stay on another five years after his mentor, Franklin Harbour, persuaded him that his job as deputy director NCS, the national clandestine service, needed him more than ever. America had come under attack-it wasn't a time for retirement.

"Approximately two hours ago. Yes, the vessel on fire was Zach Greer's boat the agency leased. It doesn't appear in the next picture, so it is presumed sunk. But when we enhance the picture's edges, there are reflections of the fire on two boats and what looks like a tracer round. See that, on the left of the frame?" Elle asked.

"Have we heard from Zach? If it's twenty-one hundred hours here, it must be three in the morning there. Have local authorities been alerted?" Shaw asked, concern and anger rising within him.

"Yes, we notified the Italian State Police, the carabinieri, and our local station in Milan. The closest asset we have is in Rome, a good two to three hours away: Agent Marcella Antonelli. She's been with the agency for six years—no field work, no tradecraft skills. She's about an hour from there at this point. There's no moon to speak of, but the locals have dispatched search boats." Elle let her last sentence trail off. She wasn't hopeful.

"Where's Ratani's yacht now? And what's the link with Ratani?" Shaw asked.

"Circumstantial, but obvious. Zach was following Ratani's boat out of the harbor. It happened so close to the harbor it would be too coincidental if an unrelated attack was made on him. It looks like they knew they were being followed and ambushed him. The Napoli harbor master reported no other vessels departing or returning within an hour of when this occurred. It was late, after midnight there. Ratani's vessel was reported into Capri at one-thirty local time and is there now," Elle said.

"Okay. Let's coordinate with the Italians on the search. I want divers down to that boat...ballistics...anything we can get. We'll reconvene at zero eight hundred local time; that's seven in London, one a.m. here. Have Richardson from Special Activities in the meeting and all analytics on what we have on Ratani," Shaw ordered.

CHAPTER 4

NAPOLI

Zach knew he couldn't be more than five miles from shore. He'd swum farther, but that was ten years earlier in college. He had stripped off his shirt and trousers and socks and was only in boxer shorts and a T-shirt. Resistance was his enemy, and wet clothes offered no protection against the cold. He was on a steady pace, his anger fueling his determination and giving him strength.

As he was lifted on a wave, he could see a cargo ship coming out of the port and headed to that location. He recalled a long seawall on the edge of the marina below the Castel dell'Ovo, where he'd started tonight's journey from. The sea wall protecting the main shipping port would be the closest landfall.

Hours passed. His luminous dive watch read 4:40; he had been swimming for over three hours. His mind turned to that day at Glen Canyon in Arizona when the terrorists nearly brought down the dams along the Colorado River. He had been there-they had killed the terrorists and transported the small nuclear device into the desert away from the dam before it detonated. Denying water and electricity to the American southwest would have killed millions. Instead, they had been lucky that the cell only managed to disrupt electricity and transportation infrastructure on a localized scale in Los Angeles. The death toll still approached one-hundred thousand. Across the country, a similar suitcase nuclear device designed to eliminate New York City's water supply had also been thwarted with only seconds to spare but that cell's conventional attack in downtown Manhattan had killed scores, mostly young kids. It had been a horrible day for America dubbed the May Day by the media. One good thing had come of it; he had met Sandy. He'd convinced her to leave the National Park Service and marry him; to follow him from the FBI to the Agency and from Arizona to Europe. It had only been six weeks since he gave her the vow that he would never leave her standing before the minister. He was determined to keep that commitment and to bring those responsible to justice.

He could see the red light of the harbor entrance and hear a bell clanging in the wind. The city's lights lit the water around him. He was going to make it.

By surprise, the seawall suddenly was there. He banged his arm against a blackened rock, sending searing pain that nearly made him lose his breath. The wall's seaward side shielded the city's light. The jetty was a jumble of car-sized concrete and stone blocks, slimy with algae and blackened by a hundred years of bilge oil. Every reach and step slid him back into the water, compounding his exhaustion. Finally he got a handhold and pulled himself onto the seawall, collapsing in the cold air. He had to continue moving. He could feel the numbing sensation and the effects of hypothermia. His mind slowed, as if he was in a stupor.

A paved empty road led toward the city along the wall's crest. He walked what felt like a kilometer to the first long one-story building built centuries ago on the seawall. That building turned into a long, narrow three-story building. No lights were on, and no one was around.

"Dove sono i tuoi pantaloni! Avete bisogno di aiuto?" the old man exclaimed, looking at Zach's nearly nude, muscled body.

Zach's Italian was rusty, but he understood that the man had asked him why he had no pants and was offering help. "La mia barca è affondata. Io ho freddo." Zach tried to explain that his boat sank, and his chattering teeth told the man he needed warmth.

The old man rushed him into a door of the building, turning on a light. It was a large warehouse, likely a transshipment storage house, Zach surmised. The man opened a closet, extracting a set of dark-blue overalls and handing them to Zach.

"Grazie. Grazie," Zach said, stripping off his wet boxers and T-shirt pulling on the warm overalls. Nothing had ever felt better. His senses were returning. He needed a phone. "Un telefono per favore."

The old man smiled, pulling a very old flip cell phone from his back pocket. "Ecco qui."

Zach dialed Elle, but the call didn't go through. The man's phone plan obviously didn't allow long-distance calling. He dialed 113 and was connected to the Polizia. "Do you speak English?" Zach asked.

"Yes, of course; this is the police," the voice answered in a King's English accent. "Do you need help?"

"My name is Zachary Greer. I am an American. My boat sank and I have just swum to shore. I need help please."

"Did you say your name is Zachary Greer? There's a search on for you. Tell me where you are." The man was excited as Zach explained where he was and put the old man on the phone to give instructions.

Zach sat down, and almost at once, the adrenaline began to wash from him. He was overwhelmingly tired. Three hours of swimming in cold water had exhausted his reserves. Even in 70 degree water, people succumbed to hypothermia. Water literally extracted the body's heat. The body burned calories in a struggle to maintain 98.6 degrees. And he had been swimming for hours.

The old man brought over some water. Zach smiled his warmest smile. "Grazie mille." They sat in silence until the sounds of sirens approached.

Stepping out of the warehouse, four Polizia cars and a sleek black Alfa Romero with carabinieri markings stopped. Two carabinieri approached in their smart Armani-designed uniforms. "Mr. Greer, I am Lieutenant DiIanni, and this is Sub-Lieutenant Rispoli. We've been briefed on your situation by a Mr. Shaw Ellis, who we understand works for your government. You are a lucky man. Can you tell us how your boat sank?

A woman pushed forward. "Excuse me; I am Marcella Antonelli, from the US embassy. Before we have Mr. Greer answer questions, I think he needs to be seen by a physician. He may be in hypothermic shock."

The Carabinieeri insisted. "Yes, of course; we have an ambulance on the way. Please. Mr. Greer, while we wait, tell us was anyone else on board?"

"No, just me. I started taking on water not far out of the harbor. It all happened so quickly," Zach said.

"Yes, of course. But why did you not radio for help?" Lieutenant DiIanni politely asked. "Certainly you had time to do that. No one reported a distress transmission."

"I was down below and walked up to the deck and saw the engine over-heating. The next think I knew, I had no lights, no electricity. The radio was out; my lights were out. I couldn't even locate a life vest or flashlight; it was moonless, or nearly so. Then the boat started sinking. It all happened so very fast. It was quite terrifying. I didn't think I would make it," Zach said, his eyes meeting the lieutenant's.

"I see." The lieutenant stared into Zach's eyes, which gave nothing in return.

Covered in a blanket, Zach was ushered into the rear of the ambu-lance. Marcella Antonelli pushed her way in ignoring the EMT's protest, exclaiming, "I'm from the US embassy and will ride with Mr. Greer." The EMT shrugged and shut the door behind them.

As the ambulance pulled away, Zach looked over at Ms. Antonelli, who was slowly moving what looked like a small radio around him. "I'm making sure there are no bugs in here," she whispered.

Zach watched, saying nothing. She was young: late twenties, he guessed. Dark hair tied up. She was short: no more than five feet and of slightly stocky build. He assumed she was an embassy liaison for the agency.

She nodded and said, "I'm Agent Marcella Antonelli, assigned to the embassy in Rome. Elle Hardwick was quite insistent I not let you out of my sight. Langley tracked the boat you were following to the Marina Grande in Capri. Do you have any idea who attacked you?"

Zach thought for a moment. "I am sorry, but I don't know you. I'd prefer to leave any questions until we get to a place that is secure and where I can communicate with people I know. I know you are doing your job, and I appreciate your help, but tonight's escapade calls for an abundance of caution."

Agent Antonelli pursed her lips, unable to hide her displeasure, nodded, and responded. "Very well; I would do the same. I'll make arrangements at the hospital for you to communicate with Langley. I'll explain you need to call your family."

The ambulance pulled into the Ospedale Santobono. Two orderlies helped Zach to a wheelchair and wheeled him through the sliding doors into the crowded waiting area and directly into a treatment room, closing the door behind him.

After several minutes of silence, the door opened, and a man in his late thirties introduced himself. "Bouno Notte, io Doctore Marzini." He glanced down at the chart and smiled. "I am sorry; I didn't see here that you are an American. I am Doctor Marzini. I want to run some tests—blood, oxygen absorption—and of course, check your vitals. You appear to be in surprising shape given your ordeal. Do you have any injuries I should be aware of? Any allergies to medications?"

"No, doctor, just tired and a little cold. Other than that I'm fine. No injuries," Zach said.

"That's to be expected. We need to stabilize you and raise your core temperature before you can be released. It says here you were in the water for over three hours. The water temperatures were around thirteen degrees... that's Celsius. I've ordered some warm zuppa, which should help." A nurse brought heated blankets and placed them on Zach's lap and across his shoulders as he sat in the chair. "You should be able to be released within an hour if your core temperatures stabilize and the tests come out okay."

"Doctor Marzini, I'd like to make a phone call to my family. Let them know I'm okay. My cell phone is gone; is it possible for the lady from the embassy who came in with me to join me?" Zach asked. "She offered to let me use her phone."

"Yes, of course; I'll ask her to come in. You are a very lucky man, Mr. Greer. Please stay here and keep warm and I'll ask the woman to come in. Good night and call me if you have any numbness or tingling in your extremities." Doctor Marzini gave Zach his card, shook his hand, and walked out the door.

The door opened and Agent Antonelli walked in taking the small device from her purse and slowly walking around the room. "It's secure. How are you? What did the doctor say?"

"I'm fine. Let's call Langley on your phone. I assume it is secure?" Zach said as Agent Antonelli nodded and pulled out her phone and dialed the saved number.

"Marcella Antonelli. Rome. Zulu, Harriet, two, six, zebra," she said into the phone. A few seconds later, she was connected with a person. "Agent Antonelli; Shaw Ellis please." Seconds passed before she continued. "Mr. Ellis, Agent Antonelli here. I have Mr. Greer. I'll put him on." She handed Zach the phone.

"Zach here."

"Zach, good to hear your voice. You had us concerned. You okay?" Shaw said.

"Yes sir, I'm fine. A little tired and cold, and a whole lot pissed. It was Ratani. Couldn't have been anyone else. They were on to me less than fifteen minutes after I left the harbor. They must have been waiting just outside the harbor. Two zodiacs—one shooter and one pilot per boat. The carabinieri know something is up. I might need some help with them. Where's Ratani now?" Zach asked.

"Capri. He went straight there. We don't have any assets there. Agent Antonelli and you are it for now. Reinforcements will be there inside twenty-four hours. Good news is they think you're dead. Bad news is that they evidently have no reservations about ensuring that. Were you able to see who left with Ratani?" Shaw asked.

"Hecox and another man were on the boat when it left Napoli. The other man was midfifties, European, perhaps Italian. Dark-brown hair, five foot six, a bit overweight, maybe a hundred eighty to a hundred ninety pounds. Dark, heavy glasses. It matches Foltz's description, but I didn't see his face," Zach reported switching the phone to speaker so that Agent Antonelli could hear the instructions he knew Shaw would make.

"Your notoriety with the polizia and carabinieri means you can't just take the next ferry," Shaw explained. "We have to assume they will be watching that. We'll develop a story that the embassy is flying you back to Rome out of Naples. The plane will take off, but you won't be on it. We'll make a switch, and the car will take you to Sorrento. We'll arrange transport from there to Carpri's Marina Piccola. It's across the island from the main marina and isn't staffed. A small craft can get in there. Agent Antonelli can take the ferry to the main marina and meet you."

"Mr. Ellis, I have a girlfriend who has an apartment in Capri. She is in Milano this time of year. I can call her and ask to stay in her place. It is less conspicuous than a hotel," Agent Antonelli said.

"Excellent. When you get confirmation, we can use the apartment from your friend; give us the address. You can meet Zach on the island and take him there," Shaw said.

"Yes, sir. I'll make the call now," Marcella said.

"Zach, I'm guessing you've been up for twenty-four hours. You've depleted your reserves swimming all night. I need you fresh in Capri. I'll have an embassy car pick you up in an hour, which will take you to the private air terminal in Naples. Wear some kind of hoodie you can exchange with a double who will be in the car. Your double will get on the plane. The car will take you to Villa San Sorrento, where we will have a room for you under the name Richard Ellington. A boat will pick you up in Sorrento at fifteen hundred. That should give you a few hours of sleep. Agent Antonelli, get to Capri as quickly as you can and keep eyes on the yacht. That's all for now, guys. Watch your backs," Shaw cautioned.

Zach looked at Agent Antonelli. "I guess I owe you an apology...and I never thanked you. We'll be working this together. I need your cell number. When I get one, I'll text you my number under that same name, Richard Ellington."

"Dick. Dick Ellington. Yes that's appropriate. I understand you Americans assign Dick as a nickname for Richard," Marcella said with a very slight upturn to her lip.

Zach managed a laugh. "I guess I had that coming."

The door opened and Lieutenant DiIanni walked in in his crisp black uniform adorned with its signature white leather and braided cross belt and red stripe down the pant leg. "Mr. Greer, my supervisors have been informed that we are to extend every courtesy to you. Your embassy will have a plane dispatched here within the hour. You must be a man of importance." He paused before continuing. "I just have one question for you. You said the boat caught fire and forced you over the side so quickly you were not able to radio for help. The boat's owner says that it was equipped with a state-of-the-art Halon fire-suppression system. Why do you suppose that didn't extinguish the fire?"

Zach looked into the man's knowing eyes. "All I can tell you is the boat took on water fast. I'm not a boat mechanic. It obviously didn't function or I wouldn't have left a perfectly good boat at night to take a swim."

Lieutenant DiIanni stiffened. "Why of course you wouldn't. I am sorry you had an unfortunate experience here. Perhaps you will come back and visit Napoli again." Lieutenant DiIanni clicked his heel against the white marble floor, pivoted, and walked out of the treatment room.

Marcella looked at Zach without expression. Her phone rang. She listened and then replied, "Benne. Capisco, mille grazie." She hung up. "The plane is fifteen minutes out, and the car will be here in a few minutes. I'll see what I can do to get you discharged. We'll see if we can find some sort of sweatshirt in the gift shop." Marcella left the room.

CHAPTER 5

LANGLEY, VIRGINIA

"Elle, Shaw here. The White House's national security advisor, Kate Helmsworth, just called a meeting for tomorrow afternoon. The Joint Chiefs will be there. It looks like a run-up to action. They asked for our intel on Hezbollah command and control in theater and assessment of Hezbollah directional elements in the US."

"Unless they are seeing something we aren't, that's insane. There's no solid link. If strikes are ordered against Hezbollah, that means strikes against Iran are part of the package. We don't have anything to support that," Elle said.

"Agreed. But it's been eighteen months since terrorists detonated two nukes on US soil. We almost lost half the Southwest *and* New York City. As it was, nearly a hundred thousand of our countrymen are dead. The economy is teetering on recession. And it's an election year. Some form of action is a given. Our job is to find out who was behind the May Day attacks and get that information to the president before the Joint Chiefs and congress lash out against the wrong target," Shaw replied.

"We know the funds that incubated the New York attack were sent to the Milan cell from IVS Bank's branch in Zurich. The Swiss have been cooperative, giving us the account holder's name. The account that wired funds was registered to KZT, Ltd. in Berlin, a German company. You'll recall that a company by that name wired funds to the Russian arms dealer, Ivan Romescki, in the Caymans, which we believe funded the purchase of the two Soviet-era suitcase nukes," Elle recited, pulling up a screen with markers geographically placed in Zurich, Milan, and Grand Cayman.

"What's Ratani's involvement with KZT?" Shaw asked.

"Nothing, as far as we can tell at this point. We know Ratani has numerous investments financed through Hecox's hedge funds and Hecox's large stakeholder interest in IVS. And we know Hecox also places large sums for Middle Eastern interests, but that's not unusual for hedge funds. We don't see a pattern or connection for now besides Javier Estaban being his stepbrother. You recall, Estaban was one of the New York cell attackers. What we do have now, though, is the attempt on Zach Greer's life. With both Ratani and Hecox on the yacht, there has to be a connection with that attempt. We need listening devices on that boat," Elle replied.

"I'm sending Ramsey Turner and John Vargas to back Zach and Agent Antonelli up. Ramsey is ex-SEAL. He can provide another dimension now that we know they are staying on board. Nobody is better at surveillance packages than Vargas. Vargas is already in Kiev. Ramsey leaves Andrews Airbase within the hour. They'll both be in Rome by the end of the day," Shaw added.

"I'll have a briefing package for Zach on his arrival in Sorrento. Vargas will bring secure communications for the team. I'll make sure we have a place for them. They can't all stay at Agent Antonelli's friend's flat. It's perfect for a man and woman, not three men and a woman. I'll put Turner and Vargas up in a highbrow hotel, give them alias as friends on vacation... maybe *close* friends." Elle tried to interject some levity as her fingers flew across the keyboard, never looking up at the screen from where Shaw's worried face stared down on her.

"We have to slow the White House down. Get them a list of Hezbollah command-and-control targets—all the ones we know of in Beirut, but tell them we need time to get what the Israelis have. Get me Mossad—Joshua Marcus's whereabouts and a contact number for him. And pull together what we have on Ratani; I'll need to brief the president," Shaw said.

CHAPTER 6

TEL AVIV, ISRAEL

"Joshua, it's Elle Hardwick. I hope I'm not disturbing anything," Elle said.

"Good to her your voice, Elle. No, I was just headed out for some lunch. What can I do for you?" Josh knew there had to be something up for Elle to call him directly on his encrypted cell. "I'll send you an encryption code. Call me back in thirty seconds, and I'll enter the companion code," Josh said, hanging up.

Elle dialed the phone and then entered the digits at the tone and waited. The line came on, and she began to speak. "What are you hearing on the link between Hezbollah and the attack in New York? We have a briefing with the president, and we are checking all boxes."

"Do you want the official version or the truth?" Josh replied.

The bluntness of the answer was a surprise. "I'm not sure I understand. Are you saying Israel is delivering information you do not agree with?" Elle asked.

"What I'm saying is that Israel's official position is that Iran and its proxies are behind the May Day attacks on your country and has no evidence to contradict the White House's assessment to that effect. And I am saying it is in Israel's *interests* to see that your country eliminates Iran's nuclear threat and rise in influence," Josh said stressing the word "interests."

"But you don't agree with that assessment?" Elle asked.

"I have not seen any direct link between Iran or Hezbollah and the attacks that occurred against your country. My sources in Iran and Lebanon are adamant that Iran was not behind the attacks. I would say it is somewhat pleasurable to see them frightened, which they most definitely are. They feel they are being framed and are quite certain we, Israel, have had a hand in orchestrating that. We did not of course. But the fact remains, if Iran was not behind the attacks, who was and what are the motives to set up Iran for the blame? I am in a very small minority here that believes an attack on Iran by your country would not be in Israel's *interests*." Josh again stressed the word "interests."

"Have you ever heard of the German company KZT, Ltd.?" Elle said in response.

"Yes, we know it funded Romescki's Cayman account, but it's a shell corporation. We traced its organization to KZT Holdings in Lichtenstein, and from there the trail simply disappeared. We learned the management was listed to three brothers who died in East Germany in the nineteen-sixties; obviously their identities were stolen," Josh said.

"Who were the brothers? Who did they work for? What connection do they have?" Elle asked, her brow deepening.

"No connection as far as I was able to tell. Their last name was Braun: Hans, Felix, and Idor. They died in a building collapse. They were each masons—you know, bricklayers. They were forced into service to hastily build the Berlin Wall. The East Germans cannibalized brick from neighboring buildings to build the wall. One of the buildings collapsed on them in December of nineteen-sixty-one. Apparently it was an accident," Josh reported.

Elle sat back staring out the window, trying to pull the pieces together before speaking. "We traced KZT intercepts to an Italian company, Aqualine ZT in Milan. That company appears to have been a shell also. It has no assets, no reporting, and no place of business. It was registered to an entity by the name of ASL. We were unable to locate any entity, organization, or person with that name or initials. We are still working it," Elle reported to Josh.

"ASL, Aqualine ZT, KZT," Josh repeated. "I'll run them through our data bases."

"Do it quickly. Folks here are getting trigger happy. Even the president's own party is calling for action. I don't have to tell you how DC gets in an election year," Elle said.

"Understood. I'll get back if I find anything. Call me on this line and use the same encryption code. I can't stress enough that there are those here that would love to see Iran targeted and hand your president the blame," Josh said, disconnecting the line.

CHAPTER 7

MOSCOW

Aleski Tuperof stood at attention in the Kremlin's Tainitsky (or "secret") Garden. He was one of twenty or so officers and guards awaiting President Putin's helicopter, and the only one not in uniform. Putin had ordered the heliport to be constructed to enable him to commute to the Kremlin from his residence in Novo-Ogaryvo, just outside Moscow.

The men's breaths were visibly torn from them as snow flurries were whipped by the frigid wind. The sound of the MI-8 chopper could be heard echoing off the walls of the cathedrals and palaces within the Kremlin, making its location and heading a mystery. The massive chopper suddenly appeared, its blades chopping at supersonic speeds, vibrating the pavement beneath his feet. Its bulbous form was designed over fifty years ago under orders of the envious President Khrushchev after observing President Kennedy's Sikorsky helicopter.

As it sat down on the helipad, the air was churned into a blinding whiteout. The men surrounding the pad stood fast, chins held high, hats under their left arm. Aleski chose to tighten his heavy coat high around his neck, holding it with his free hand, the other arm clenching his briefcase under his armpit.

The chopper idled down, its rotors spinning slower until they stopped. A uniformed captain opened the door, walked down the three steps to the pavement, and stood at attention. Vladimir Vladimirovich Putin, president of the Russian Federation, walked down the steps without saluting. His face showed no emotion. His eyes fixed on Aleski, nodding. Aleski fell in behind the president walking to the black limo. The door was opened and Putin turned, whispering to Aleski.

Aleski sat in the back seat with the president of Russia, his throat dry. He kept his hands fixed solidly on his thighs and briefcase to keep them from trembling.

"The Americans are going to attack Iran. They will destroy the reactors we delivered. Iran will be looking to us for assistance. A response is to be developed. What have you learned from your sources in Washington?" President Putin calmly asked.

Aleski knew his response needed to be perfect. Romescki had been an FSB agent turned arms dealer who sold the two suitcase nukes used on America. The FSB's counterintelligence directorate failed to expose his activities. The FSB's foreign intelligence directorate had also overseen Russia's failed Syrian strategy. Two dramatic and public failures. A wholesale purge, reminiscent of the Stalin era, removed scores, leaving Aleski Tuperof in charge of the counterintelligence directorate. Before Putin, such positions were reserved for Russia's elite. Putin, who rose within the ranks of the KGB to become a lieutenant colonel, valued results over lineage. He made his loathing for entitlement known. He touted his mother as a factory worker and his father as a conscript in the Soviet Navy as proof that family relations did not dictate reward in the new Russia. Aleski knew his response needed to be direct, devoid of hesitation or doubt.

"Sir, Russia cannot accept another failure of intelligence. But we must be careful. Our response must be clear and with a long-term goal of making America a pariah in the Middle East, but we must look to the Americans as though we are not militarily aligned with Iran. The Gulf States' rulers, mostly Sunni, fear and loath Iran. But the common Muslim will feel America's attack on Iran is an attack against Islam. That is the message that should be pushed. For Russia to come to the aid of Shia Iran would increase sectarian tensions and appear like the old Cold War–era pattern of proxy warfare. Russia would be seen as the same as America...and such a response invites a dangerous showdown between Russia and America. I remind you there are those within the American intelligence community that are convinced that Romescki was sanctioned by FSB and are pushing to reinstate the Cold War. Our economy cannot withstand that. No, we must be smarter," Aleski said, his brow narrowing and his confidence growing.

Putin sat silent, thinking. Aleski thought for a second and proceeded. "Sir, our goal must be to lessen the influence of America and Israel while inciting Muslims across Europe against America. The recent aggressiveness of NATO can be dulled if there is discord within Europe. If Europe is preoccupied by counterterrorism activities within its borders, its cohesiveness as a force against Russia will be stifled."

Putin spoke. "How do you see this strategy being implemented?"

"Sir, I do not wish to establish he mechanics of a strategy without careful thought and planning. I will have an outline of the elements to you shortly. This is too important to hastily devise," Aleski said in a confident tone, which concealed his anxiety.

"You are wise to do so. Your predecessors operated, as the Americans say, 'on the fly.' Your observations are sound. I look forward to the details," Putin said, expressing no emotion.

Aleski's mind raced. He stared out at the swirling snow, all manner of thought and emotions mixed as if roiled by the same wind.

CHAPTER 8

NAPOLI

The drive from the airport to Sorrento was only an hour, but it was the first time Zach had been alone since coming onshore hours ago. The adrenaline had dissipated, and he was overwhelmingly tired. He stared out of the Mercedes limo's tinted windows as they drove in traffic along the A3 autostrada. On his left Vesuvius dominated his window. Vesuvius had erupted over three dozen times in the twenty-one centuries since destroying Pompeii and would do so again. He was captivated by the rawness of the landscape and its history. To his right lay the Gulf of Napoli, with Capri in the distance. His anger simmered as he remembered last night. Ratani had made a mistake not killing him.

Zach dozed in and out of sleep along the way. The car slowed and began to wind along narrow streets. Zach wiped his eyes as the car eased along the narrow Via Luigi de Maio, a street that wound its way down to the edge of the sea before coming to the hotel. Zach stepped out with the driver, who pretended to accept money for a fare. Zach grabbed the rolling duffel out of the trunk that had been packed for him. He glanced forward toward the sea, a busy parking lot separating the hotel from the ferry dock. He turned back and walked toward the hotel's front steps. Like many European hotels, this one appeared to have been two buildings joined—one cream, the larger coral in color. He took a few steps and was met by a doorman.

"Buon giorno signore. Benvenuti al Hotel il Farro," the young doorman said. The boy couldn't have been over eighteen, Zach thought.

"Boun giorno. Lei parla inglese?" Zach asked.

"Yes, of course, sir. You are American?" the boy asked.

"Canadian. I have a reservation under the name Richard Ellington for one night only," Zach replied as he walked into the lobby.

A young woman stood behind the front desk a few feet away. "Yes, Signore. Your office made a reservation for you earlier today with an early check-in. You will be staying with us just the one night I see. We have you in a wonderful camera vista mare...ah...I mean a room with a view of the sea. May I have a credit card and your passport please?"

"Yes, of course, but I'd like to hang on to my own passport. Take down any information you wish, but I make it a practice to never have it leave my sight. I also would prefer to pay you cash for the room to keep my credit card bill down. I'm a little bad with credit cards," Zach said with a self-deprecating smile.

The woman narrowed her brow. This was unusual and she resented the implication that the passport was not safe with the front desk. These North Americans were always thinking of what bad could happen, she thought. "Yes, sir, I will just make a photocopy of it and run your card only for incidentals in case you do wish to charge anything. The one night will come to...one hundred twenty-two euros."

Zach handed her the cash. She stepped into a back room and walked out a few minutes later, handing a receipt and his passport back. "You are in Camera three-thirteen. The elevator is to your left. Would you like Fabrio to assist you with your bag?"

"No, thank you. I can handle it. Grazie." Zach smiled as warmly as he could and walked to the elevator.

He stepped out of the elevator as the doors opened. His footsteps on the polished white travertine floors echoed off the hard white walls. He came to his room and opened the door. Stepping inside, he shut and locked the door behind him. Before him was a spartan room: two single beds pushed together with a thin blue bedcover that revealed the uneven levels of the two beds. A small desk and single wooden chair sat next to a window, with a small bathroom off to the side. He walked to the window and opened it. The view from the window was breathtaking. Capri lay off in the distance, as did the ferry dock that he would use in a few hours. The breeze was cold, scented with the lemons, sea, and flowers that grew below his balcony.

Zach placed the duffel on the bed and opened it. He would have two hours of sleep before leaving for the dock, but he needed to know what the agency had sent him. A phone, two shirts, a navy blazer, one pair of jeans, a pair of slacks, underwear, socks, toiletries, and a leather case. He opened the case to see a Sig Sauer 9 mm Elite with threaded barrel, suppressor, and combat night sights. Four magazines were included, two of which appeared to be armor piercing. Nice, he thought.

Washing his face never felt better. He laid down on the bed and set his alarm to 1:45. The driver had instructed him to be at the dock at 2:40. It would give him plenty of time. He fell asleep, it seemed, the instant his head hit the pillow.

It felt like he had just closed his eyes when his phone alarm went off. He reached for it and silenced the alarm. Sun was streaming in the partially open window with the sounds of the busy ferry dock and bus drop-off below. He showered and was amused to find sand and salt in his scalp. Last night seemed so long ago. He put on a new T-shirt, overshirt, and jeans. He packed everything back in the duffel, keeping the 9 mm in the duffel's outer pocket. He walked down the back stairs and exited the hotel's side door. Better to not be seen checking out two hours after his arrival.

Opening the door out into the side gardens, he walked across Via Luigi de Maio, through the waiting buses to the harbor beyond. There were two docks: the main ferry dock, filled with lines of tourists, and a second, smaller dock, empty of people. He walked to the smaller dock, where he sat his duffel down and sat on the dock. His watch read 14:36. The on-shore breeze was cool, perhaps 65 degrees, and the warm sun felt good. The whitecaps outside the harbor glistened as he looked out at Ichia far off in the haze.

A small boat approached, perhaps eight meters in length. Zach unzipped the side pocket of the duffel with one hand. The man on the boat waved and yelled in a strong Napoli accent. "Signore Ellington? Sei Signore Ellington?"

Zach waived and stood up. "Yes, my name's Ellington. Are you for hire today?" Zach waited for the proper response.

The man replied in broken English. "No sir, I already have customer today...from Banff."

It was the required response. Zach replied to confirm. "I live in Banff part of the year. I believe I am your fare."

The boat moved along the edge of the dock just long enough for Zach to throw the duffel to the man and step onto the boat. Zach shook the man's outstretched hand.

The boat captain this time spoke with an English accent that had no trace of an Italian accent. "I'm Guiseppi Spanno; call me Sep. Shaw sends his regards. Place your duffel in that waterproof case; we will get some spray going over to Capri. You should put this rain poncho on and sit here... it will be the driest place. We need to get going; it will take an hour, and I have several of these trips today. I'm picking up your backup, Turner and Vargas, here at seventeen hundred hours. I'll drop them at the main harbor. I'll drop you off on the other side of the island."

Zach settled in behind the windshield as the boat made its way past the jetty. For the second time in thirty-six hours, he was back in the Gulf of Napoli. This time they didn't know he was coming. For that matter, they were sure he was dead. Seven nautical miles ahead lay Capri with its twin high plateaus. The higher Anacapri just beyond the plateau that held most of the population and the City of Capri.

The vessel cut through the low waves as it neared the craggy limestone cliffs. The water was cobalt blue. The boat swung around the south shore of the island to the Marina Piccola, or small marina. There were a dozen or so small boats at anchor, and tourists could be seen on the rocky beach.

Sep dropped an anchor over the bow and eased the boat back until it caught. It would swing on the anchor with the light breeze blowing toward shore. He lowered the small two-man dingy from its hoist off the back and tied it off the stern.

"Get your bag while I start the motor," Sep instructed.

Zach stood in the open aft door panel and leaned over, placing his duffel in the middle of the small dingy. Sep got the small outboard motor to start on the third pull. Zach then took a seat at the front of the dingy, and Sep pulled away from the boat. A small dock, not more than twenty feet long, extended out into the shallow water. The water was crystal clear. The rocky bottom was strewn with white-and-black limestone boulders, visible in the crystal blue shallows. As the boat approached the dock, Zach reached up and held onto the dock above his head. With one hand he swung his duffel up onto the dock, and then twisted and pulled himself up.

"Thanks for the ride. Take care of yourself. Probably a liability to be seen with me," Zach said as Sep nodded with a smile and backed the dingy away.

"Be careful yourself. Go up to the bar in the hotel. El Merendero is its name; right there," Sep said, pointing to a tan stucco building with bright umbrellas planted in a row. He turned the dingy around and began to motor off.

Zach walked up the rock steps to the hotel, past Italian and German tourists. He walked into the hotel and heard a familiar voice. "Signore Ellington! It is good to see you again." Zach turned to see Agent Marcella Antonelli dressed in white cotton slacks, sandals, and a sleeveless coral blouse and large sun hat. Her olive skin revealed a small dolphin tattoo on her shoulder. She looked nothing like the Agent Antonelli he saw last night. She was radiant—not beautiful but sultry, oozing a sensuality he hadn't detected before.

"Boun giorno, sinorina," Zach said, amazed at her transformation.

"I have a taxi waiting to take us to town. You'll like the apartment. It is centrally located," she said as they walked to the taxi. They looked like a perfect tourist couple.

He paused and asked, "What do I call you? What name are you using?"

"My own. I want the neighbors to know I am here. Remember, I'm borrowing the apartment for a getaway. It would be bad form to have a stranger in a borrowed apartment," Marcella said.

Zach stared out of the cab as it wound its way up to the town. After a few turns, they were on Via Camerelle, where cars could no longer enter the city. "It's four blocks up, but cars are not permitted beyond this point. See, you can just see it, ahead on the right, above the linens store," Marcella said.

He looked around as they walked. It was perfect: a two-story building with one staircase on the side of the building accessible through a walled courtyard. No one could approach the flat without being seen. "Who's place did you say this is?" Zach asked.

"A girlfriend of mine owns it. Her parents left it to her. She uses it two months a year each summer. She's let me stay in it once before. Her younger brother lives on the island and takes care of it when she doesn't use it. He lives with his girlfriend down by the marina and will be of help to us," Marcella said.

The street was filled with tourists, shoppers, and locals on their way to and fro. The street was narrow, pedestrian only with the exception of a few electric carts that shuttled goods and tourists. Everywhere lemon trees showed early fruit. The scent of salt air, lemons, and flowers had a calming effect. No wonder people came from all over the world to Capri.

"What do we know about Ratani? Is he still on his yacht?" Zach asked.

"Yes. Peter is the brother I told you about. He operates a guide boat down at the marina that takes tourists to the Blue Grotto. He welcomed the opportunity to make some money watching the yacht. His business is slow as it is still a little cool for the tourists to venture out on the water. His boat is docked across from the yacht. I told him I was a writer doing a piece on the lifestyles of the superrich and their yachts. It seemed to excite him," Marcella said.

"Ratani won't hesitate to kill him if he knows he's being watched," Zach said.

"I told him as much. I told him the boat was Mafiosi. Peter knows what that means. He learned from one of his friends who works at the dock that the yacht is scheduled to be in port for at least one more night," Marcella replied.

"I want to pick up some dark glasses and a hat. They think I'm dead, and I'd rather have them continue with that thought," Zach added as he opened the gate to the apartment staircase.

The flat was beautiful: One bedroom, a bath, and combined kitchen living area. A window looked out on the street, and another larger one and a door to the rear led out onto a balcony, which captured the view of Anacapri's cliffs and the sea. Zach had never seen anything like it. He wasn't here for the sights, he told himself. That said, Turner and Vargas weren't scheduled to arrive for another few hours.

"Reinforcements arrive tonight. We need to get Turner down to the dock, where he can slip into the water. He will place a listening and tracking package on the hull of the yacht this evening. I want to get down to a place where we can take some pictures of the harbor, the yacht, and vantage points. It will be dark when Turner and Vargas arrive. They are going to need to see the lay of the land from photos...I'm also famished," Zach added.

Marcella laughed at this last comment. "Allora, Capri has some of the finest food in all of Italy. I know a place where we can do both. Ristorante l'Approdo: it overlooks the luxury yacht moorings. Taking pictures there is common," Marcella said with a bit of excitement in her voice, adding, "and their frutti di mare is the best on island."

Zach's emotions were mixed. They were talking like tourists when they should be focused on Ratani and the end game. No wonder the culture of Italy focused so much on the aesthetic and culinary—it was impossible to escape. "It might be our last meal for a while once things get dicey. We do need to eat. There's not much for us to do except take the photos before Turner and Vargas arrive," Zach said, rationalizing.

They left the flat and started the walk down to the Piazetta, where they could get a taxi down to the marina. The Piazetta was bustling with outdoor diners and tourists milling in the warm sun. The famous clock tower set against the edge of the cliff overlooking the blue Tyrrhenian Sea towered over the square. It was surreal—too beautiful for Zach's mind to accept as real. Zach pulled the brim of his new hat lower, touching the wraparound sunglasses he had purchased.

The drive from the town of Capri to the restaurant was less than five minutes. The restaurant sat immediately above the marina. The maître d' sat them on the veranda overlooking the harbor. Zach looked through the iron railing down at the *Gulf Vision,* which was backed into the edge of the harbor below him. The vantage point was perfect. He could look into the aft of the 108-foot yacht. Its third deck's white sun sofas were filled with three sunbathing women taking advantage of the last light, who were opting for a no-tan-line look. They didn't seem to care whether they were visible to the buildings that lined the harbor.

No sign of Ratani, Hecox, or Foltz. Zach steadied the iPhone on the railing, taking pictures of the yacht, surrounding boats, jetty, and access points. "Which boat is Peter's?"

Marcella looked around. "There: second boat in on the right side of the fifth row from the harbor entrance. White power boat with blue canopy."

"Yes, I see it. It has a pretty limited view of the yacht. A person could leave the yacht and not be seen from that angle," Zach observed.

"Peter said that. He has been over at the café across from the boat most of the day. He reports that one man, an overweight, shorter man, left to go up to Capri," Marcella replied.

"That would be the Italian, Foltz. With him onshore and the women on the sundeck, it doesn't look like they are moving anytime soon," Zach observed, taking one last glance at the women on top of the boat.

The waitress came over, offering them menus and asking if they wanted a beverage. They ordered agua minerali to the disappointment of the waitress. "Please order for me. I can't read a thing on the menu...probably some pasta for carbs. We might be up late this evening," Zach said.

"Capri's charm and fine food has been celebrated almost on a mystical level since Caesar Augustus. I don't believe anyone in that time but you has selected a meal on the basis of their energy requirements. You Americans really need to appreciate the life that surrounds you," Marcella said, smiling and with a kidding tone.

Zach nodded. She was right of course, but his mind was on the boat, not the menu. "One day I'll come back under better circumstances. The island really is beautiful." Zach's mind wandered to Sandy. He resolved to himself that one day he would bring Sandy here. Until then, he needed to stay focused. He needed to know what Ratani's game plan was. Ratani didn't do anything without a purpose. He was in Naples and Capri for a reason.

CHAPTER 9

MILAN, ITALY

Elle strode into the foyer of Veneto Zaparo Banco, a securities house in the banking district. Nearly every major international banking institution had offices within these four or five blocks on Corso Venezia, the financial epicenter of Italy. Her six-foot frame was elevated by five-inch heels. With her black hair, black leather pants, and a long gray cashmere wrap, she exuded wealth and commanded every man's eyes to follow her.

"Signorina, posso aiutarla?" a short impeccably dressed man said, rising from his chair at a desk marked INFORMAZIONI.

"Scuza. Non parlo italiano. Lei parla inglese?" Elle asked the man.

"But of course. You are English? American?" the man said in a formal English accent.

Elle smiled. "I'm from London." Elle was still amazed that nearly everyone in Europe who spoke English did so with a noticeable high King's English accent, since the English teachers were, of course, from England. "Can you tell me if Niccolo Attino is available?"

"He is here. I will check to see if Signore Attino is available. Can I tell him the nature of your business?" the man said.

"I was told he is in charge of wire transactions. I will be opening an account requiring a number of wire transactions weekly. He was recommended to me," Elle said in reply.

The man gave a slight bow, tipping his head, and walked around a corner. Elle looked around at the camera placements. She removed a lip brush, holding it vertically to her lips while she turned nearly 270 degrees. The lip brush was of course more than lipstick: it contained a ten-megapixel camera that took high-speed pictures that could be stitched together later to form a high-definition panorama of the entire inside of the bank's lobby. The soft application of lipstick to her moistened lips ensured that every man's eyes were still on her, giving her perfect full-frontal images for face-recognition software to analyze later.

A medium-built, handsome man in his thirties approached. "Signorina, I am Niccolo Attino. I am told you wish to open an account. That is normally done by one of the tellers, but I would be pleased to do it personally for you. Please let me show you back to my office." Signore Attino pointed the way in a manner hoping to impress the beautiful woman who he noticed wore a large diamond on a finger on her right hand. Divorced, he noted.

As they entered, Niccolo Attino held a chair for Elle, who sat, crossing her long legs encased in soft leather. Attino was mesmerized. He sat down behind the desk and tried to act as professional as he could. "I am sorry; I did not get your full name. Would the account be opened under your name or an entity?"

"Andrea Hollinger. The account will be opened under one of my trusts, the A. Q. Hollinger Family Trust, a Canadian trust registered in the United Kingdom," Elle said, pulling out a checkbook and iPad from her leather bag. She slid a business card before Niccolo, who proceeded to type information.

"You can open the account with as little as one hundred euros. What amount would you like to deposit to open the account?" Niccolo asked.

"I'll open the account with a thousand euros. Once you give me wiring instructions, I'll have my London bank wire an additional five hundred thousand euros. I will be doing business in Milan and Rome, so I will need to make regular wire deposits and outgoing wires. Will you be able to help with this?" Elle asked.

"Consider me your personal banker. Whatever I can help you with would be a pleasure. You may call me on my personal line." Niccolo rose, handing her his business card.

Elle wrote a check and handed it to the banker, who excused himself, rose, and went out the door, returning with a receipt and wiring instructions. Elle rose, extracting her lipstick once again and rotating it slowly against her lips. "Thank you, Signore Attino. I do have one more question. I have not been in Milan in more than a decade. I am staying at the Park Hyatt in the Galleria Vittorio Emmanuelle. Can you recommend a restaurant near there that is quiet and suitable for a woman to have dinner alone without being disturbed?"

"Why yes. I do not recommend the restaurants in the Galleria, or those that front on the Duomo; they are for tourists. There are three in the area that I recommend. Ristorante Cracco-Peck is two blocks away on Via Victor Hugo. Carlo Cracco is probably the finest chef in Italy; I am not sure you can get a reservation, but you should try. A few doors down the street is Via Spadari, where the store Peck is located. It is the finest gourmet food shop in the world and has a restaurant by the same name; it is not to be confused with Cracco-Peck. There is also Trussardi alla Scala a few blocks away near the Opera House. Among the three, Cracco has the best food, but Trussardi, being the designer, as you might imagine has the best décor. I hope you don't think me forward, but I would be pleased to meet you for a drink at your hotel and walk you to any one of them. You can arrange for a car to pick you up whenever you return." Niccolo knew the moment he said it that he shouldn't have. "Sono italiano," he said to himself. He *was* Italian.

Elle deliberately placed her sunglasses on, looked directly at the shorter Niccolo Attino, and paused deliberately before speaking. "Thank you for the recommendations, but I wish to dine alone and can have the hotel car take me." She turned and walked the three steps to his door, turned, and with deliberation said, "Perhaps another time." Elle knew a glimmer of hope would cause the degree of anxiety she wished upon the banker.

Once out of the bank, she walked over to the waiting sedan, opened the back door, and got in. "Let's go. The bait is out. Get me a line to Langley please," Elle said to the driver, Mike, an agency case officer assigned to her.

"Ms. Hardwick, line 1," Mike said, hitting a button that rolled the glass panel up between the back seat and the front seat.

"Zero, zero, foxtrot, nine, nine, echo, hotel. Elle Hardwick. Shaw Ellis," Elle said after the tone. The line resounded with a series of loud clicks, then a human voice came on.

"Elle, Shaw here; what do you have?" The CIA's newly promoted director of the National Clandestine Service Division, NCS, spoke.

"I met with Niccolo Attino and opened the account," Elle responded.

"Did he take the bait? What's your read?" Shaw asked.

"He's Italian. He invited me to dinner," Elle said musingly.

Shaw's smile broke wide. Ah, Elle—no one can resist her wile and charm, he thought. "Good work. We don't have a lot of time. How long do you think you need to turn him?" Shaw asked.

"Today's Tuesday. I would say Friday would be a reasonable expectation. I'll work with Mike to get it done. Any word from Zach and the Capri team?" Elle asked.

"Zach's on the island. Turner and Vargas are due there in under two hours. I assume you placed the bugs in Attino's office. Upload the panoramas of the bank when you get to a secure platform," Shaw instructed.

"Roger that. The bugs are under his desk, under the guest chair I was sitting in, and under his office hardline phone. He was nice enough to leave the office for me. We should be able to hear any office or phone conversations. I'll keep you informed; we are pulling up to the hotel now." Elle hung up as the car approached the Via Tomasso car portico at the Park Hyatt.

Mike stepped out and opened Elle's door as she swung her long leather-encased legs out of the black Mercedes. The doorman held the door as she walked into the small lobby desk. "Andrea Hollinger; I have a reservation for four nights."

"Yes, of course, Signorina Hollinger. I am Letitia Rispani, and this is my assistant, Marcus. Welcome to the Park Hyatt. If I may see your passport and a credit card please?" The front-desk couple were young, attractive, and efficient. Elle loved Park Hyatts, particularly in Europe. It wasn't a hotel chain the agency usually booked for their employees.

"You will be in room two-oh-two; it is a quiet deluxe king room. Your bags will be brought to the room. Is there anything we can get for you?" the woman asked, handing the passport, key, and credit card back.

"Is it possible to have you get me a reservation around eight o'clock this evening for just me and have a car take me to Ristorante Cracco?" Signorina Hollinger asked.

"I will see if that can be arranged. If there is a problem getting a reservation at Cracco, I can ask the concierge to recommend another restaurant. We will leave a message on your phone. Our courtesy driver can take you and come back for you whenever you are ready. The restaurant is only four blocks from here," the young woman said.

Elle followed Marcus, the male desk attendant, to the room. She entered to find her luggage already in place. Shutting the door behind her, she looked around at the rich, warm, modern interior. Travertine walls, rich leather upholstery, and a king bed pulled tight in white linens greeted her. Hmmm, I could get used to this, she thought.

She looked over to the phone with a small, flashing red light. She picked it up and asked for her messages. There were two. The first one was from Niccolo Attino. She listened. "Signorina Hollinger, I must apologize and hope you did not think me forward. My intentions were to make sure you were comfortable and safe here in Milan. It is a beautiful city but has some elements that, like any city, should be avoided. In any event, I hope you have a good evening, and I look forward to our business relationship."

Elle smiled, deleting the message and moving to the second one, which was the concierge advising her that he was able to get her into Ristorante Cracco at 7:30 if that was acceptable. That was a big "get" she thought and reminded herself to stop by the concierge desk and leave a sizable gratuity.

She removed her lipstick, unscrewed the end, inserted a cable, and attached it to the USB port on her laptop. It downloaded the panoramas of the bank, which she loaded into the proprietary software for encryption and hit the send button transmitting the data to Shaw.

With nothing to do for two hours, she decided to run a bath in the over-sized tub. On the counter were fruit, cheese, and a half bottle of wine, a 2007 Tenuta Caparzo Brunello. A note accompanied the wine: "Benvenuti al Park Hyatt," signed by the manager. Elle marveled at how some people lived.

She opened the wine and poured a glass. She sat on the edge of the bed, kicked off her red-soled Christian Louboutin heels, and peeled her supple leather pants off as if they were a second skin. She removed her cashmere sweater and reached back and unfastened her bra. She was completely naked as she closed the drapes and walked into the travertine bathroom. She sat the bottle down on the edge of the tub and took a sip of wine, looking at herself in the mirror.

At thirty-four her skin was still taut—no imperfections in her six-foot frame. Her 34C breasts were full, defying gravity. She worked with a trainer three days a week religiously; her toned body showed her dedication. She had treated herself several years ago to full laser treatments eliminating any and all body hair. Her shoulders and back were defined and toned, her olive skin smooth and flawless, with not a mark on it save for the small tattoo on her right hip at the bikini line she obtained one night in Moorea: a small blue-and-pink dragonfly two inches in length.

She reached over and checked the water temperature; it was perfect. She perused a selection of oils and bath salts, selecting one packet, and stepped in. The water enveloped her. She swilled a sip of the wine, letting the flavors register and mix with air: tastes of spice, leather, tobacco, and a hint of vanilla. Between the room's luxury, the bath, the wine, and the time to herself, it was a moment to savor.

She allocated herself fifteen minutes of downtime but after five was already thinking, planning her approach with Niccolo. She knew she could seduce him, but such indiscretions for married men were not as embarrassing in Italy as they were in other countries. An affair in Italy was not blackmail material; it was a right. After all, it had seemed over the years that a prerequisite for the highest job in the land was a penchant for lurid and indiscriminate tastes. No, she had developed a far more convincing embarrassment, one an Italian, married, Catholic businessman could never allow public. She sipped the last from her glass, savoring the plan. It was time to get out, to set things in motion.

She rose from the tub and reached for a towel. The towels were heavy and soft. She placed one around her and stepped out of the tub before the mirror. Letting the towel drop, she opened one of the body oils from the counter. It had a faint smell of lavender and honey. She applied it first to her arms and then cupped a generous portion in the palm of her hand and spread it across her breasts and flat stomach. It glistened on her tight breasts, made her deep brown nipples hard. She stood allowing the oils to absorb, to nourish her skin, as she looked at her body in the mirror. It was a view men and an occasional woman had seen but no lovers had embraced. She had no time or need for a true relationship. That would come later, perhaps if she secured the station chief position in London. Shaw had intimated it was a possibility the last time he was in London.

She blotted herself with a second towel and walked into the bedroom, opening her suitcase. She had brought three outfits with her: two for the evening and one daytime, plus the outfit she traveled in. She selected a black dress with four-inch leather heels that came to the ankle. She put on hose and then the dress. Her short hair meant she could be ready in far less time than when her hair was to her shoulders.

After a few minutes, she finished getting herself ready, checked the compact Beretta 3032 in her purse, and stepped out of her room, where she walked to the Cupola Bar in the hotel. She assumed Niccolo would have a contact or employee in the hotel he would pay for information on her. At least that was what she would do. There were two businessmen in suits sitting down at a small table and a couple in their fifties having martinis. She walked to the crescent-shaped bar with its eight leather bar stools as the sole waiter walked behind the bar. It was seven; she had time for part of a glass of wine. She ordered and the waiter poured her a sangiovese.

A man and woman in their thirties walked out of the elevator and into the bar. The woman looked at Elle, and a few minutes later Elle saw the man give her a glance through two vertical mirrors on an adjacent wall. There, a second look by the woman. They were watching her—perhaps admiring her, perhaps wondering what a single woman was doing at the bar, or perhaps more.

Only one way to find out, Elle thought to herself. She took the glass of wine and walked toward the door, disappearing around the corner. She turned, pulled out her phone, and waited. After a few moments, the woman walked around the corner and hesitated in her stride seeing Elle on her phone. She walked past and to the bathroom. The hesitation in her step told Elle everything.

After a minute or two, she returned to the bar where the man glanced at her and then back to the hall his companion had walked to. The waiter asked whether she wanted a menu and Elle replied, "No, thank you. I have a dinner reservation in a few minutes at the restaurant inside Peck." She knew she had said it loud enough for the man to hear. The woman appeared a few minutes later whispering to her companion.

She signed for the drink she had barely touched and walked out to the waiting car. The courtesy car was a black Mercedes Benz S550. It dropped her at Via Victor Hugo 6, half a block from Cracco. She tipped the driver, telling him she would call for her return trip. She backed up into a door front, appearing to look at a window filled with shoes, when a cab appeared. The man and woman from the bar got out and walked into the Peck store. Yes, her intuition was right. They had been a tail. It would be a matter of time before they returned to the hotel and realized her true dinner destination, but the ruse had proven useful. She knew she was being followed. She turned and walked next door and into Cracco. Niccolo could not have arranged a surveillance package so quickly; he would have just tipped an employee, a doorman, for information. So who was tailing her? she wondered.

CHAPTER 10

DUBAI, UAE

Burj Khalifa towers over the city. The world's tallest building is an address coveted by global concerns vying for a piece of the region's wealth. Rawan Jalabi stood gazing out the window toward the sea and the vast orchestra of high-rise hotels, office buildings, and residential towers that had erupted in the last ten years along the waterfront. He recalled his first trip to the city ten years ago enrolled as a student here. His parents had insisted he should become educated, to escape the poverty that enveloped all that were not of class lineage. His father had achieved modest success having developed a business of maintaining and purchasing oil-field trucks. His parents' hard work and frugality allowed him opportunities he didn't waste. He could remember his father's oversized, weathered knuckles stained by years of oil, grease, and tobacco. Those hands patted him on his shoulder at his graduation, and he had held them two short years later when his father took his last breath.

Rawan achieved not one but two degrees. After graduating engineering school at NYU/Abu Dhabi, he attended the University of Tulsa's petroleum engineering graduate school, one of the finest in the world. A degree from a prestigious American university served him well. He was back home, being recruited by a pillar of the country. The floor of the office lobby was deep, rich brown plank wood, a building material shipped from far away. The walls were a pebbled granite from Saudi Arabia adorned with rich fabric from China.

It was unusual...he didn't know why he had been asked to come to the office. Job interviews were conducted many floors below. The courier had merely presented a letter to him and left after obtaining his signature. The letter requested his presence for an employment opportunity fitting of his accomplishments, giving a date and time. It had been signed by M. Khouri, president of Arabesco, Ltd.

A door opened at the end of the lobby and a young woman, replete with hijab that covered her hair but left her beautiful face to be seen, walked toward him. "Mr. Jalabi, Mr. Khouri will see you now. Please follow me." She turned and walked back through the open doorway.

Two men sat at the end of a massive conference table surrounded by more than thirty chairs. On one side of the room were floor-to-ceiling windows commanding a view of the Gulf. On the other side was a low credenza stacked with all manner of fruit, pastry, juices, and tea. Above the forbidden buffet were a series of three framed photographs, each nearly five feet in length, showing refineries, and a fourth frame exhibiting a map of the Gulf region.

"Good afternoon. My name is Mr. Khouri. Please, sit down where the water glass has been poured for you." The man at the end of the table gestured.

"Good afternoon, sir. Thank you for inviting me here," Rawan managed to get out.

"We have asked you to come here today to discuss a potential employment opportunity with Arabesco. I have read your resume and done a little background checking. You have no negatives on your background and a great many accomplishments. Your parents, they are from Bahrain?" Mr. Khouri asked.

"My mother lives now in Abu Dhabi. She moved there after my father died two years ago. She has a sister there," Rawan responded. "Sir, if I may, what type of job are you considering me for?" he asked hesitantly.

The man who had not spoken rose. "Arabesco is establishing a division that will revolutionize refining through a computerized adaptive refining program. Efficiencies will be enhanced by over seventy-five percent increasing production output. We are looking for the best minds in petroleum engineering, computer programing, and mechanical engineering. We would like you to be a part of this. We are prepared to offer you eighty thousand AED per month."

Rawan was stunned. That was more than twice what he had hoped for. His expression told them that they had him. "I accept; when do I start?" Rawan managed to say.

The men smiled warmly. "We would like you to start immediately. Tomorrow at eight please report to the thirty-seventh floor, and they will get you started," Mr. Khouri said.

As they rose, the door opened behind them at the end of the conference table. Two large men held the door. A holstered gun was visible under the sport coat of one of the men who glared at Rawan. They seemed out of place—not the type of men who would be in an executive office. It was a brief distraction from the feigned giddiness Rawan projected as he went out the other door to the elevator.

Downstairs he saw the man who followed him out of the elevator. It would take several minutes and a walk through the Mall of the Emirates to lose the follower. Rawan walked back into the dressing room at the Kenneth Cole store where he had left the phone under the dressing-room bench and dialed with the ear bud in. "Joshua, I'm in. They hired me. I start tomorrow."

CHAPTER 11

CAPRI, ITALY

Turner eased into the dark water. Zach and Marcella strolled as lovers on the dock, making sure no one would see him slip beneath the surface. A single light bulb had lit the dock, which Zach had unscrewed before Turner walked down the dock with the mesh gear bag holding a rebreather, weight belt, mask, fins, and the surveillance package Vargas developed for him.

The equipment was heavy above the water. Below the water, Turner switched on the night-vision monocle fitted into his dive mask. The green light showed hulls of the boats as he made his way down the dock to the channel. From there, he would descend to the bottom of the channel, ten meters deep for the thirty-meter swim to the other side of the dock where the yacht was moored. Buoyancy control was the key—as deep as possible without disturbing sediment that might make it to the surface. The rocky bottom shouldn't have loose sediment but he dared not risk it.

The water at night was pitch black as seen through one eye and soft green without any shapes by the other. He kicked methodically—thirty-four, thirty-five, thirty-six, he counted his leg kicks. By his estimate it would take him fifty to sixty kicks to make the distance. He pulled the equipment bag that swung below him just off the surface. There, a shape—yes, his directional navigation was perfect; he saw the bow of the large yacht protruding out beyond the other four large moored yachts.

When he was below the bow, he adjusted his buoyancy to be neutrally buoyant and still. He slowly turned 3 degrees, observing the bottom of the yacht, looking for security cameras. There it was: a security camera protruding two inches midhull; he assumed there would be another near the aft to monitor the props. He then scanned the vessel's hull for motion detectors or magnetic transmitter coil sensors that would detect metal. Much like an airport security wand, a metal detector would send a magnetic charge around the vessel hull that would induce an electrical current in a metal object near the hull. A weight belt and rebreather tank would be more than enough to set off an alarm. After several minutes of scanning, he decided there were no detectors or they had been shut off while in the harbor due to the close proximity of the yachts anchored several feet away on each side.

Turner removed a canister and pulled the cord; black dye flooded out in a cloud drifting beneath the vessel. He slowly followed it coming up to the obscured camera port. He slid a half moon shaped pliable cover over the port. To the person monitoring the camera, it would appear like the black bottom; there would be no indication of anything until daylight and by then the cover would be gone. It was designed to dissolve after several hours in salt water. He repeated the action at the aft security camera port. He then went to work. He attached several GPS tiles to the rudder and another to the anchor line where it joined the anchor. He then applied a thin film, perhaps three feet by three feet, to the bottom of the hull well forward of the engine compartment.

Two more packages to install. He slowly ascended to the waterline with no movement. He rotated a thin telescoping arm with a clear sensor that resembled a piece of glass with an undulating, uneven shape no more than two inches in length and raised it the four feet to the lower fixed window and pressed. He disengaged the telescoping arm. He repeated this on the next window above. Both windows were fixed and above the waterline—they could only be cleaned from the outside—and to someone casually observing from the inside, it would look like a drop of seawater or salt-water stain. In reality, they were high efficiency voice detectors with a built-in transmitter. Voices that caused sound waves to strike the glass would be transmitted up to three miles away for ninety-six hours, when the engines weren't running.

Turner then slipped back under the surface. He had been in the water for nearly two hours. The rebreather would allow him to stay down longer than his body would; hypothermia was the limiting factor. He couldn't use a bulky dry suit. Even with a four-mil wetsuit, he was beginning to feel the effects of the cold water. At sixty-one degrees Fahrenheit, the water was nearly forty degrees colder than body temperature. The dense water was literally pulling heat from him. His heart's pumping converted calories to maintain the temperature of his organs, weakening him with every minute that passed. When the body's core temperature dropped eight to ten degrees, confusion, misjudgments, and dizziness began to occur; any misstep could be fatal.

He focused and repeated the mantra to himself he used whenever he was in a life-threatening situation. "Please, God, don't let me fuck up. One, two, three, one, two, three, focus, focus, OORAH." He methodically repackaged all of his implements and fixed them to his belt and began the fifty-two-kick swim back.

Zach and Marcella had strolled away from the dock awaiting the sign to return. They watched the big yacht from a bench. "Look, the large boat with the two men on the tail moored three boats down. It's a tender for Ratani's yacht...and it has two black zodiacs on the tail," Zach said.

Marcella looked down the dock. Yes, she could see it; it was bristling with antennae, radar domes, and two satellite dishes. The boat's black hull was topped with a light gray superstructure two stories above waterline. It appeared about two-thirds the length of Ratani's yacht. She could see two men pacing around the edge of the boat—obviously guards. She assumed there were others onshore with eyes on the harbor.

Zach put his arm around Marcella and leaned closer, whispering in her ear. "They have to have surveillance on the harbor. It's going to be difficult for Turner to get out of the water. When he signals, alert his comm; tell him to make his way underwater to the far side of the service dock; that will be out of eyesight from the boats and probably outside of their surveillance zone. Now, when I pull away laugh in case we are being watched." As he withdrew, Marcella tossed her hair back and gave a laugh.

Zach knew Turner would be exhausted. He'd been in the water for a long time. Telling him to swim another two hundred meters was not going to be welcome. They started walking from the bench toward the service dock, halfway between the yacht and the ferry dock. They walked along a paver-lined path when a man approached them. Zach bowed his head, tipping the brim of his hat down low.

The man spoke in Italian. "The harbor and dock area is now closed; the last ferry has arrived; you will have to leave."

Marcella replied in Italian. "The harbor does not close at night. Who are you? You are not a police officer or harbor official, are you?" The man looked first at her and then at Zach, and his eyes met Zach's. A moment of realization in his eyes. Zach struck his Adam's apple with his right hand's knuckles. The man's horrified look revealed surprise, pain, and resign. Zach caught him as he fell. Zach pulled him behind a cart; he would die soon, his brain starved for the air that was unable to pass through his larynx. As the man gasped his last breaths, Zach checked his pockets. A 9 mm Beretta, wallet, cell phone, and compact binoculars. Zach removed money, credit cards, and a driver's license from the wallet. He carefully wiped the wallet clean of fingerprints. He needed this to look like an ordinary mugging. Zach began to strike him to the head, face, and chest.

"What are you doing? He's dying," Marcella exclaimed.

"It needs to look like a mugging. A single blow would look like a professional did it," Zach calmly said as he pocketed the cell phone and Beretta. "We'll bury the credit cards where they can't be found. Come here and place your arm around me. There will be another one looking, particularly when this one doesn't check in. Look at his cell phone recent calls and see what the timing is between the last three calls coming in and going out. My guess is that it will be the same number. We need to know how much time we have until this place gets dicey."

Marcella put her arm around Zach's waist as they walked, and she scrolled through the phone log. Her phone vibrated. It was Turner's signal. She texted back:

EXFIL 1 COMPROMISED EXIT SERVICE DOCK-EXFIL 2

She hit SEND and then returned to the man's phone. Just as Zach said, there were five calls in and five out. The log showed the same number called the phone every twenty minutes, the last call occurring twelve minutes ago. "You're right. Looks like we have eight minutes before the next call."

"Okay, it will be tight. Let's get to the service dock. It'll take Turner eight to ten minutes to get there. This place is going to get real busy in about ten minutes," Zach said as he put his arm around Marcella and they stepped up their pace away from the private dock. Zach kept his head down and leaned into Marcella. The dock was crowded with people, tourists walking along the cafés that sat next to the dock. He didn't see anyone take notice but assumed the other would be elevated in an overwatch position. The hillside was crowded with buildings, restaurants, and thick vegetation.

When they got to the service dock, Zach ducked behind a panel truck and threw the man's Beretta into the water. They then strolled down to the end of the service dock to a low platform used to winch motors. It was high tide and the water level was no more than a foot below the platform. He slowly removed his daypack and swung it around in front of him as they stood together gazing out at sea.

Suddenly, almost imperceptibly, the water surface broke and a very tired Turner surfaced and pulled himself up onto the service platform. Zach dropped the daypack down the five feet or so to the platform. Turner peeled out of his wetsuit, filled it with his mask, fins, and weight belt, and let it sink under the dock. The rebreather he placed in the pack as he withdrew the dry clothes, shoes, and jacket. Zach turned sideways to Marcella and placed his lips next to hers, murmuring, "Let's get out of here." To anyone watching it would be a romantic kiss at the end of a dock.

Zach and Marcella walked the length of the service dock arm in arm. At the end of the dock, they walked to a taxi and got in. Looking down the dock, they saw a sole man walking slowly from the end of the pier, backpack over his shoulder.

As the taxi began to move, Marcella exhaled a deep breath. Zach looked down at her hands on her lap shaking almost uncontrollably. He reached over, his large hand over hers. "Are you okay?"

Marcella's eyes, wide, swelled as if to tear. "I'm okay. I haven't done field work before. Damn! I'm shaking."

"It's normal. It's the adrenaline leaving your system. You did great. It's done. It's now up to Vargas and Turner to monitor them for the next six hours. We'll relieve them then and do a six-hour shift. Let's go back to the apartment and try to get a couple hours rest," Zach said, removing his hand from hers.

Turner knocked three times and then entered the second-floor door of a warehouse on the edge of the Piazza Angelo Ferraro overlooking the harbor. Vargas sat behind a single monitor where six images were scaling across the screen. Two of the six inset screens showed the yacht from different angles. One was from a distance where the harbor was shown in scale to monitor both the yacht and tender. The other image showed a close-up from a high-powered lens looking straight into the back of the yacht's main deck and flybridge. The remaining four screens showed scaled sound and voice monitors. Vargas looked up long enough to give Turner a thumbs up. Turner dropped down on the stained sofa, peeling the damp socks off his feet.

"So, do you like to be called John or Vargas?" Turner asked, sinking back in the sofa.

"Vargas is good."

"What kind of name is Vargas, anyway?" Turner asked.

"Latino. Mexican actually. My parents came into the country in the seventies from Jalisco—you know, where they make tequila. When I was born, they gave me an English name, John, not Juan. They insisted I'd have more opportunities with John; they wanted me to have everything they didn't. I guess that's pretty much what every parent wants," Vargas replied before continuing. "What about you? Where do ex-SEALs grow up?"

"An hour west of Wichita. The only open water around was stock ponds. Played a little football at Texas but mostly went wild...first time in a city. I spent more time in the bars on Sixth Street than in class. One day I walked by a recruiting window and saw a poster. A few tours in Afghanistan later, here I am," Turner replied.

"Living the dream and being all we can be I guess," Vargas quipped.

"Have you confirmed whether Ratani is onboard?" Turner asked.

"Yeah, voice recognition on him—Hecox also. Foltz is onshore; the kid confirmed he took a taxi from the boat a few hours ago. Bunch of female voices. These guys know how to live," Vargas said without looking up. Vargas straightened up, looking at the screen and listening. "All hell just broke out on the tender. They must have found their boy's body."

Turner got up from the sofa, walked to the window, and looked between the slats with binoculars. "Yeah, I count two on the fantail of the yacht and another three along the dock. Lights, probably police where Zach said he left the goon."

Turner watched the two on the fantail of the yacht touch their ear-pieces at the same time. They seemed to be scanning the dock. The lights were out in the room but a faint blue glow from the computer monitor dimly it the room. He froze and slowly dropped down. He could see the two looking directly at where they were, nearly a hundred yards away. If they were scanning the buildings with binoculars, it was possible—not likely, but possible—they could see someone standing at the window. He walked into the other room, where no lights and no computer screen were on, and edged toward the window. Standing five feet back from the window, he looked through binoculars. Only one man stood on the fantail of the yacht. He was looking in his direction through binoculars. He couldn't see any of the other three that had been on the dock. He knew they would be there, but it bothered him they weren't in his view.

Turner thought a split second and made a decision. "Break it down. Now. We're compromised. We're relocating!" Turner barked at Vargas. Vargas knew better than to not trust intuition. They scrambled to pull cords from the monitor, audio bank, and wall. Vargas roughly placed the components in the foam cutouts in the black aluminum rolling bag. Turner went out first, gun drawn, and motioned Vargas to follow. They went into the neighboring office and through the wall board Turner had cut open behind two file cabinets, and then Turner slid the cabinets back in front of the opening. They walked briskly though the office to the back of the building. Turner went down with the steel staircase first, motioning all clear to Vargas. They walked down the alley and into a back door two buildings down from where they started. Once in, Turner closed and latched the back-door lock.

"Go set up in the alternate space; I'll keep eyes on down here for a while," Turner said. Vargas walked up the staircase, past an apartment where he could hear a TV playing behind a closed door.

Turner walked up the staircase to a window overlooking the alley they just had been in. Two men, one with night-vision headgear, went into the building they had just been in. Not good, he thought, walking up the stairs.

"Is it possible for someone to backtrack our surveillance feed to track our position?" Turner asked Vargas.

"No. I mean, it's possible but it would take a hardline analyst hours to do that. No way it could be done in this time period and here on this island," Vargas said while he deftly reassembled the monitoring equipment.

"Then someone tipped them off. A team just went into the space we were set up in. Don't turn your monitor on without a blackout hood over it," Turner said peering out the blinds. He could see two other men milling in front of the building they had been in. He surmised he had been followed or observed, or perhaps they had eyes on the entire harbor area. Just then he remembered: the wet socks. He had taken them off and thrown them down on the floor next to the sofa. They already knew they were there, but he cursed himself for being careless.

Turner stood in the dark near the window. He bent down and removed the Panther Very Small Aperture Terminal satellite communications

manpack (VSAT) and put the headset over his ear. "Virginia One, this is
Indigo Tango Alpha One, over."

Immediately the earpiece resonated. "Indigo Tango Alpha One,
Virginia One, read you clear."

"Virginia One, we need SAT coverage our position. Position one compromised, moved to position two. Need oversight our position, over,"
Turner recited.

A familiar voice came over the sat line. "Indigo Tango Alpha One, what
do you mean compromised?" Sarah Tashkent's voice was immediately
recognizable.

"The security team received a communication and directly looked at
our position. Someone keyed them to us. Had it been their harbor oversight, they would have hit us earlier. They learned about us *after* we were
in position. They went straight to our position," Turner reported. Turner
knew the chances of him seeing that had been one in a million and knew he
had used up another life.

"We have SAT eyes on your position. We see two tangos outside position one building, another one in the alley. The one in the alley is checking
doors, walking toward your position," Sarah said.

"Roger that," Turner said. He chambered a round and went back to
a position at the stairwell. He crouched, waiting. They would use flash-
bangs—it would be what he would do. He closed one eye and waited.

The locked door rattled at the attempt to open it. Turner waited for
the door to be breached. Faint voices now in the alley, Italian. Then, "Alto,
policia." A staccato of gunfire erupted in the alley.

"Local officers down; suspects down. Turner, stay put. Other police in
vicinity. Hole up for now. We're not sure what went down, but your location will be swarming with the locals," Shaw said, grabbing the headset
from Sarah.

"Roger that. No one is scheduled back into this building until Monday, so that gives us a few days. Indigo Tango Alpha One out." Turner crept from the staircase back into the room and closed the door, draping a rug near the door to block out any light or shadows that could be visible from the hallway.

"What the hell happened?" Vargas excitedly asked.

"We got lucky. We're here for a few days; cops are swarming around outside. Stay away from the window and use the hood when the monitor is on. This place has to look and sound empty...*real* empty," Turner whispered.

CHAPTER 12

MOSCOW

"Aleski Tuperof, Counter Intelligence Directorate, FSB. I am here to see the president." Aleski introduced himself to the stately woman behind the desk. The woman was petite, young, lean, with high Russian cheekbones. Her dark hair was swept back in a single short braid. Her soft complexion was in contrast to the cold look she gave Aleski.

"Please take a seat. The president is expecting you, but he is running late," the woman said, motioning him to sit.

Aleski had been up most of the night. He had a plan, but it wasn't perfect. He went over the plan and its variables and contingencies over and over while he waited. He knew it was rushed and cursed himself for promising a plan on such short notice. It was based on many moving parts, none of which were certain and all of which were dependent on those who hated both Russia and America.

The Middle East was slipping into a long sectarian war from North Africa to Iran. It was inevitable. Russia had allied itself with the Shi'a minority and the Shi'a had shown its dominance under Iran in the past year. Hezbollah controlled Lebanon and the West Bank. Iran had fostered Shi'a movements in Sudan and Niger. Shi'a rebels had, for a while, pushed the US-backed moderate Sunni power structure from Yemen, and Iraq was increasingly looking to Iran for support against ISIL after America had abruptly withdrawn. Despite being a minority, the Shi'a were becoming dominant due to Iran. For this reason, Iran could not be allowed to fail at the hands of Israel and America. First, America would have to be convinced that neither Russia nor Iran had any part in the attacks against

America. Second, Europe would have to back away from its newfound resolve to wean itself from Russian energy supplies. To do that required both an understanding of those attacks and a demonstration.

CHAPTER 13

MILAN

The timeline was compressed. Elle decided Niccolo needed to be turned tonight, not in two more days. She picked up the phone and dialed. "Niccolo Attino por favore."

The call was placed on hold while Signore Attino was notified. "Niccolo Attino, posso aiutarla?"

"Niccolo, Andrea Hollinger here," Elle announced. "I hope I'm not catching you at a bad time."

"Not at all, Ms. Hollinger. What a pleasure. How may I be of assistance today?" an excited Niccolo responded.

"I'm glad I caught you before you left for the day. I find myself in town two more days. I am going to make an additional transfer into my account in the morning and will have two wire transfers out tomorrow. I am wondering if I can email or fax you that information? And by the way, I enjoyed Cracco; it was an exceptional restaurant; thank you very much for the recommendation. I may need to solicit your advice for another for this evening," Elle said, letting the last sentence seductively trail off.

"Yes, of course. Please fax the details of the transfers. My personal fax number is on the business card I gave you. It will come straight to my desk. As for dinner, I recommend either Giacomo or Armani Nobu. Giacomo is fifteen to twenty minutes by cab and is a quiet place with some of the best seafood in the city. Armani Nobu is more lively and is perhaps a five-minute cab or ten-minute stroll from your hotel. It's on the edge of the shopping district at Via Manzoni and Via Monte Napoleone. The Armani Lounge is private, but I have a membership, and should you wish to go, I believe I can arrange for that," Niccolo said, not wanting to make the same mistake of seeming too forward.

This time, the response was unexpected. "You know, Niccolo, I've been traveling now for nearly three weeks and eating either alone or in my room. I think I would prefer 'lively' tonight. If you are free, maybe we could meet for a drink or dinner and you could show me the Armani Lounge," Elle said.

Niccolo's mouth opened but no words came out. "I...I would be pleased to meet you. That would be very nice indeed." Niccolo's left thumb subconsciously fiddled with the bottom of his wedding band. "Perhaps half past nine o'clock I can swing by Nobu and meet you. I'm sure your hotel can get you a reservation for nine or so for dinner; they have an excellent sushi bar area as well."

"Thank you; I look forward to it. I'll send over the wire instructions in a few minutes," Elle said and hung up. She sat back, smiling to herself. This was almost going to be fun, she thought.

Elle then dialed Shaw. "Shaw, Elle here. We're set up for Attino tonight. I have a tac-team set up at an apartment in the Galleria, which can be accessed from the Park Hyatt. We should be to the apartment around midnight local time."

"Elle, be careful. Whoever we are on to is good. We almost lost a team in Capri. Watch your back." Shaw hung up.

Elle was now not as sure as she was before the call. She sat thinking of the plan—choke points, alternate routes, and whether anything should be changed. She decided her plan of going alone to dinner was too exposed. She would have one of the team shadow her at the restaurant and have another be in the bar. The club would be more difficult. It was exclusive. That would be a challenge. And she checked her weapon. It wasn't going to be concealable in what she had planned to wear for Attino.

Elle rose and set the privacy lock on her door. She turned the TV on to CNN International. A reporter with a strong British accent stood outside the White House on the sunny lawn. "The president met with his top advisors for nearly two hours. In attendance were Secretary of Defense Hartert, National Security Advisor Helmsworth, and the Joint Chiefs. Eighteen months after the May Day attack, the deadliest terrorist attack in history and the detonation of two nuclear warheads in US territory, it's clear that some form of action is now on the table. President Putin of Russia, President Xi Jinping of China, and UN General Secretary Ban Ki-moon have called for restraint."

The London anchor cut in. "I don't see how the United States can exert restraint under these circumstances. Two nuclear devices were deployed within its borders and another two conventional attacks. Had it not been for a combination of sheer luck and fine work by America's counterintelligence community, the damage would have been catastrophic. As it was, damage has been in the hundreds of billions to the US economy and nearly a hundred thousand fatalities linked to the attacks. It is unrealistic to assume the US would stand down from taking action once those responsible are identified. And for more on this crisis, we turn now to Matthew Hurst in Tel Aviv."

"Night has fallen here in Tel Aviv and the country is on edge. Israeli Defense Forces have called up reserves, and a dusk-to-dawn curfew is in effect in the West Bank. In the past when such measures were instituted, Hezbollah and Hamas have retaliated, but it has been eerily quiet here for two nights, as if no one wishes to provoke the conflict they know is coming. In a rare move, the reclusive leader of Hezbollah, Hassan Nasrallah, spoke in Beirut, urging his followers to not provoke conflict and calling for calm across the Middle East. It is obvious Hezbollah's strings are being pulled tightly by Iran, which fears it is in the crosshairs. Matthew Hurst, Tel Aviv." The camera panned behind the reporter, showing a blackened skyline.

Elle knew there was little time to spare. Washington was marching toward war, whether they had the right target or not. Franklin and Shaw had made it clear that they had precious little time to learn the identities of who, or what, was behind the attacks. Once hostilities ensued, culpability would be immaterial.

CHAPTER 14

LONDON

"Honey, its Zach. I'm okay. Sorry, I have been out of touch. It's been...an interesting thirty-six hours. How are you?" The sound of Zach's voice soothed Sandy's anxiety.

"I'm okay. I had a ten-hour day. A lot of logistics and red tape. I'll be glad when I'm doing something on the ground. Actually looking forward to getting to Tel Aviv. The weather is so dreary here. I miss sun," Sandy said, exhaling and curling into the sofa.

She was trying to adjust to the new life, Europe. It was so different from her rural roots—so different from her education and training as a National Park Service officer. She preferred the solitude of the desert, the expanses of nature. But this was the trade-off she had made to be with Zach.

"Sandy, I want you to get back to the States. I can't say why; I just think now isn't the time to be in the Middle East, anywhere in the Middle East." Zach's voice had a tone she hadn't heard.

"I can't. I'm scheduled to leave for Tel Aviv in two days, to be in Jordan in less than a week," Sandy said. She was resistant but hesitant. She had never heard Zach worried before.

"Honey, I'm assigning some security to you. They will be there within the hour. They will introduce themselves as being from Arizona. The agency will fly you and your team back to Dulles tomorrow night. Things... well, things are occurring. You've heard the news. The Middle East is going to explode, and if it explodes, Europe ignites. You're the wife of an

American intelligence officer. You could be a target. Please, do as I say. I love you. I'll see you in a few days. I love you, I gotta go." Zach's voice was soft, carrying.

"Okay, I'll go back for a few weeks, till this blows over, I promise. Be careful. I love you." Sandy hung up, her eyes swollen and her breath short. There was worry in Zach's voice. She knew he wasn't safe and wouldn't have insisted if it wasn't serious.

She started packing again, although this time, she unpacked the carry-on's assortment of conservative beige and brown clothes and began repacking it with clothes more accustomed to New York or Washington. The small apartment was cluttered with gear—clothing, books, easels, notebooks. She decided to leave it all, to just take clothes, enough for two weeks. She resolved she would be back, when the doorbell chimed and a voice came on the intercom.

"Ms. Heller? This is agent Brooks and Howard from your husband's office."

Sandy pushed the wall intercom. "Come up please; Zach told me to expect you." Sandy depressed the button next to the intercom, releasing the lock on the door two floors below.

Sandy opened the door, watching the two men as they walked out of the elevator. The shorter, younger one smiled and extended a hand. "Ms. Greer, I'm agent Brooks; this is agent Howard. The office sent us over to give you some additional security. I'm sure it's just precautionary; may we come in?"

Sandy, closed the door behind them. "May I get you water, tea, anything?" The blinding pain knocked her to the rug. She woke a few seconds later; her ear was throbbing from the hit she didn't see coming. She felt the soft Persian rug against her cheek, laying as still as possible, trying to understand. She knew the fault was hers. They never mentioned Arizona. Dammit, she thought.

She could hear the men talking. She heard the short one. "Get her up; put the shroud over her head. Make sure she can't see anything. She acted as limp as she could as the man shoved a gag in her mouth and placed a black shroud over her head, and everything went dark. The man smelled of cigarettes, garlic, clove. She tried to memorize everything she could as her training had told her to do.

She felt herself lifted, carried over the large man's shoulder, head down, swinging against his back. The shroud parted enough that she could make out the floor, then the elevator. Certainly, she thought, somebody would see them, help her, report it.

The elevator door opened, and she was carried through what seemed like a boiler or equipment room; she could hear machinery and see the concrete floor. A door parted and she could feel the cold air, smell recent rain. She was outside. The large man stopped, swung her around, and laid her down. Then a sound...and movement. She was in the trunk of a car, and panic crept through her.

CHAPTER 15

LANGLEY, VA

"How did this happen? Get Sarah working with Scotland Yard's camera complex." Shaw was in overdrive. He knew they had limited time before they changed vehicles. London has the most number of public surveillance cameras in the world, an estimated half a million. That would be a godsend now.

"Shaw, I have Scotland Yard on; they are tasking all cameras back thirty minutes in the area of Mrs. Greer's flat. Sarah Taskent's fingers flew across her keyboard as she managed four screens in front of her. She was Langley's best, perhaps the one who had made the most difference nearly eighteen months ago, when the terrorists were on US soil.

"There. The alley behind the flat. Only one car had been in and left the alley in the last thirty minutes. A black Mercedes, E-class. Partial license plate Seven Alpha One...three characters I can't make out. Fast forwarding now. There, the car is parking westbound on St. Johns, appears to be stopping in front of a warehouse in the Hounslow District, intersection of St. John and Wooten. Building on the southeast corner. Real time," Sarah repeated.

Shaw knew they were lucky...damn lucky. Zach had asked for protection, and the team was enroute to her flat when she was taken. The answer of how was elusive. No one knew Zach was alive outside the agency, Sandy, and a handful of Italian authorities. "Get me Inspector Fabrizio at Carabinieri Gruppo Speciale," Shaw told the room.

A few minutes later, Shaw was on the phone. "Inspector Fabrizio, Shaw Ellis here in Langley. We have an agent who was nearly killed two nights ago in Naples. Your men questioned him after he swallowed a large portion of the Mediterranean. There was an agency close-down on that information, but the word's gotten out. Less than a dozen people in the agency knew he was alive, perhaps that many on your end. We believe this may have something to do with the May Day attacks. That agent's wife was just kidnapped in London."

Inspector Fabrizio put the glass of chianti down and pushed away from his lunch at Armandos near the Pantheon. "Mr. Ellis, I will consult our people here and can assure you that you have our complete cooperation and attention. Can I ask you what your agent was doing in Naples?"

"Sir, he was following several parties who have financial links to accounts we believe may have a relationship to the terrorists behind the May Day attacks. It was a long shot until the attack on him and now, the kidnapping of his wife in London, a few minutes ago. No one outside a very small circle knew he was alive. She wouldn't have been taken unless they knew he was still in play," Shaw said.

"His wife? I will personally attend to the investigation. Let us know how we can support you." Inspector Fabrizio was deeply disturbed that the Americans had not involved him, that his office could be compromised, and even more that this was happening again on Italian soil. The terrorists who had struck America had come from Marseille and Milan. He hated what had happened to his Europe.

"Sir, video surveillance cameras show the vehicle is parked. Scotland Yard and MI5 are developing an action plan. There is a one-kilometer security blanket around the building. Drone is fifteen seconds out."

They watched the screen as the British surveillance drone showed real-time images of the building. The two-meter, battery-driven drone was nearly silent; the pictures were crystal clear. The drone dropped down to nearly roof level.

Shaw scanned the tactical plan that appeared on the screen. On a companion screen, schematics of the building appeared. The building was an open warehouse purportedly housing office paper products. There were very few internal walls, which would help the snipers who were gaining access to the third floor at this very moment. Time was on their side. The perpetrators would never expect to be located so soon, and never expect an operation to be mounted so quickly.

"Base One, Oversight One. Have taken up position above the main warehouse floor. One suspect in sight; woman is not visible. Repeat, captive is not located," the MI5 sniper team reported.

"Base One Oversight Two, two tangos in sight, no sign of the woman," the second sniper reported. Rule one was that eyes on the hostage was required before any assault could be planned.

The MI5 team arrived and began scanning the building for heat signatures. Three signatures were visible on the ground floor, another on the second floor. "Chances are the single signature is the hostage. If it isn't we can eliminate one threat without the others knowing. We can access that floor from the building next door; the rooftops adjoin. From there we can take this staircase to level two," the burly, red-haired MI5 Tactical Team Chief said, pointing at the schematics of the building floor plan. The other three operators looked over the floor plan and nodded. As if in unison, each started checking his weapons and gear.

Shaw watched the screen from 3,500 miles away. The distance resulted in a brief audio delay that made it more nerve wracking. Everyone in the office stared silently at the screen. It wasn't a normal operation. It was a dependent of one of their own on the line. It was personal, and they each knew it could happen to any of them. They watched the red heat signature and three blinking dots slowly walking down a staircase; those would be the tactical team members.

They could see the tactical team on the screen outside the door, and then nothing. Silence. Shaw could hear, no feel, his heart beating in his temples, when a voice came over the speaker. "Tango down, not—repeat not objective." Taking the body they proceeded back up the stairwell, hiding the body to avoid alerting the others.

"That means the objective has to be with the other two signatures," MI5 reported. It would be a blind assault. Flash bangs and stun grenades to disorient the hostiles. They were all in one room; it should go smoothly. They had trained for it a thousand times.

The team returned down the stairwell, this time branching into two teams of two, approaching the room where the heat signatures were from either direction. One operator slid a small camera on a flexible hose, no larger in diameter than a pencil, under the door. Retracting it he gave the sign of two hostiles and the captive.

Once again Shaw held his breath.

A kinetic battering ram breached the door and bright explosions erupted, followed immediately by gunfire. "Mrs. Greer. Mrs. Greer. British security forces. You're safe!" a voice far off seemed to say. Sandy's ears were ringing, and her vision was blurred by smoke.

"I'm okay. Oh dear god, thank you. I'm okay," Sandy muttered rubbing her eyes. "I need to talk with my husband. Can I talk with him?"

"Ma'am, Mr. Ellis of the CIA is on the phone. He'd like a word with you." The young operative handed Sandy a phone.

"Sandy, Shaw here. Are you okay?" Shaw asked.

"Yes. Yes. I'm fine. I need to talk with Zach, to tell him I'm okay," Sandy sobbed.

"Sandy, Zach isn't aware you were abducted. He's in the field. It all happened very quickly. He doesn't know. But without his intuition and request for your security, we would never have known you were abducted. We got lucky." He hoped his words would calm her. He knew she had been a trained national park ranger before meeting Zach. Law enforcement was a part of her training—even though, it was an ordeal she had been through.

"Shaw, they spoke in Arabic until one received a call. He spoke English over the phone. I think the person on the other end was a woman. He called her Marwa. She seemed to be in control. He deferred to her. She did most of the speaking." Sandy tried to remember any other details.

"Marwa? Okay, got it. Anything else you can recall, however insignificant it might seem, call me. For now, we are putting you up at the embassy. You'll be safe there. Sandy, I'm sorry this happened," Shaw said.

"Is it starting again?" Sandy said, her words trailing off.

"Starting? I think it never ended. You're in the middle of it because Zach is close to them. Close to bringing them out into the light. They're scared or they would never have gone after you...that, and Zach and you ruined their plan to cripple America two years ago. You'll be safe at the embassy. I have to go. Call me anytime," Shaw replied, disconnecting the call.

Shaw stared at the screens. They were close, but to what, to whom? "Get me Zach on the line," Shaw said. He heard the clicks of the encrypted satellite connection in his headset and then Zach's voice.

"Zach here."

"Zach, it's Shaw. First, she's all right. Sandy was abducted less than an hour ago. MI5 rescued her unharmed a few minutes ago. She's shaken up but otherwise unharmed."

Zach sat down, staring out at the sights of Capri. His mind was going in a thousand directions. "They know I'm alive. How? The Italians? First they try to kill me, now this. We must be close—no. *I* must be close, but to what? Did they capture any of them alive?"

Shaw replied. "No. One it seems shot himself rather than be taken. Zach, have you ever come across the name Marwa?"

"No. Not ringing a bell. But Shaw, think about it. According to Turner, Ratani's men received a call and looked directly at their concealed location. Someone tipped them off. Less than a handful of people know I survived. We can't ignore the possibility that they have someone on the inside. Remember the FBI mole two years ago. They've done it before, quite effectively," Zach said.

"Okay, let's assume that's the case. Let's flush them out. Who there knows you are in Capri?" Shaw asked.

Zach thought. The list was short. "Turner, Vargas, Marcella, Elle, your Langley team, the driver from the Rome consulate who took me to Sorrento, the boat captain who took me from Sorrento to Capri." Zach thought for a second. "Shaw, the Italian officials had no idea I was headed to Capri. As far as they are concerned, I got on the plane in Naples."

Six people, all trusted CIA employees. No way, Shaw thought. Both Zach and Shaw had arrived at the same deduction. "Zach, watch your six," Shaw said.

CHAPTER 16

Shaw sat waiting in the outer office. He hated this task. Franklin had warned him this was part—no *the*, most important task he had...briefing, nurturing, and controlling the White House. How in the world had Franklin done it? Four presidents. This was his first, and Franklin told him, his hardest. A president who for his first two years in office avoided foreign policy whenever he could now sought to control every element of it. On his watch two nuclear detonations on US soil. If he had any hope of completing a second term, he had to act decisively.

"Mr. Ellis, the president will see you now," the matronly secretary to the president said, walking him to the opening door.

"Shaw, good to see you again. You remember Director Tankersfell of the FBI; Admiral Weams of the Joint Chiefs; Kate Helmworth, my national security advisor; and of course Director Harrence, your boss." The president introduced Shaw to the room. He, of course, had met with and knew well everyone but Admiral Weams, the new chairman of the Joint Chiefs.

"Shaw, Director Harrence tells me that you have some recent developments? Where are we on nailing down Iran to the May Day attacks?" the president asked.

"Sir, your question assumes a point my information doesn't support. Our information points to a group other than Iran. It..." Shaw's words were cut off by the president.

"Not Iran? We aren't on the same wavelength here. *All* of our information points to Iran. The money transfer to the Caymans came from a man with Hezbollah ties. The ringleader of the Arizona attack was filmed with the former action commander of Hezbollah in Beirut. And our friends in Israel have linked the Milan cell that attacked New York to Iran's Quds brigade," the president said, pacing in front of the Oval Office's window.

"Sir, I've read the reports and don't find them supported. The Israelis want us to attack Iran. They are scared to death that Iran will get a nuclear weapon and even more scared of a preemptive attack on Iran alone. The picture of Akmed Halabi with Hezbollah's operational commander in Beirut was taken over a decade ago; bedfellows change alliances overnight in the Middle East. And the financial link to the Caymans came through London, where it could have been rerouted through any number of accounts. It is all too convenient. Our sources in Tehran, who to date have been very reliable, emphatically assure us that Iran is being set up. And Russia would love us to disenfranchise Islam," Shaw explained.

"Of course Iran's denying involvement; they want to live," National Security Advisor Kate Helmsworth said. "This is a distraction. We're here to authorize retaliatory strikes on Hezbollah and Iran under the congressional mandate we received over a year ago. Israel and Great Britain have been briefed. We are meeting with congressional leaders in the morning. The new moon is day after tomorrow. We will not have another opportunity to get our strike aircraft over these targets for another month."

Shaw calmly continued. "There's more. In the past twelve months, we've uncovered a previously unknown organization that isn't Shi'a in nature, which we believe is based in the Gulf...the Emirates or Bahrain."

No one in the room spoke; each pondered the implications. Admiral Weams spoke first. "The Gulf states clamp down on radical groups. How is it that they have been undetected? Who are they allied with, ISIL?"

"It's early in our investigation, but we believe they are *not* a radical Islamic group. There is reason to believe they have economic and geopolitical goals. They are using—perhaps manipulating is a better word—radical Islam for the goal of compelling us to strike Shi'a interests, Iran. People we have traced to this group include non-Islamic industrialists and financiers in Europe and the Middle East," Shaw replied.

The president walked to a couch and sat. Everyone waited for some word, some direction. Director Harrence looked to Admiral Weams, then the president. Kate Helmsworth sat, her mouth slightly agape. An awkward silence pervaded. Shaw knew he should continue. "We have been shadowing a billionaire prince from Bahrain who now resides in Abu Dhabi, who is connected with an Italian industrialist and a commodities trader in London. Two days ago we believe they tried to kill our agent who was watching them. He escaped. Earlier today his wife was abducted in London. MI5 rescued her. We believe that they have a mole in our agency security apparatus...precisely as they did eighteen months ago when they struck before."

FBI Director Tankersfell winced. It had been his agency the last time. "What are they after. What is their end goal. Who are they aligned with? Iran?"

"We aren't sure. The prince is Sunni, we have two intercepts between him and an Imam in Qatar who urges the destruction of Iran and is virulently anti-Shi'a. In those intercepts the word Twelver was repeated. It can be a derogatory term against anyone Shi'a. And the commodities trader has been making numerous currency and oil trades. Right before the attacks on the US, he shorted the dollar. Billions were made for his clients. He would have made even more if those attacks had fully succeeded. Recently he's been making trades against the ruble and deutsche mark."

"This is about money?" the president asked, rising from the sofa.

"It's too early to say, sir. They may be using the trader to finance the group's aims, which may well be religious-based terrorism. What this leads to is caution—caution in rushing to conclusions as to who was behind the

May Day attacks. Iran may well be the perpetrator, but if it isn't, attacking Iran without confronting the real enemy may be catastrophic, and precisely what this group has orchestrated," Shaw said.

"Sir, this is just a theory," Kate Helmsworth reminded the president. "We have actionable intelligence from the Israelis, a photograph of one of the attackers with a Hezbollah commander, and DNA tying one of the dead attackers to a brother now serving time for terrorism charges in England. If we don't get the go order in the next twenty-four hours, we will miss the attack window for another thirty days, and our forces are all ready and on-station."

The agency's director Harrence spoke up. "Sir, we need to flesh this out. The Israeli intelligence should be weighed against their overriding goal of seeing Iran prevented from obtaining nuclear weapons. There is sufficient doubt in my mind to suspend the operation and let the agency do its job."

The president's youthfulness was gone. Gray hair, which peeked out from his temples two years ago, now dominated. He stared out the Oval Office window, looking at the lawn and the Washington Monument in the distance. He heaved a sigh and turned to face everyone. "Mr. Ellis, you have three weeks. After that, we go with what we know. Admiral Weams, withdraw forces where you can, tell others they are on exercises...buy us another month. That's all, gentlemen."

CHAPTER 17

MILAN

Elle's security team took up positions in the restaurant, one at the far end of the bar with his back to the wall and the other dining alone in the restaurant section. Elle arrived a few minutes later and walked to the bar. She was dressed in her black leather pants, heels, a sleeveless black top, and a dark gray suede jacket with black leather collar and sleeves. The jacket concealed her compact Sig Sauer P239 weapon. She was hard not to notice.

The bartender came over immediately. "Prego signorina."

"Grey Goose on ice with olives please," Elle, now Andrea Hollinger, said, as she surveyed the restaurant in the mirror behind the bar. She saw her team and relaxed a bit.

"Welcome to Nobu, signorina. You are here on vacation?" a slightly built bartender asked.

"Business. I come to Milan frequently, but this is my first time at your restaurant," Elle responded.

Two men in overcoats entered the bar and looked around carefully. One held his hand under his coat, obviously having a weapon. The other appeared to speak into a microphone he held at his wrist. Elle's security team member at the bar held his weapon under the table, eyes fixed on the two. The door burst open, and four young girls in impossibly tight, short cocktail dresses and heels came in dragging a short, portly man of fifty into the bar. The man was grotesque: overweight, with a bulbous nose and pockmarked complexion. "Ne tyanite, devochki," the man barked in Russian and three of the girls let go. The other slid under his arm, a difficult task given his height.

They walked past the end of the bar and down a set of stairs in the corner of the bar. "Russians. They have no class. Please excuse them," the bartender said in a tone of distain.

"What's downstairs?" Elle asked.

"Armani Prive. It's a private club. Very expensive and very exclusive. If you wish I can ask my manager if you can see it," the bartender replied.

"Thank you. I am meeting someone for dinner that I believe is a member," Elle responded. She knew her team would not be able to protect her there. She would have to change her plan. She glanced over at her protection in the bar, who had reholstered his weapon and was again mastering a set of chopsticks.

The door opened and Niccolo entered the bar, smiling as he saw "Andrea." "I hope you haven't been waiting long. I had a bit of difficulty finding parking," Niccolo said.

Elle stood and asked the bartender, "Can you transfer my check?"

They walked to the maître de station. "Signore Attino. Ho una prenotazione alle nove per due. "

The Asian woman nodded and showed them to a table in the center of the restaurant directly in front of the other half of her protection detail. Good news, bad news, she thought. It would be hard to slip him something and flirt in the center of the restaurant.

"Thank you for letting me join you for dinner, Ms. Hollinger. This is one of my favorite places in Milano. Not Italian but with Armani fashion," Niccolo said.

"Please, call me Andrea. You can tell the Armani influence by the colors and textures. It is much different from the other Nobu restaurants I have been in."

They engaged in small talk as several courses were set in front of them. The restaurant was full when they sat down. She could see several tables had left for the downstairs night club. The waiter poured another glass of Biondi Santi Brunello. "I must excuse myself for a moment. I need to visit the restroom," Niccolo said.

Finally, she thought. He walked out of the room into the bar. Elle opened her purse and reached in the pocket for her lipstick. She removed a coated pill and dropped it into Niccolo's wine. It was manufactured to instantly dissolve with no residue, bubbles, or sediment. Far more sophisticated than flunitrazepan, or ruffie as it is called, this drug incapacitated gently as if a person was overwhelmingly inebriated and tired, with none of the incapacitating and amnesia effects.

She watched Niccolo stroll back to the table. "How about some dessert. They have a wonderful tiramisu here. It has an Asian influence. Or would you rather have a drink downstairs in the club? Armani Prive is a very special place. Excellent people watching," Niccolo said as he sipped his glass of wine.

"Dessert sounds perfect. Then perhaps the club if we are both feeling like it." She figured ten, maybe fifteen, minutes and the drug would take effect.

Dessert was finished, and he was still seemingly fine. She began to wonder whether the drug was going to work. "And now, we go to the club. All right?" he asked.

She would be alone at the club—no protection and no way of handling him when the drug kicked in. On the other hand, she needed him to drink more if the drug wasn't going to work. She figured it would take another fifteen minutes or so before the bill came and was paid. Hopefully by that time the effects of the drug would be felt. "All right, perhaps one drink; should we get the bill?"

"I already took care of it," he said, rising from his chair. He held her chair out, and she walked past her protection in the bar who looked at her with a slight frown.

They walked past the bar to the stairs that were carefully guarded by two men, a large bouncer-looking man and another slight, well-dressed man. Bouncer and fashion police she thought. One had to make the grade to get into this club. The men took one look at Elle and opened the felt barrier, never asking for Niccolo's membership card. They walked down the glass-and-steel stairs to the space below: a light-colored stone tile floor, modern aluminum décor with mirrors on every wall, and a series of roped-off seating areas along one wall with unreserved seating facing the reserved seating. Two of the young Russian girls were grinding against each other on one of the tables looking at themselves in the mirrored wall. An oversized bottle of Stolichnaya Elit Vodka sat on the other table before the grotesque Russian, who had the other two girls draped over each arm.

Elle looked at the booth next to them where two couples, each in their twenties were laughing and conversing with British accents while staring around at everyone else. One of the men at the table nudged the other, nodding for him to look at Elle. She smiled. "How about here." She sat down on a sofa across from the two couples.

The place was loud as music reverberated and all manner of entertainment surrounded them. The hip, ultrawealthy, and entitled. A waitress in white satin shorts with hose underneath stood in front of them with a drink menu. "Grey Goose please, rocks and olives," Elle said. Niccolo ordered grappa.

When their drinks were finished, Niccolo leaned over to speak. "Would you care for another..." His sentence faded, his right eye closed, his lips parted, and he slumped against her.

Elle threw fifty euros down on the table next to the drinks and caught the eye of the man sitting across from her who had not stopped staring at her. She yelled the six feet or so across to him. "Can you help me? My boyfriend is jet lagged and shouldn't have drunk. Can you help me get him upstairs? I don't want a scene."

The girls laughed while both men came to Elle's aid. Niccolo kept murmuring. "I'm sorry. I'm so embarrassed." Elle thought he should be proud; the drug and alcohol would have hit any other man long before this.

Niccolo struggled to stand and was supported by the two men and Elle. They walked back to the staircase and took the elevator. The elevator rose the one floor and the door opened. The bar was nearly empty. The security detail was waiting as they shoved Niccolo into the back of the waiting Fiat. "Thank you very much. His brother here and I can take it from here," Elle said to the men who turned and walked back to the elevator.

Elle got in the back with Niccolo. They pulled away for the Galleria.

Back at the Galleria, they pulled into an alley, and the larger one threw Niccolo over his shoulder, taking the steps to the third floor. They went to a room that had been set up with cameras and photographers' lights lining the bedroom. By now Niccolo was out cold.

They undressed him and placed him in various compromised positions with Renee, a transgender informant they often used in Milan. In Italy things were different. The traditional honey-pot scheme of blackmailing a husband's indiscretions with another woman didn't work. Affairs were expected. But an affair with another man, a man undergoing transgender sex-change surgeries—well, that was quite another story. He'd turn on Ratani and disclose the financial transfers; that was a certainty.

The next step was to get him dressed and back home. He'd wonder what happened in the morning, would remember bits and pieces and see his car out front, which he would assume he had had driven home.

Elle was exhausted. "You boys can take it from here. I'm hitting the sack. Tomorrow's a big day. I'll go to Niccolo's office in the morning when he arrives at work to show him his Oscar-winning film." Elle walked out and across the interior courtyard of the Galleria to the entrance of the Park Hyatt.

The team was just finishing dressing Niccolo when the first stun grenade went off, followed by a burst of silenced gunfire. The protection team was down, along with the agency photographer, Renee, and Niccolo. It was over in less than five seconds. Mark, the senior member of the team, managed to activate his microphone before taking his last breath.

Across the Galleria, Elle had just opened her hotel-room door when she heard the ear bud erupt in static, and then what sounded like a muffled groan. Then the sound of a unfamiliar, accented voice: "Make sure they are dead. Where's the woman?" Elle froze. Then in a burst of action, she threw her passport and what she could in fifteen seconds into a large over-the-shoulder bag. She put her black Puma workout shoes on and stuffed the heels she had been wearing into her purse and zipped it. She drew her weapon and looked through the security port and opened the door. She saw the elevator readout and saw the elevator car climbing to her floor and dashed for the stairwell, where she went up from the third to the fifth floor.

Getting to the hallway, she looked at her options. Rooms on each side and a maid closet across from the elevator. It was 01:45 and the hallway was quiet. She went to the end of the hallway and climbed out the window. One window over was a fire escape shared with the neighboring building. She threw her bag over to it and edged out on the ledge. She hated heights; she tried to tell herself not to look down. She made it halfway to the fire escape's railing when she heard voices in the hall she had just left. She leaped to the fire escape. The sound was deafening in the empty Galleria. She grabbed the railing and swung herself over, picking up her bag.

Suppressed ricocheting shots could be heard. She broke a window in an empty office with her bag and jumped in, falling hard on the floor covered in broken glass. She ran to the door, down the hallway, and down the stairs. It seemed forever before she reached street level. They would be waiting at the street. She threw the door open, crouching in a firing position. No one. She ran out the alley to the Duomo. There, a few people were still walking in the plaza. She briskly walked to the taxi stand and jumped in the first taxi. "Hotel Principe di Savoia, por favore." It was the first place she could think of and probably the last place she should go.

She texted Shaw. *Team attacked, all down, incl NA. On the run. Need extract. Will call in 15.*

The taxi drove down Via Manzoni, past the Armani store and Nobu where tonight started...when she had been in control. Think. Get a plan, she told herself. She slipped out of her running shoes and back into the heels that were in her over-the-shoulder bag, which carried everything she now had. It was okay, she told herself. She had her leather travel portfolio with her passport, cash, and credit cards. They would be hunting her. Using the cards would lead them to her, and they likely had bulletins to all hotels, which meant she couldn't use her passport to check into a hotel.

They'd be watching the US consulate. She knew she needed to stay ahead until the agency could get her out.

The taxi swung around the Plazza della Republica and pulled up to the ornate facade of the hotel. A doorman opened her door as she paid the taxi. "Mille grazie," she said in her best Italian. She walked up the steps and into the lobby, past the elevators, and into the main seating area. There she turned and walked out a second door back to the doorman. "Una taxi por favor." The doorman looked quizzically but whistled a cab.

Once in the cab, she told the driver, "Four Seasons por favore." She then Googled Expedia, which allowed her to search hotels by star rating. She'd pick a two-star hotel. They would only glance at her passport, and paying cash would not arouse suspicion. There, the Hotel Parco Sempione. "Scusi, l'hotel Parco Sempione por favore." The taxi driver shrugged and turned at the next light, never bothering to look back.

Her phone rang. "Elle, Shaw here. We have a team inbound. ETA two hours. You know what to do. Remember your training. Stay alive."

"I plan on it. I'll call you back on a land line in twenty with my location," Elle said, hanging up. With that, she removed the sim card from her phone and dropped it out the window.

Elle watched everything. Her senses alive, she looked in the rearview mirror for anything in the facial expression of the taxi driver. The taxi approached the Parco Sempione with its manicured grounds. She could see the hotel in the next block; she glanced behind her. No cars. She paid the taxi driver and got out at the park, a half-block short of the hotel.

The man behind the desk had greasy black hair and a stained shirt from what looked like tomato soup that was in a bowl next to a filled ash tray. "Prego, una camera con bagno." Elle hoped she remembered the words for a room with a private bathroom.

"Settanta euros," the man replied, leering at her. He hadn't seen a fine-looking woman in the hotel before. The women here were usually old... or hardened and rented. Elle handed the man seventy euros, and the man handed a key marked 43.

She walked past the elevator and up the stairs. She needed to see all points of access and egress, visualize escape options. At the fourth floor, Room 43 was two doors from the stairs. She opened the door and was struck by the stale scent of tobacco and musty carpet. The room was clean but dim. A single bed, desk, and wooden chair. The desk had a phone and old tube TV on it. The phone had a label in English, Italian, and German that read: *Local calls 3 EU. Long distance—charges plus 50% added to room.*

Elle dialed the number Shaw had dialed from. "Shaw here; you okay, Elle?"

A flood of emotions came over her. Exhaustion, anxiety...she teared up. This was unfamiliar to her; she was the one always in control. "I'm okay. They're all dead. Attino, the team. Two minutes earlier and I would have been there. I keep going through things, trying to find out how, when the breach occurred. The only thing I come back to is the night before I was followed from my hotel to where I had dinner. By a couple, male and female in their late twenties, early thirties. Pretty sure they were Russian."

"Russian? What else. Who could have come into contact with you tonight, perhaps planted a locator on Attino or you?" Shaw asked.

Elle thought. If it was after Attino met me at the restaurant, it had to be the men that helped me get Niccolo out of Armani Prive. "Niccolo did a face plant on me, and I solicited help getting him out of the club. There were two couples at the next table. But I was the one that initiated that. They couldn't have known I would sit there, or ask for their help," Elle said, thinking.

"First Zach, then his wife, now the team and you. This is beyond what the SVR would dare do. No, the Russians know this would escalate into hostilities. Whoever is doing this is *hunting* our agents...and they have exceedingly good intelligence. To do this requires surveillance methods and logistics that only a sophisticated nation-state intelligence apparatus possesses. Iran, Russia, China...not a terrorist organization," Shaw said, thinking out loud.

"Shaw, I want to stay in country. They know who I am and they want me. If I stay and am protected, it may be the only way to lure them out. They want me dead; they'll try again," Elle said, wondering to herself why she said it almost before her words were complete.

Shaw didn't say a word. He sat thinking. "Elle, I can't protect you. If we place enough security around you to protect you, they'll know it. You don't blend well. You're six feet tall and pretty noticeable. It's not like you can effectively go under the radar. You stand out in a crowd. It's better if you come out."

"Shaw, if I come out the trail ends. Right now they don't know what I know, what Attino gave me. It could be our only play," Elle said softly, almost pleadingly.

Shaw agonized. He knew they were both right. Shaw decided reluctantly. "The extraction team will stand down—all but one. Jay Setter is an operator in that team. He's Special Activities. Before that, he was Delta. He's your protection. He'll come to you. He will introduce himself with the line 'Are you Alice?' You are to reply, 'No, but I saw the rabbit.'"

Elle managed a laugh. "Seriously?" Shaw knew how to make her laugh even in the most dire of times. She needed that. For the first time in her life, she was scared. She had never been in real danger. Her life was in the London station or Langley. She'd been in the field before but never at any serious danger—certainly not when agents were being actively hunted as they had never been since the early days of the Cold War.

"Stay safe, Elle. Jay is the best. Do what he says and you'll get through this," Shaw said, disconnecting the call.

Elle sat on the edge of the bed, watching her hand holding the phone shake. She was trained. She knew what to do. She locked the door, checked the window, and was relieved to find no ledge anyone could use to get in that way. She placed two chairs in front of the door, obstacles to anyone storming the room. They weren't there to block, just to give a moment of hesitation—a moment she could use. She then turned off the lights and positioned herself on the floor in the far corner of the room, back against the wall. From there she could see the light in the hall under the door. If she saw a shadow, she would close one eye as she was told in case flash bang grenades were used, which could temporarily blind. The closed eye would be all she would need. She sat with her weapon and two spare clips, her eyes and ears alive to any sound or movement.

CHAPTER 18

LANGLEY, VA

Vladimir Vladimirovich Putin had neither looks nor height. At five feet seven inches, he was a dour thin-haired man outwardly projecting little. But charisma and ruthlessness have over history made men larger than life, made men followed. He had ruled Russia with the power of new money in a symbiotic relationship with oligarchs who he allowed to amass great wealth and who in return sponsored him.

But dynamics shift. A trifecta of low global oil demand, domestic energy independence in America, and tepid economic sanctions imposed by the West threatened this balance. The oligarchs were unhappy with the impact of sanctions and the siphoning of the budget to rebuilding Russia's military. And to this unease, Vladimir Putin was now doing what every ironfisted ruler of Russia had done before him: interjecting firm control. He had created an image of virility, of a bare-chested warrior...and to that he would remind those that challenged him of the days of Yuri Andropov's Fifth Directorate, which suppressed dissent through assassination and exile. First one, than another, of Putin's opponents were assassinated on the streets of Moscow.

Thirteen assassinations in as many years. Thirteen investigations. Zero trials and convictions. The message was clear: dissent would not be tolerated. Blame was of course assigned to various external causes, but people knew better: Dioxin poisoning of Victor Yushchenko, the anti-Russian candidate in Ukraine. Polonium 210 radioactive poisoning of Alexander Litvinenko on the streets of London, a former Russian spy and outspoken critic of Putin. As the Russian economy worsened, fear replaced money as the weapon to combat dissent. Putin's charisma and methods had elevated him far beyond his modest stature.

"There has been a noticeable shift here in the past eight weeks. Putin has replaced authoritarianism with dictatorship, whether people acknowledge it or not. The people we have always done business with are increasingly silent...or disappearing. I don't like it, Shaw. Things are...unpredictable. A year ago when the White House asked whether Russia was behind the attacks in the States, I scoffed. I'm not sure any more," William Staten, the agency's Moscow station chief calmly said over the secure video conference.

"Is there anything you've seen or heard to support the theory that Romenski was sanctioned by Moscow when he sold the nukes?" Shaw asked.

"No. Nothing," Staten replied.

"Any connection between Moscow and Ratani?" Shaw asked as a follow-up.

"Nothing we've seen. It also doesn't fit. Moscow has shifted to the Shi'a side. That wouldn't support a connection with Ratani. But what we are exploring is Moscow's assistance to the Quds. Word we have is that Russia's intelligence service, the SVR, is providing direct intel to Iran's Quds on US strategic planning, deployments, and targeting platforms. Maybe the White House's and Joint Chiefs' conclusions are sound. The cells did have a tie to Hezbollah," Staten added. It was a point that struck a chord. Iran's special forces arm, the Quds Force, had been suspected of intelligence sharing with Moscow.

Shaw wasn't prepared to make that leap. The facts were weak, the connections tenuous. "Two of our agents were attacked in the past two days in Italy. One reported that she was followed by a Russian-speaking couple the night before. We lost an entire security detail—four murdered. If Russia is behind this, it is beyond anything we have ever seen from them since the fifties. The implications are obvious. Tell your people to get us information and tell them to be careful." Shaw pushed back from the desk as the video conference went black.

"Sarah, where are we on placing Elle? Before we let the bad guys know where she is, I want a location that is impregnable. If she's going to be bait, we can't let anyone have a clean approach to her...and we can't let anyone get to her. Traps and double traps, everybody. Get on it," Shaw said to the room.

"Shaw, Joshua Marcus is on the line. He says to interrupt you. Line three," the intercom announced.

Shaw picked the line up. "Shaw here. What's happening Josh?"

"I'm in DC. We need to meet. What I have to say can't be said over the phone. Can you meet me in an hour? Café Milano, Prospect and Wisconsin. You know the place?" Josh asked.

"Yes, I know it, but we are in the middle of something here. I can't break away," Shaw said.

"I know you are. I heard about your people in Milan. Sorry. This is related," Josh replied.

Shaw's mind raced. How did Mossad know about Milan—so quickly? And what was related? "I'll be there."

"Sarah, get me a detail. I'm going to Georgetown. The OP in Milan stands down for two hours. That should give time to set up a site and strategic plan there. Tell Jay to keep Elle locked down. Get a minidrone from Aviano on station in two hours. And tell the Capri team to go silent till I return," Shaw ordered.

Everyone in the room was stunned. To leave at this moment, when so many balls where in the air, defied comprehension.

Shaw met his detail in the tactical room. It was a typical detail: a lead SUV with two protective agents and a second SUV driven by a third agency protective agent. They weren't expecting trouble, but after what today had shown, no chances would be taken.

The twenty-minute drive turned into forty. There had been a time, not that long ago, when the trip down 123 to the GW Parkway took fifteen minutes, when the public bus system dropped people off at the front door of the CIA. Those days of innocence, when our enemies were across oceans, were over. DC had become a transit nightmare.

Two black suburbans crossed Key Bridge and made their way down M Street. Shaw looked out, recalling the old days when Georgetown was a series of small bars and boutique shops. Now, it had lost its character; it was no different than any mall in any city. The same shops, the same storefronts one could find anywhere, in any city, any suburb. It had lost its uniqueness, its quirky avant-garde culture. The lead SUV carrying Shaw made a left off M Street at Wisconsin past the Apple store with its throngs. Shaw thought of the horrible day nearly two years ago when the bomb went off in the Manhattan Apple store killing hundreds, mostly young.

The cars came to a stop in front of Morton's Steakhouse and Café Milano, with its chic outdoor dining. The second SUV checked in at the valet parking stand, and the agent presented his credentials. The young attendant saw in large blue letters *CIA*. The attendant quickly cleared a space for both vehicles parked in front. One of the agents stayed with the cars while two went in with Shaw, taking up positions discreetly removed but within close proximity of their charge.

Joshua sat near the back of the dining room, away from windows, his back to the wall. Ever the cautious one, it was likely the reason he was still alive. "Josh, good to see you. I hope you haven't been waiting long," Shaw said, shaking Josh's hand. Josh's five-foot-ten-inch frame was fit, extremely fit for a man in his late forties. His squared jaw and green eyes telegraphed he wasn't just a handsome man, but a man of strength.

"Thank you for meeting me on short notice. I've taken the liberty of ordering for us as I need to get back to my embassy. I hope you like Maine lobster with linguini. I order it every time I get to DC. Your country's lobster can't be equaled," Josh said, pouring Shaw a glass of Les Charmes Meursault. "I've only ordered a half bottle; we have business to discuss, but I'm afraid you may feel as though we needed the full bottle after you learn what I have to say."

Josh continued. "One of our assets in the Emirates is looking into one of the major oil production and refining companies, Arabesco, Ltd. A number of its workers, young promising engineers, have been disappearing at an alarming rate. They are working on an industrial process to increase oil-refining efficiencies. Ordinarily that wouldn't be dangerous or even noticed, but a second asset in Berlin has been investigating a commodities and currency trading software platform being developed by a company you may be familiar with, KZT. A very large deposit, nearly four hundred million euros, was made by Arabesco, Ltd. to this KZT. You may also be interested to know that those funds originated from a London account managed by William Hecox for the benefit of Amir Ratani."

"Do you know what the trading platform is for and who it is designed to be used by?" Shaw asked.

"No, but the Arabesco employee claims that Waleed Muhannad al-Najm has paid two visits to Arabesco's offices in Dubai in the three weeks that he has worked there," Josh said.

"Waleed Muhannad al-Najm, in Dubai? He's ISIL's banker. He also has a five-million-dollar bounty on his head. What is Mossad doing with this?" Shaw asked.

"Nothing. That's the point. I'm bringing this outside of normal channels," Josh said, pausing as the waiter served them, and then continued. "There's more. Two brothers, who served in the Russian army, to be exact, in the Spetsnaz Vostok unit, are reportedly on Ratani's payroll as security and intelligence consultants. They've been mercenaries and now it seems are running a family business for hire. Mossad tracked them to Milan; they arrived there two nights ago. There's reason to believe they are the ones who killed your team."

"Are you tracking them now? Do you have a location on them?" Shaw asked.

"No. We tracked them two days ago from Bucharest to Milan, where they went into a café and never exited. We found later that they paid a waiter to exit the back door, telling the waiter that one of the men was being followed by a jealous girlfriend. They disappeared. Their pictures and background files are on this thumb drive." Josh handed the drive to Shaw.

"Again, I find myself thanking you. Is there anything I can do for you?" Shaw asked handing the waiter a credit card.

"Perhaps an apartment in your fair city if my superiors find out we've met on this. Our people are intertwined. There are those in my country who would withhold this information if it served Israel's interests. Withholding this information would be a betrayal that would rupture forever our countries' bonds," Josh said, swirling the Meursault and admiring its subtle taste of peaches and minerality.

Shaw sat thinking, quiet. He signed the check and rose. "Thank you, my friend. Perhaps the next time we can just sit and enjoy more than a glass."

Shaw walked toward the door, his two bodyguards closing to open the door. Once in the vehicle he inserted the drive in a laptop and called Langley. "Sarah, Shaw. I'm sending you files. Get them to Jay and Elle. The two men on the drive are their attackers. I want at least one alive. Have the tact team stay concealed two blocks away. These guys are good; I don't want the trap blown."

CHAPTER 19

MOSCOW

Vladimir Putin stood at the window staring out at the lifeless trees, their bark painted white from the wind and the snow. Even by his standards, Aleski Tuperof's plan was daring. If successful, it would lead to the accomplishment of his legacy, the reconstitution of the Russian empire, and the marginalization of American influence. If it failed—well, the consequences for Russia and all those involved could be fatal.

The West had not acted when Russia seized Crimea; and it had not acted when Russia invaded eastern Ukraine. Europe's resolve was weaker than its appetite for cheap natural gas. After fifteen years of war, America's will for confrontation was broken. But he knew history. The winds of sentiment changed quickly in America. If ever there was a time to act, it was now when America was withdrawing around the world.

"Aleski, your plan is bold, but very dangerous. Russia must support Assad at all costs; there must never be a Gulf States natural-gas corridor through Syria; it would break our control over Europe. Iran is an unknown. They are not predicable, not controllable. Russia is a large trade partner, but Iran's strength in Lebanon, Yemen, and Iraq may embolden it to break away from our control. Iran must understand that Russia is its only defense against Israel and America," Putin said, pacing.

Aleski Tuperof said nothing, watching Putin, listening for any inflection in his voice that would provide insights into what he was really thinking.

"Care must go into the most dangerous element: distracting NATO. There can be no linkage with Russia. How is it that you intend to accomplish this?" Putin studiously asked.

"Agreed, Mr. President. The Americans are focused on Iran as the origin on the attacks on their country. America's withdrawal from Iraq has caused a vacuum Iran has filled. There are some in America who believe that the nuclear weapons that Romescki provided to the terrorists were sanctioned by Russia. And there are those that believe Russia has acted with Iran. We must act to direct the Americans away from Iran and Russia. This can be done by creating linkage with Sunni elements, ISIL in particular. That fits well with our goal for NATO; NATO countries must be distracted by the threat of terrorist events within their own borders," Aleski said.

CHAPTER 20

CAPRI

Zach had slept for nearly four hours. He woke to the smell of coffee, startled...looking around for familiarity. Slowly it came to him. Capri, with Marcella. "It's getting to be daylight. Vargas and Turner must still be locked down with Ratani's men around them. The observers are now captives. We have to break that lock, get them to a more secure location *while* we keep an eye on Ratani."

"Here, take this." Marcella handed him a caffé, two shots of espresso. "I have an idea. There's a small bar close to Ratani's yacht. It seats no more than ten. I have been there before at night. It has large speakers and is a place people go for a wild happy hour. For a few euros, I am sure the bartender would blare music early this morning. It would be met with complaints by those on the dock and Ratani's men. It should be enough for Vargas and Turner to exit their position in the commotion and reposition themselves. What building are they holed up in?" Marcella asked.

"It's worth a try. How long was I asleep? Have you heard from Langley or London?" Zach asked, his thoughts clearing with the infusion of caffeine.

"Yes, Vargas has been in contact and they're fine. Ratani's been seen on the back of the boat, as has Hecox. Vargas said the electronics are operable, but so far nothing has been heard as to their plans or destination. If they decide to embark before we hear that, we will still have their locator transponder but no audio when their engines are operating and they're underway," Marcella said as she washed the espresso machine and wiped the sink.

They straightened the apartment to remove evidence of their stay and walked out. A crisp, clear day. The sun was clearing the Capri cliffs, warming the stone surfaces it touched. The cool air smelled of flowers and lemons; lemon trees were planted seemingly everywhere. A few shopkeepers were arriving at their businesses, rolling up metal grates, unlocking doors, placing wares out. Several early-rising tourists strolled about, peering into the closed shops.

They walked to the square where taxis sat waiting to take departing tourists down the hill to the ferry. Marcella directed the driver to the café. Zach called Vargas. "We're coming your way. You like music?"

"What, you going to sing for me?" Vargas responded.

"Just get ready to exit. We'll meet at a trattoria a hundred meters or so west of your location. It has a sign in the window you'll recognize as home." Zach smiled to himself.

"Roger that, Sinatra." Vargas disconnected. "Get packed up, Zach's going to serenade our way out of here," he said to a puzzled Turner.

Zach saw three of Ratani's men as he stepped out of the taxi: one on the aft of the yacht, one in the café behind the yacht, and another thirty meters further down the dock standing next to a vendor who was setting up shop. He pulled the brim of his cap down low and put his arm around Marcella's shoulder, strolling past the yacht and the café where the burly man sat. Two doors down he saw it: a bar with three bar seats and three tables in front. "Bar Pompeii" the sign said. No one was there except a young man behind the bar in his midtwenties with a week-old stubble of a beard and short black hair. He was cutting lemons behind the bar, no doubt setting up for what he hoped would be a busy afternoon.

"Boun giorno, vorremmo parlare con voi?" Marcella asked as she leaned forward and whispered to the young man.

The man looked back quizzically and replied. "Five hundred euros. They might shut me down for a day; I could even lose my job," the kid said in perfect English, adding, "This is for a video?"

"Five hundred it is. Wait fifteen minutes; we'd like to go get our camera set up," Zach said, handing the young man five crisp bank notes.

Zach started to turn and leave when the bartender asked, "What music do you like?"

"Anything, as long as it's loud and sudden. Heavy metal maybe," Zach replied.

Marcella and Zach once again strolled back, past the yacht and the scrutinizing eyes of the men. Zach again pulled his hat's brim down against the top of his dark glasses. He saw Marcella stare at the man on the stern of the yacht and whispered in her ear. "Don't make eye contact. Don't look at them."

Marcella whispered back. "To go past such a yacht and not look would be more suspicious."

Zach considered her reply. It made some sense, perhaps more sense... still it was an unnecessary risk. They finished walking the length of the small dock and walked toward the trattoria when the quiet dock erupted to Van Halen's "Jump." Not exactly heavy metal, but it'd do, Zach thought. The man on the stern of the yacht went down on one knee, gun drawn. Everyone on the dock was staring in the direction of the bar, including all of Ratani's sentries.

They walked for a tense, very long minute to the restaurant when the music stopped as abruptly as it started. Marcella laughed, looking at Zach. "I wonder if the local police silenced him or if Ratani's men shot his speakers up?" Zach responded with a big smile as they entered the Trattoria Casa.

Turner waved from a table near the back. They walked back as Turner stood. "That was slick. We were getting pretty tired of being stuck in that building. A couple of Ratani's men were stationed below us in the next building literally sitting in the doorway. Vargas here crept down and bugged the hallway where they were. They are evidently pulling anchor at 20:30 hours. Sunset is at 19:15 tonight, so they must be thinking they won't be visible to satellites."

"The locator beacon is in place on the hull, right?" Zach asked.

"Yes. We'll be able to track them for the next four days, then the batteries give out," Vargas added.

"Well that gives us the day to figure out what they're up to and position assets. Are the audio receivers on the hull giving us anything?" Zach asked.

"No. They're functioning; we hear small talk but nothing of detail. It's almost as though they know not to talk when we they go down below. The conversation appears...I don't know...staged," Vargas said.

The waiter came over and each ordered a large lunch, salads, zuppa, and pasta. Turner ordered a beer.

"I'll talk with Langley, but this seems like we aren't getting anywhere. I say we grab either Hecox or Foltz when they go onshore. Convince them to work with us or end up on an extended vacation," Zach said.

Turner shrugged mild approval while Marcella sat mouth open before speaking. "You're not serious are you? Kidnap a well-connected Italian industrialist in Italy? A man that has regular lunches with the Italian Prime Minister?"

"He's also on a terrorist's yacht, a yacht that tried to have me killed. And yes, he is the one I would target. He's older, out of shape, privileged, and has no family, all of which taken together means he would be the most vulnerable. Hecox is arrogant; he'd feel like he could control his situation," Zach replied.

Marcella sensed he was right, but the idea of capturing someone like Foltz was incredible. "Don't you think we should run this by Langley first?" she asked.

"Yes, I *think* we should...but I'm not going to. I know what they'd say," Zach replied. He stared into Turner's eyes, who knew all too well what would be involved if this idle talk materialized into action.

Vargas brought them to reality. "Listen, this is outside my field. I'm just an electronics kind of guy. But we *are* on an island. If something doesn't go as planned, we have limited options. Maybe now...or rather, *here* is not a good place."

Zach knew he was right. Without a plan and additional assets in place it was risky. "Okay, what other options do we have? These guys are going God knows where in a little over nine hours. We can't very well follow them around the Med while they bang young prostitutes on board their super yacht—sorry Marcella. We don't have time. DC is marching to war, and something tells me it's against the wrong player. I'll talk to Shaw."

Zach walked outside to make the call. Just outside the door, he saw Foltz. Alone. He couldn't believe it...he was walking toward him, with no one in tow. Zach called Turner. "I'm outside the restaurant. Foltz is walking toward me from the dock. He'll be next to me in sixty seconds. I'm not shitting you! What's the call?"

Turner jumped up and went back through the kitchen and out the back door, to the shock of the staff. He looked at the alley and went to the back corner of the building. "No joy, it's too public. Follow him down the block. I'm in the alley walking parallel; let me see what I see." Turner called Vargas and filled him in.

Foltz walked by the trattoria and Zach, who was leaning against the building talking in English into his phone. "Yes, honey, I'm really where we were in Capri just last year." Zach put headphones in one ear and dropped his phone into his pocket, slowly following behind Foltz. He stopped and looked in a storefront surveying behind him and across the street. Unbelievably Foltz was on his own...unless these people were really good and Zach missed his tail.

Zach's phone rang, and the familiar sound of Turner's voice came alive. "Zach, there's an alley coming up. I'm in it. Only one storefront, and it's a tailor; no one out front. If we're doing this, it happens here. There's a dock across the street. If we can get him to a boat, we can get him out of the marina."

This was beyond risky. But it was sudden and bold...and time was running out. Zach made the call. "Do it. No one's behind me. I'll push him into the alley; get ready."

Zach saw the alley coming up and increased his pace. He timed passing Foltz with the alley. He brushed against Foltz right as he walked across the alley, pushing him into Turner, who instantly had his left hand over Foltz's mouth and his right hand over his flabby throat, applying pressure to his carotid artery. With blood flow stopped, Foltz fainted into Zach's arms, going down softly to the ground.

"Son of a bitch, this guy's heavy!" Zach said.

"Too much fine living. Help me get him up and behind this dumpster," Turner said. They carried him behind the dumpster, and Zach took off his shirt, then his undershirt. He ripped the T-shirt into two strips, tying the smaller one as a gag and the other around his wrists. He removed his belt and cinched his feet tightly together, finishing as Foltz began to recover consciousness.

A wild look appeared in the man's eyes: fear as he hadn't ever experienced. Turner saw it and smiled at Zach before confirming Zach's call to target Foltz. "Right call, man."

Zach looked at him sternly. "Calm down. Cooperate and you *may* live. Struggle, yell out, or try to escape, and this will be your last day on earth. Capisci?" The man nodded, his eyes wide with fear.

Turner's earpiece came alive with the sound of Vargas's voice. "I've got a boat. Two docks to the west, third slip. Blue-and-white twenty-one-foot cuddy cabin."

"Okay, here's what we are going to do," Turner said, his teeth clinched in Foltz's face. "You and me, we are going to walk across the street to a boat. If you do anything, say anything, I'm going to shove this knife into your left lung, which is going to produce two things. First, it's going to be incredibly painful. Second, your voice will stop instantly as you gasp to fill your punctured lung with air. You'll live for a while, but just long enough for you to tell us what we need to know."

Foltz's wide eyes teared as he nodded he understood. Zach walked back to the restaurant, leaving Turner in the alley. He paid the bill and told Marcella to come with him. He grabbed an open bottle of wine from behind the bar and walked out.

Marcella and Zach walked down the block, turning in the alley. Marcella's eyes went wide seeing Foltz. Not having an earpiece, she had no idea what had been going on. "Who's that?"

"That's Mr. Foltz," Zach replied. Marcella stared, speechless. Zach bent down and removed Foltz's gag and ties, replacing his belt. "I'm going to walk out across the street, the two of you are going to take this bottle and walk across the street to the boat. It's already been explained to Mr. Foltz what happens if he utters a word. Here, Foltz, you carry the wine," Zach said. Turner pricked the side of Foltz's ribs with his knife, who reacted in terror.

Zach walked across the street, watching each way. He whispered into his mike, "All clear. Remember, one big, happy party; now walk." With that, Turner yanked Foltz close, the three walking out of the alley so close to each other they stumbled, looking the part of drunk tourists. Turner had one arm around Foltz, the other with the knife pressed against his side. Foltz stumbled in fear, holding the bottle.

Zach scanned the people on the street; a few glanced in disapproval of their public inebriation. They walked down the dock and onto the small boat, where turner shoved Foltz's pudgy body through the small door of the cuddy cabin. "Give me a hand; take in the lines on your side of the boat. Then get down low in the boat, just Vargas and me visible; everyone else take a seat low in the boat or the cabin," Zach told Marcella.

Marcella did so as Vargas started the engine and backed the boat out of the slip. They idled out of the small harbor, within sight of Ratani's massive yacht and adjacent tender, bristling with men scanning the harbor and shore. Zach hoped the boat's owner was not looking as the small boat made its way past the jetty. They were most vulnerable now, idling out of the marina. They would never be able to outrun the tender's zodiacs, and Zach didn't want to try to elude them a second time in broad daylight.

The small boat accelerated up the coast around the northeast edge of the island to get to the Piccolo Marina Zach had landed on just a day before. They were winging it, and that concerned Zach. It would only be a matter of time until the boat was reported missing, and with only two harbors— well, it wouldn't take long to find them. First a body in the marina and then a boat gone: the locals would scour the channel between the island and mainland. They had to switch boats or get ashore quickly. Vargas was talking with Langley on the satellite phone. He could tell by the one-sided conversation there was some displeasure on the other end of the line.

Vargas hung up and swung the boat to port toward Sorrento. The windswept waves' whitecaps sprayed over the small boat as they made for open water, as he turned his head and yelled to the others. "Change of plans. The agency's asset in Sorrento is being dispatched to meet us. I think he's the one that ferried you here, Zach."

"Good, but that's an open boat, no cabin. It's going to be difficult to get Foltz on shore," Zach replied, realizing that they hadn't thought through the plan.

They motored for nearly an hour before another boat was seen on a course to intercept them. Zach recognized the blue boat as it approached, slowed, and came alongside. Vargas threw two bumpers over the edge and tied the boats together. The boats wallowed violently on the swells as Turner transferred Foltz to the other boat. Then each boarded the other boat. "We should scuttle the boat so it's not found," Turner said.

"No. Stand here and take the wheel. A man's boat is his livelihood," Sep said as he boarded the smaller boat. He tied the steering wheel to the throttle housing, aiming it back at Capri, then straddled the two boats, one foot on each boat's railing and instructed the others. "When I say, untie the two lines at the same time." Turner untied the lines from the two cleats and held the boats fast together with one line. "Now!" Sep yelled as he moved the throttle into forward, stepping back onto the larger boat. The small boat started slowly motoring back in the general direction of Capri.

No one said anything as the boat made its way toward the cliffs of Sorrento, turning south along the coast and around the Scoglio a Penna, the northern tip of the Amalfi coast. The air had warmed and the sun accentuated the beauty of the shore. Red-azalea-covered cliff estates perched high on the edge of the cliffs. The Amalfi coast was perhaps the most picturesque in Italy and seemingly the most difficult to land on.

After another hour the boat approached a small beach with fine graveled shore. No more than ten meters wide and five meters deep, it resembled a small oasis set against towering, steep cliffs. The boat waited until the seas calmed and rode a small wave into shore, easing bow first onto the pebbled shore. "I'll hold the boat in place; no place to dock it. Everyone off here, hurry," Sep yelled over the sound of the waves washing against the rock cliffs precariously on each side of the small boat.

They pushed Foltz toward the bow of the boat as Turner jumped down onto shore. He reached up to give a hand to Foltz, who stared around and down the four feet to shore. He froze. "It's too far; I can't jump. I have bad ankles," Foltz said. Zach pushed him off from behind. Foltz rolled when he hit the ground. He reminded Zach of a sea lion wallowing onto shore. Zach reached up and helped Marcella down. Her bag fell off her shoulder and into the small surf. She yanked it up but it was too late, its contents soaked.

Looking around, they saw five steps cut into the cliff leading to a small cave. Inside the cave were a table, stacked beach chairs...and an elevator. "Well, that's damn convenient. Zach, come with me. Everyone else stay here," Turner remarked.

Zach and Turner stepped into the small elevator, which was adorned with a mural of the Amalfi coast, and pushed the single button. They could feel the elevator rising. One side of the elevator had an ornate metal grate allowing a view of the wall of the limestone shaft as the elevator rose through the hollowed-out cliff. The elevator slowed. Turner's and Zach's weapons were drawn, waiting for the door to open.

The door opened as Turner stepped out gun drawn, sweeping left to right. They pivoted around the circular foyer. White walls were adorned with paintings of different regions in Italy. The floor was white Carrera marble. A two-story ornate domed ceiling rose above them with a huge crystal chandelier.

They moved room to room slowly, pausing at every choke point. Going through the kitchen, Zach opened a door onto a large empty garage. "Doesn't look like anyone's home," he whispered.

"Hell of a safe house," Turner whispered back. They walked up a flight of stairs. Six large bedrooms each with verandas perched out over the sea below. Another set of stairs led a half floor up onto an open terrace where a large infinity swimming pool sat on the edge of the cliff. "Okay, I'm impressed. The agency must really like you, Zach!"

Zach smiled. "I'll go get the others."

As the elevator door opened, Marcella stepped out, followed by Vargas, who dragged Foltz out of the elevator, dropping him unceremoniously on the marble foyer. "Wow, this is more like it!" Vargas said.

Zach walked out of the elevator last just as his phone vibrated. Shaw's familiar voice came on the line. "Don't get used to the place. And don't damage anything...it's on loan from a friend in Rome. We'll have an extract for you tomorrow, but in the meantime, you should be safe there."

"Thanks, sir. Sorry for all this but Ratani was scheduled out tonight, and we don't have time to play cat and mouse with him. The opportunity just...presented itself," Zach said. He was rather certain the agency was none too pleased with his initiative.

"I don't disagree with your decision, although I am in the minority on that here. Foltz is well connected. His abduction is sure to result in a manhunt for him. More importantly, it may well tip off Ratani and make him go to ground," Shaw said.

"I've thought about that. But Shaw, Foltz will break. He's scared out of his mind. He pissed in his pants for God's sake. He knows what Ratani's up to...I guarantee it," Zach said.

"Okay, get to work on him. You have till the morning. We'll start developing a plan to reinsert him in a way that doesn't spook Ratani," Shaw replied and hung up.

Zach looked around the posh mansion, walking into where Turner and Vargas stood at a French door that led out onto a veranda draped in flowers. "We're good here for the night. Extract tomorrow. We have until then to get Foltz to talk. He doesn't sleep; he doesn't eat. Water only. Physical persuasion to a minimum; no marks. He needs to be reinserted. He's scared; exploit his fear. I'll take the first shot. Turner, set up a defensive plan just in case. Vargas, you play good cop," Zach instructed. "Where's Marcella?" Zach added.

"She's checking things out upstairs. Foltz is restrained in the upstairs east bedroom," Vargas said.

Turner saw that setting up a defense was going to be difficult. The mansion was set into a rocky hillside. A gated driveway no more than thirty feet long led to a garage and front door. The house was open to the rear overlooking the sea, but the only access besides the elevator down to the sea was the front door. Keeping that secure required someone to be outside the home on the rocky cliff the home was built into.

"It's three hours till sunset...I'll take first watch. Vargas, you relieve me at eight; in the meantime get some food and sleep," Turner said, unlocking the front door and walking out.

Zach walked upstairs and saw Marcella sitting in one of the bedrooms at a desk. "You all right?" Zach asked.

"Yes, just going through the contents of my purse. It fell in the water. My phone's shot," Marcella responded, she sounded frustrated...angry.

"No phones is better. Get rid of the sim card. Get some sleep; you'll have to take a turn on watch tonight—plan on midnight. We're on four-hour watches," Zach said as he moved down the hall to where Foltz was confined.

Zach opened the bedroom door. Foltz sat on the floor, hands behind him around a bedpost. With his ankles bound and the weight of the bedpost, he wasn't going anywhere. That restraint would never have kept an operative confined. That told him something more about Foltz.

"Giovanni. That is your name I believe. You're probably wondering why and, more importantly, who we are." Zach let that sit before continuing. "I have orders to kill you if you don't give me everything I need. Silent, you're of no use. On the other hand, you aren't important enough to be killed. That's good news for you. It means that if you talk, you live."

Giovanni Foltz sat in his soiled pants, his bulbous face bloated with fear. "I'm a rich man. If it's money, I can arrange that," he said in his thick northern Italian accent.

"I'm not interested in money. I'm interested in information. Information on the group that calls itself the Gulf Service. Information on your friend, Ratani," Zach said.

Foltz swallowed hard before answering. "I know nothing of this Gulf Service you mention. I have done business with Ratani three or four times. He invited me to his yacht to present a business opportunity."

"I'm only going to say this one last time. If you lie to me, if you are no use to me, then you will die in this room," Zach said low and in a measured tone, staring into the man's eyes. He could tell Foltz was lying: his pupils and breath revealed it. A trained individual could mask the telltale quickening of heart rate and breath, and not allow his eyes to react. Foltz had never been in this position, probably never been the one not in control. He was readable.

Zach reached out and took Foltz's hand, turning it palm up, and with his other hand touched it. "You can tell much about a man from his hands. You've never done anything with your hands; they have the tone of a baby's. Your palms are warm, moist. You aren't an effective liar. What will it be, Foltz?"

"I swear, I haven't ever heard of this Gulf Service thing. Ratani invited me to Napoli because he said he wanted to discuss a business venture in Italy. He and I were both investors in a hotel project some years ago in Milano, and we've kept in touch. That's all," Foltz said pleading, tears welling up in his eyes.

"I'm going to step out for a few minutes. Take that time to reconsider your choices. If I don't have the answers I require in two hours, then I'm done with you...another man walks through that door. That man is experienced in...what's the nice name for it...*enhanced* interrogation. We both know you won't be able to endure that. And after he's done—well, my ability to reinsert you into your normal life will be gone. I'll let him carve you up for the fish," Zach said turning and walking out, closing the bedroom door behind him.

Zach walked next door into the adjacent bedroom, where Marcella was staring at a laptop, which showed a fidgeting Foltz in the next room. "Are you really going to kill him if he doesn't talk?" Marcella asked.

"He'll talk. Sooner than later. He's not the type to withstand pain, physical *or* mental. I'll let him sit for thirty minutes and go back in. My guess is that the moment Turner walks through the door, he'll talk. You should get some sleep before your watch tonight," Zach said, staring at Foltz on the screen.

Zach walked into the kitchen and opened the large stainless refrigerator. Whoever owned the place hadn't been around in a while. Canned juices, bottled pesto, butter, pressed garlic—not much else. He opened the freezer: three boxes marked *salciccia*. Ahh, he thought to himself. If only... He walked into the pantry and was rewarded with two stainless canisters filled with tagliatelle pasta and a six-litre can of crushed tomatoes. Two birds with one stone, Zach thought.

He found a large pot and filled it with water for the pasta, adding salt as the water filled. He then found another large pot and heated some olive oil, garlic, and the large can of tomatoes, and placed an entire box of salciccia in the pot and covered it, turning the stove on low. He knew the sausage would unfreeze and while doing so fill the residence with an aroma that would torture their fat captive even more. No one had eaten all day; everyone but Foltz would at least have a good dinner to replenish for whatever tomorrow would bring.

Zach walked back into where Foltz was. "Okay, Foltz, what have you remembered about Ratani?"

Foltz hung his head down, not looking at Zach. "He's from Bahrain but lives now in Dubai and Switzerland. I think he came from wealth but has amassed a large empire based in the Gulf: oil transshipping, petrochemicals, fertilizers, I believe. He has very serious security that is all around the boat and him. He's devout Sunni...doesn't drink, doesn't smoke. As far as I can tell, he doesn't even partake of women. I arrived in Napoli two days ago and have been treated like a king on his yacht, but so far he's not mentioned anything about why he invited me. I swear, that's all I know about him, and I never have heard of this *Service* you describe."

"Let's start with who contacted you and when. Did he call himself, use an intermediary, what?" Zach asked.

"His financial advisor, who I've dealt with in the past, extended the invitation," Foltz said.

"William Hecox?" Zach asked.

Foltz raised his head, surprised at how much Zach must know. "Yes, he's from London. He called me three or four weeks ago and told me of the invitation. He said Ratani had a very interesting proposition that would increase my holding company's revenues by over fifty percent. Naturally, I was interested."

"What do you know about Hecox?" Zach asked.

"His fund averages high returns: well-connected, arrogant, and can't be trusted. Whatever you make on your money, you know he's made more. St. Andrews graduate, I believe; Oxford financial degree of some sort. His fund is heavily weighted in commodities, oil, currencies, agribusiness...the things no one can do without," Foltz said, relaxing a bit.

"What's the relationship between Hecox and Ratani?" Zach continued.

"They do a lot of business together. Hecox places a lot of Ratani's money in his fund and I believe, what's the word, *directs* even more in other funds and investments run through his investment house. That's all I know, I swear," Foltz said.

"That's a start. But I know you've been working—investing, or whatever—with Ratani and Hecox for at least two years. Money has been passing between Berlin, London, and Milan...money you have knowledge of. Right after the attacks on America, large sums were transferred from Hecox to accounts you have control over in Switzerland and the Caymans. So I'm going to ask you one last time, tell me everything you know about the Gulf Service," Zach said with an icy detachment.

Foltz stiffened; he paused before responding—just enough of a pause for Zach to know what Foltz was about to say wouldn't be the truth. "Hecox trades much of my company's money. I'm not aware of what or how much he trades on a day-to-day basis. I look at annual returns, that's all. If you say Hecox transferred large sums into my account, then it had to be a trade he arranged. He is the one you should be talking with."

Zach looked into his eyes, turned, and shook his head, before responding to Foltz on his way out the door. "Good-bye, Mr. Foltz. You can die with your silence—you are of no use to me."

Zach closed the door and walked back into the kitchen. The pasta water was boiling, and he opened two packages of pasta and dropped them into the water, stirring the sauce, which by this time had married with the slow-cooked sausage. The aroma pervaded the residence. Vargas walked into the kitchen. "Damn, that smells good. It woke me up! How long till it's ready?"

"It's almost ready; you take the first bowl. I wanted to get it done before the next watch so everyone can eat," Zach said, glancing down at his watch before continuing. "Turner can have his when his watch is over."

"Oh man, that's good. I haven't eaten all day. Zach, you missed your calling. You could've been a chef!" Vargas said, never looking up from his bowl.

Zach watched Vargas devour the pasta. Just then Marcella walked in. "I didn't know you were such a cook. By the smells, it seems you have mastered Italian cuisine!" she said.

Zach smiled and responded, "You haven't tasted it yet."

"Any progress with our guest?" Vargas asked in between bites.

"A bit. Says he was invited by Ratani, through Hecox, to be introduced to a new deal. Claims he doesn't know anything about the Gulf Service. He's withholding. He knows a great deal more. I told him he was of no further use without more. I'll let him worry about that some and have Turner go to work on him," Zach said.

Zach began filling bowls for Marcella and himself.

"Vargas, when you get done, I want you to take the next watch. Send Turner in for some food. Marcella, you relieve Vargas in four hours, then wake me. Turner and I have some work to do with Foltz," Zach said.

A few minutes later, Turner was sitting at the table, head down and focused on his pasta. Looking up he commented to Zach, "This place is a defensive nightmare. If someone hits us, we have only two options: fight room to room or get down the elevator to the beach and let them come to us. The problem with that is once we go down, we are trapped down there with no boat."

"Langley seems to think we're safe for the night. You and I need to work on Foltz," Zach said. Turner finished the bowl of pasta and nodded to Zach to get on with it.

Turner entered the room alone. Foltz looked up expecting to see Zach and was at once terrified. Turner walked over to him without saying a word and cut the flex cuff, pulling him to his feet.

"What are you going to do? Where are you taking me?" Foltz managed to say.

Without saying a word, Turner took him out of the bedroom and onto the stone veranda with the Mediterranean far below. Turner pushed him against the ornate wrought-iron railing before finally speaking. "Climb over and fly."

"Fly? What...what do you mean?" Foltz blathered.

"I mean jump," Turner said staring into the sobbing man's eyes.

"What! No, I can't," Foltz sputtered.

"I was hoping to avoid picking your fat ass up and throwing you over," Turner said in a growl. He reached for Foltz and grabbed one leg, raising it off the ground.

"Wait, wait! I'll talk, I'll talk. I have information—let me talk to the other man!" Foltz screamed.

Zach stepped out of the bedroom's French doors onto the veranda. "I'm listening."

Foltz dropped to his knees, crawling away from the railing. "Ratani's a member of a group. They call themselves the Twelfth Gulf Service. They're very powerful. They control governments. They're using markets and groups to get what they want."

"What do you mean *markets*, and what groups?" Zach asked.

"ISIL. Al Qaeda. They use them. They use them to gain advantages in commodity markets. They've even used Russia. Most of the time those being used don't even know they are being used. The group has members all over the world: Europe, China, Middle East, even your country. Twelve members." Foltz rattled on excitedly.

Zach interrupted him to ask. "Twelvers doesn't refer to Shi'a?"

"It does in a way. The same way there were twelve disciples of Jesus, twelve Olympians of Ancient Greece, twelve tribes of Israel, the twelve knights of King Arthur's roundtable...they view themselves as above any national or international law—outside looking in."

Zach considered the answer for a few seconds before asking another question. "Are they an Iranian-sponsored group?"

"You're not listening. They aren't under the control or direction of any nation-state. *They* control nation-states," Foltz responded.

"What is their goal, their mission?" Zach asked.

Foltz thought for a moment, pondering the question, and then looked into Zach's eyes. "Power, money...maybe it's just their mind-set...you understand? When someone has been doing things in a certain way for so long, they perceive their actions to be accepted, a moral and business standard."

"Are you saying they have been around, operating for years?" Zach asked. This time it was his eyes that were wide.

"Decades; in some cases, a generation or more. I understand its origins were during the waning days of the Second World War," Foltz said.

Zach looked at Turner when he asked Foltz, "How is that we are just now discovering them? No group can remain under the radar that long."

"As with all organizations, leadership changes. In the past ten years, a more aggressive leadership has taken over. The world's nation-states are declining in influence. Business, allegiances—they are global now, no longer nation-centric. They're filling that void," Foltz said.

"Who are they? Names, locations?" Zach asked.

"Before that, I need written assurances—guarantees that my assets, my family, and I will be protected. Their reach extends into every country, every government," Foltz said glancing at the railing and sea below.

Zach grabbed Foltz's arm and walked him back to the bedroom. This time he attached one wrist to a bedpost with flexi cuffs so Foltz could sit in a chair next to the bed with some comfort. Zach motioned for Turner to come with him.

They stood outside the bedroom door, which was open just enough to allow them to keep Foltz within view but outside of earshot. "I think he's telling the truth. What do you think?" Zach asked.

"I think it's insane. A mysterious group formed during World War Two controlling governments? Doesn't this sound like a grade-B Bond movie? No group could remain unknown with that influence for three quarters of a century," Turner replied.

"I know, but he's scared out of his mind, and an industrialist with the clout he has being that scared tells me some or all of what he's saying is true. Two years ago terrorists purchased nukes on the black market to attack the US, not just to cause maximum casualties but economic devastation. Shortly after that huge sums of money transferred between Hecox and accounts all over the world. We're about to launch an attack on Iran, and someone is leaving just enough fingerprints to direct us to Iran. Ratani and his operations are in the Gulf States; they have no love for Iran...and neither does Israel," Zach said.

"Zach, when something walks like a duck, quacks like a duck, and looks like a duck, it might actually be a duck. It likely *is* Iran," Turner said.

"I don't want us going to war on a '*likely*'—and this war would be like no other we've faced since World War Two. It would be generational," Zach replied before continuing. "Let's talk to Langley—we need a priority exfil...this can't wait, and if he's right, we might be far more exposed here than we or Langley thought."

Turner knew just how vulnerable the property was. "I think we should all move into the back foyer where the elevator is. If trouble happens outside, it will only be seconds till the house is breached." Turner knew that whoever was standing watch would die within those seconds.

"Agreed, but what do we do down at the water? We can't swim for it. They'll for sure have a water exit covered," Zach said.

Turner and Zach thought, and then the obvious came to them both. Zach said it first. "We need to move. Now."

"I'll get us transportation. There's a town half a kilometer down the hill; I saw it from where I stood watch," Turner said. Zach nodded.

It took Turner fifteen minutes to get to the small town center, and that included removing the license plates from two cars parked in a driveway along the way and reinstalling one of the car's plates on the rear of each vehicle. The loss of a front plate would likely go unnoticed for days. When he got to the town, it was hardly more than a small square with two restaurants on it. He walked a block away from the square and spotted a Renault Megane rental car parked in a small hotel parking lot. That would do. He opened the hood and disabled the alarm and then broke the small vent window. He reached in and opened the door and hot-wired the ignition. The antitheft gear on the car was far less than the average American sedan. He drove away and back to the villa.

Zach had told Vargas they were moving and was now searching bed-room by bedroom for Marcella, whom he finally found in a study on the floor below. "Get up; we're leaving," Zach said to Marcella.

"Leaving? I thought we were safe here. Is that wise?" Marcella replied.

"We'll be okay; we're getting out of here; come with me," Zach said. She had a look of exhaustion, fear, and raw nerves. She wasn't used to field work and he knew it; he just hoped she could hold it together.

As they reached the top of the stairs, Turner burst into the house. "Let's go! I'll drive. Zach, you ride shotgun." Vargas grabbed the last bowl of pasta, handed it to Marcella, and grabbed Foltz, pushing him into the middle of the back seat. He handed him the bowl of pasta, which he clutched as if it he was in a rugby scrum. Too bad: the agency would get grief for leaving the dishes, Zach thought.

They flew out of the driveway and made it nearly to the square where the car was taken when Vargas remembered. "Wait! We need to go back. I left the duffel with our surveillance gear. We can't leave that behind!"

They had to get the duffel. It couldn't fall into anyone's hands, and they might at some point desperately need it. Turner swung the car around and raced back the short distance up the hill. Nearing the villa, Turner yelled, "Shit—get down!" Both Zach and he saw it at the same time: two black Range Rovers, parked in the driveway of the villa, with one man standing next to the vehicles, an assault rifle in his hands. The door to the villa was breached.

Turner maintained a constant speed past the villa saying out loud what was on nearly everyone's mind. "Three minutes, tops...that's the margin for us breathing." A pause, and Turner continued. "How did they know?"

"I'm not sure, but for now, we're on our own. Everyone, get rid of all cell phones and all laptops except Vargas's secure tablet, now! Keep just the sat phone," Zach said.

"Where to, Zach? North to Rome or south along the coast?" Turner asked.

"Rome. I have friends, an apartment there. It's a big city, easier to hide in a crowd," Marcella said.

"No, they know you're with us. They'd know we might try that. South to Salerno? It's a big harbor. It would be our best choice, but we have to get off this road. It's two lanes and perfect for an ambush. They must know they missed us by only a few minutes. No, we go inland and then along the coast toward Napoli. Getting to Sorrento, I saw several large marinas. We need to charter a boat. How much cash do we have? Marcella, get us there without going on an autostrade."

They dug for their money. Vargas counted. "We have $4,400 euros between us. Is that enough?"

"Not for the size of boat I would have wanted. Okay, plan B: we need to get rid of this car and get a limo. Vargas, get on the sat phone and call us a limo. Ah...tell them Mr. and Mrs. William Haper and guests, three passengers, are arriving at the private terminal at zero six hundred. We'll need a driver for a full day to tour Pompeii and the Amalfi Coast." Zach was formulating his plan on the fly. "When we get to the terminal, we'll park this car at the commercial terminal and split up, taking a shuttle to the private terminal. We'll tell the driver we'll pay him an extra thousand euros to keep the additional two passengers and our destination to himself."

"And where is our destination?" Marcela asked.

"The British embassy in Rome. No one will expect it. I have a friend there who will give us sanctuary until we find out whether the agency has been compromised. In any event, whoever these people are, they'll be watching the US consulate and embassy."

"I like it. Now all we have to do is stay alive until the morning. Where are we headed for the next seven hours in this stolen car?" Vargas quipped.

It was one part joke and one part apprehension. The airport was only two hours away at most, even going a roundabout route. The longer they drove, the higher their risk of getting caught.

Vargas had his secure tablet up, using a satellite uplink for Internet access. "The direct route to the airport has us going up E45, which is an autostrade that narrows between Mount Vesuvius and the sea. That's a perfect pinch point to set up an ambush. If we avoid that and take local roads around the back, or the north side of Vesuvius, the area looks urbanized with a lot of factories and small farms, which might allow us to park out of sight for a few hours. It's not the sort of route one would expect us to take."

"Okay, we've got nearly a full tank, which should get us there without stopping," Zach said.

CHAPTER 21

MILAN

It had been hours since she spoke with Shaw. She feared this Jay Setter was never going to show. She had nodded off several times, once for a period of time she could only imagine. She thought she heard something, a scraping sound. There—a shadow interrupted the light from the hallway under her door. She raised her weapon, staring for any movement, one eye closed as she was taught. Then she saw it: a paper slid under the door. After a long pause, she crept, low, toward the door, retrieving it and retreating to where she had been crouched. It was too dark to read. She slid into the bath, pulling the door silently shut, and turned the light on. The note read: *Alice?*

She turned the light off and walked silently to the room's door and tapped on the door, gun drawn.

A low voice spoke through the door. "Are you Alice?"

Elle forced herself to speak. "No, but I saw the rabbit."

The voice on the other side of the door replied. "Elle, it's me, Jay." Elle opened the door, her gun still at the ready. Jay looked at her. Even with dark circles, swollen red eyes, and a look of absolute exhaustion, Elle was a sight he never expected. She was beautiful. "Cavalry's here," he said.

"Why the note under the door? That scared me shitless," Elle said.

"I've done this a few times. It's been my experience that people who aren't field agents often fire first when someone knocks on a door," Jay said, grinning.

It was the first time in several days that she allowed herself to laugh, to smile. "Smart. Now what?" she asked.

"I spent an hour or so observing the building and area before coming here. I saw nothing. For now, I think we are fairly secure here. But I was able to look at the registration desk when that lump of a front deskman went out for a smoke. There are three rooms on the next floor down that are empty. At this time of night, they won't get filled. I'm going to move you just to be safe. Stay here, and I'll be back for you. I'll knock four times gently. Please don't shoot me," Jay said, which brought out a relaxed look from Elle.

Minutes later they were in the new room, directly beneath the room she had been in. Jay attached a suction cup with a wire to the ceiling and placed the wire into a small appliance no bigger than a cell phone. He inserted an earplug in that and handed it to Elle. "Put this in your ear and listen for anything in the room you were in above. Let me know if you hear *anything*." Jay then set up a slender, flexible camera tube, sliding it just even with the bottom of the door threshold. "It's a wide-angle lens. It will let us know if anyone walks in the hallway."

Elle watched Jay then lay down what looked like small boxes on the floor near the door. "What are those?" Elle asked.

"Small directional charges. They'll stop the initial assault if anyone tries to break the door down," Jay replied.

Somehow that made her feel more vulnerable. She hadn't ever been in the company of someone like Jay. He had a confidence that was disarming in the face of all that terrified her. She felt like she needed to talk. "Jay, where are you from? Is this what you do every day?"

Jay laughed out loud. "Not every day. I grew up in Waynesboro, Virginia. It's a little town on the Blue Ridge Parkway west of Charlottesville. I have a little one-bedroom cabin on Afton Mountain near there that is on twenty-five acres that is a piece of heaven. Unfortunately, I don't get there very often. Lately, I've been everywhere but the States." A hint of Virginia accent came through when his voice had a touch of nostalgia. "What about you?" Jay asked.

"Me? Uh, I guess I don't have a place of refuge. My real father walked out when I was six. My mom remarried a few years later to an air force major. I grew up in Omaha, Nebraska, and moved to Lakenheath, England, right before high school, so I stayed in England. I have no family ties left in the States," Elle said. Her face twitched and she held her ear, pointing at the ceiling.

Jay put his finger to his lips and reached for her ear bud. The sound of metal turning and a board creaking. Someone was in the room over their heads. Jay expected them to have breached the door, but they were quiet and in the room. That meant they had a key and cooperation from the obese sleaze at the front desk.

"Quietly, get in the bathroom and don't make a noise," he whispered. Jay then unplugged the floor lamp and stripped the cord, laying the bare wires on the floor between the door and the bathroom. He took the floor rug from the bathroom and held it under the sink, getting it as wet as possible, and laid it gently over the bare wires. The floor rug was next to the single metal table and folding metal chairs that someone had placed in the room decades ago. He took the end of the lamp cord and walked into the bathroom. "Hold this, but don't plug it in," he whispered.

Jay then took a position in the doorway of the bathroom, gun drawn, watching the door. He whispered to Elle, "Stay down behind me. If I go down, empty your magazine and plug the cord in. No one should make it that far, not with the explosives we set and my line of fire."

Jay knew they would have a team of six or eight. Two would stay at street level. A breaching team of three or four would come in. If they were smart, they'd know about the empty rooms. The directional charges would eliminate the first two or three into the room. He'd have to take out the remaining ones because if they got to the electrifying wet throw rug trick, he'd already be dead.

They waited, listening to every sound. It was nearly four in the morning. He opened the encrypted communications keyboard and typed in the code *Circle Alice*. Two quick-reaction teams were three minutes out, waiting for that signal. Three minutes...a hundred and eighty seconds to keep her alive. She pressed his arm and pointed at the ceiling. "I don't hear anything anymore. I think they left the room."

He turned the bathroom light off. Now the room was completely dark. He took an eye patch out of his pocket and placed it over his right eye and whispered to her. "Close your right eye. If they use flash bangs, it will temporarily blind your open eye." He recalled that there were several empty rooms on the floor above. Each would take several minutes to check out... he hoped. He knew what he would do. The reaction teams knew they needed to take as many of them alive as possible.

Jay thought he heard a noise in the hall; he raised his gun. The sound of the voice in his earpiece jarred him. "Jet One, Action One; thirty seconds out." Then he saw it. An object under the door. It would be a flexible tube camera. Hopefully not infrared. He wished he had thought to stage one of the other empty rooms. The object disappeared, retracted. They would probably check the other two empty rooms if they hadn't already. He knew they would try to breach this room first. It's what he would do—he would assume the empty room below the one she was checked into would hold prey.

A noise in the hall. A person running down the hall. Then a welcome voice sounded in his earpiece: "Jet One, Action One; two tangos down street level."

The door flew open with a deafening crack, followed by a blinding light. Instinctively, Jay clinched the detonator for the charges with his left hand, and the room erupted with an explosion and a rush of air, which seemed to pull them toward the door. Jay slid the eye patch off, searching in the smoke for targets. Then silenced gunfire in the hall and silence. "Jet One, Action One; hall clear, level three."

Jay relaxed and raised his arm to speak into the mike. "Action One, Jet One. Room secure, level three...coming out." He turned to see Elle, eyes wide behind him, pressing against his back, shaking. "It's okay. It's over. Good guys are here." She was staring past him through the smoke. He turned and saw. "Don't look; take my hand; you're okay." He rose and guided her past the shredded bodies and room furnishings that the directional charges had scorched across the far side of the room.

In the hall, two black-clad men were bent over two men dressed in dark gray overalls, administering first-aid compression on a gunshot wound to one man's thigh. The man grimaced and looked up at Elle, then Jay, saying nothing. The other man was clutching his ears, his foot turned the wrong way. Undoubtedly, the directional charge had blown his leg one hundred and eighty degrees.

A large red-bearded man came over and put his arm on Jay's shoulder, grinning. "Jeeze, Jay, you really made a mess. You might not get your room deposit back."

"Murph, this is Elle; Elle, Murph. Glad to see you, Murph," Jay said holding Elle around the shoulders, who was pressed so close to him as to make his movement impossible. He pulled her apart from him and held her shoulders. She was as tall as he, a stunning woman despite the tears and dirt. "We're okay now. I'm not leaving you." Murph stared at her, top to bottom, then raised an eyebrow at Jay. Jay rolled his eyes; only Murph could focus on a girl's figure in the midst of this.

"Sixty seconds!" Murph barked the order as the team wiped down the room for prints, secured the prisoners, and placed the bodies of the two dead assailants in body bags. They would leave no bodies behind. Within sixty seconds they were in three black SUVs in the alley.

As the large cars shot out of the alley, Jay was the first to speak. "Carabinieri have to be close. Where's Langley securing us?"

The answer from Murph was as surprising as it was chilling. "This is an off-the-books OP. Langley's not in the loop. Shaw called this one himself. Sounds like it's pucker time back home. We're going outside the city." Jay watched the other two SUVs split off in different directions behind them.

CHAPTER 22

WASHINGTON, DC

The president sat on the edge of his Oval Office desk, arms crossed, listening to the Joint Chiefs, his two national security advisors, and Defense Secretary Peters. "So gentlemen, let me cut through the discussion. You're telling me that we have two windows for an attack, one next Thursday and the following in one month, when we have the next new moon. I want to make sure each of you are on the record for the next two of my questions. First, what will Russia do? Second, are you certain we can eliminate both the Iranian nuclear sites and decapitate the Quds forces?"

Admiral Weams spoke first. "On the Russia question, we expect them to not play a direct military role. Instead, they will ship additional defensive arms to Iran, with advisors. They will try to alienate us in the Middle East, particularly with the Shi'a. We project eliminating eighty-five percent of their nuclear program in the first three days with air strikes. The remaining portion is too deep; special forces will need to act on those. We'll degrade but not eliminate the Quds structure, but they'll rebuild. And we will be fighting them for a generation, likely with attacks on our own soil at some point."

"That's not a reassuring assessment," the president said.

"Sir, with respect, war isn't a science. The only certainty is that every plan will not go as planned. We can only provide our realistic assessment. When you integrate asymmetrical warfare, variables multiply exponentially," Admiral Weams added.

A knock on the door preceded Elaine, the president's secretary, entering. "Mr. President, the director of the CIA is on the line for you. He insisted on having you interrupted."

The president stepped around the desk and picked the receiver up. "Yes, Jim."

"Mr. President, are you alone?" the director asked.

"The Joint Chiefs are in the room. Should I place you on speaker?" the president said, more a statement than a question.

"No, sir. I prefer to speak with you only for now," the director said.

The president knew it was important. There was a certain urgency in the director's voice. "All right, what do you have?"

"Sir, we now have a high level of confidence that the attacks on this country eighteen months ago were not the work of Iran. In fact, they may not have been state sponsored at all. We stirred a hornet's nest in uncovering this. Our operatives in the field are being systematically hunted, eliminated. And sir...this group has tentacles throughout certain business sectors and governments, including, it would seem, our own. For now, we have to keep a tight lid on this, so tight, even our—*your*—closest advisors and confidants must not know we know," Director Harrence said.

His muscles tensed. He tried to think. He thought of the how President Bush looked, acted, when his chief of staff whispered in his ear that a second plane had hit the World Trade Towers, that America was under attack, that September day. He spoke into the phone. "Get over here with what you have." He hung up and leaned against the desk with one hand to steady himself before speaking. "Gentlemen, Kate, we need to break on this. Let's convene again tomorrow at ten in the morning. That's all, thank you."

The room was silent, in disbelief. What could be more important that this? The color had drained from the president's face. Something, perhaps personal, thought Kate.

The president sat down on the sofa. Alone. Who to trust? Who to include? He picked up the phone on the side table. "Elaine, get me Director Tankerfell at the FBI." He'd known Tank since college. He'd received his name for the obvious reasons, having been an all-American tight end at Stanford who had a propensity for running down defensive backs. After ten years with a San Francisco law firm and another three with the Solicitor's Office, he had served as assistant director of the NSA before the president appointed him director of the FBI. If ever there was a person he could trust, who had been vetted, who had served this country, it was Tank. And his selfless refusal to participate in turf wars when America was under attack eighteen months ago had earned respect, a reputation not often seen in this town.

Elaine peeked her head in. "Sir, I have Director Tankerfell on."

The president picked up the receiver, "Director, I hope you are in town. I need you here at the White House ASAP."

"Sir, I'm on final approach to National, I mean Reagan. I can be there in thirty," the director said. He had never before heard of a president calling and asking to meet on short notice. He hung up and spoke to the two agents sitting across from him in the C-37, the government version of a Gulfstream. "Tell the men to pick us up on the tarmac, the president wants us at the White House now."

He'd respect the agency's instructions. No one but Tankerfell would be in the room. Opening the office door, he could see his chief of staff and Kate standing across the end of the next room. "Elaine, Directors Tankerfell and Harrence will be arriving. Show them in as soon as they arrive, and hold all calls."

"Sir, do you want any of the staff in on the meeting?" Chet Roundsfell, his chief of staff, probed.

"No, thanks, Chet. I'll call on you if I need you in here," the president said, shutting the door. His mind tried to run through what he had been told, tried to think of what it all meant.

Director Harrence arrived first, with Elaine opening the door and showing him into the Oval Office. "Jim, before we get started, I've asked Director Tankesfell to join us. No one else."

"Yes, sir. I know I sound a bit paranoid, but it is for good reason. I trust Tank implicitly, and he needs to hear this as well." He walked around the edge of the sofa, turned, and asked, "May I sit down, sir? I was woken at two in the morning and briefed on this and, I'm sorry to admit, I'm dragging a bit," Director Harrence said.

The president touched an icon on the panel on his desk and Elaine walked in. "Alice, please bring is some sandwiches and fresh coffee."

"While we're waiting on Tank, fill me in on why I dismissed the Joint Chiefs," the president said.

"Sir, as you know, we have a wealth of circumstantial evidence that the attacks were directed by Iran through cells linked to Hezbollah. But that's all we have, circumstantial evidence. We have yet to identify any direct evidence or link. It was too neatly packaged for us. It caused us to question," Director Harrence said.

The president began to interject when Director Tankerfell walked into the room.

"Alan, thank you for getting here on such short notice. I asked you to come because, well, I trust your assessments, and Jim here has a theory that may need more than my arms to get around," the president said, trying to interject some levity before turning to the agency's director. "Jim, why don't you brief us."

"This is happening in the field as we speak. Director, you may recall Zach Greer, is now working for us—he was with your agency a few years ago and played a pivotal role in stopping the terrorists that attempted to set off the nuke inside Glen Canyon Dam. Anyway, Greer has been working to track down a lead on those attacks by following the money trail in Europe that supplied funds to the Cayman account that bought one of the nukes from the Russian black market. He was following three powerful business-men in Naples, an Italian industrialist named Foltz, a London financier by the name of Hecox, and an oil magnate from the Gulf named Ratani; each profited substantially in the markets by shorting the dollar right before the May Day attacks."

Director Harrence took a sip of water and proceeded. "He must have spooked them because they tried to kill him off Naples on the way to Capri. Concurrently, another asset, Elle Hardwick, who also is a part of this same agency task force, was trying to turn a Milanese banker who was trans-ferring money for Ratani and Foltz. We grabbed the banker and took him to a site for interrogation. The entire interrogation team, a security detail, and the banker were killed within hours. They knew where the site was and how our security was deployed. Ms. Hardwick escaped and is on the run. Greer and his team placed surveillance on Ratani's yacht, grabbed the Italian, Foltz, and made their way back to an agency safe house on the Amalfi coast near Sorrento. Within hours that safe house was breached— our people escaped with only seconds to spare. They too are now on the run."

He let that hang in the air before continuing. "All this happened in the last seventy-two hours. Our agents are being systematically hunted with intel that can only be supplied from within. We feel it is because we are getting too close. Foltz is willing to talk, presumably because he fears Ratani more than us. He tells a story of a group, dating back to the end of the Second World War, capable of manipulating countries and markets. He called them by name, 'the Twelvers.'"

Tank put his glass of water down. It was the name given by the sole captive of the New York attack. Only a handful of people knew that name or even that a perpetrator had been caught and interrogated. They always assumed Twelver referred to the Twelfth Imam in Islam, Mahdi...to a Shi'a group. It was a morsel of intelligence that forged the belief that Iran was behind the attacks against the United States. "This Twelver group, you are saying they *aren't* an Iranian-sponsored group?" Tank asked.

"They aren't Iranian or, apparently, even an Islamic group. Foltz is saying they are a secular, multinational economic group, one with elements in nearly every major country, including, it seems, ours. And the fact that our agents are being compromised on such a level lends support to the theory that we may have a mole or spies very high within our intelligence apparatus," the agency director said.

"Geeze, not again," Tank said. He knew the damage a single mole within the FBI caused eighteen months ago.

"How does an organization like that stay under the radar for over half a century? Is there anything to support the theory beyond the word of this Foltz person, which, frankly, sound incomprehensible?" the president asked.

"Nothing concrete. A Mossad agent investigating this lead has identified a company Ratani owns in the Gulf, which has been developing refinery efficiency software. The Israeli is on his way there now to meet with an agent who has been inserted as an employee of the company. There's also the nationalities to deal with. Foltz is Italian, Hecox, a Brit...and each profited greatly as a result of the decline of the dollar eighteen months ago, through the same accounts; accounts that were linked to the same IVS Zurich account that transferred funds through London for the purchase of the nuke used on New York. We don't have all the gaps filled in, but two things are certain: one, there is no connection with Iran; and two, this group may have people in every government." Director Harrence paused, letting it sink in.

Tank rose from the sofa, staring down at the rug's great seal of America. The president waited for Tank to speak. "The bigger question is not who but why? Why would such a group manipulate us into attacking Iran? If this was their plan, it has been years in the making, and it means the attacks against us eighteen months ago were a step, not an end. And if it isn't Islamic terrorism and the group has been operating for decades, why now? We need to get this Foltz someplace safe. We need answers."

"For now, I'll postpone any military action. Get your people safe; use all resources. Whatever they planned, it was based on us taking military action. We're now in control of the timing of that. Find these people," the president said. As they left the meeting, Tank thought to himself how this president had aged in the last few years, and matured from a politician into a leader.

It was raining as Director Harrence got into the back of his armored sedan. Ten at night, four in the morning there. He dialed Shaw at Langley. "Shaw, I just met with the president and Tankerfell. They're briefed. Where are your people?"

"They've been evading. The next hour is critical. In another thirty minutes, they'll transfer to a limo that should take them to the British consulate in Rome. London's transferred a security detail there for security. I've handpicked two four-man teams with no prior involvement in the investigation to assist. They will be in place within the next hour. We will have drone surveillance over the limo out of Aviano, with a quick-reaction special activities team on helicopter standby in the Med. I'll call when we have more," Shaw reported, scanning the screens before him in the action room. He hung up knowing he hadn't thought of everything; this was short notice, thrown together, and so far, the other side had been a step ahead throughout the operation.

CHAPTER 23

NAPOLI

The night's silence dissipated with the darkness. Night gave way to a gray overcast morning; trucks and cars began to stir in the industrial zone. "It's time. We're about fifteen minutes from the airport. Everyone, keep watch; the airport will be watched. Foltz, slump down. Let's make it look like vacationers in the car," Zach said as he eased the car out of the lot and onto the road.

Zach had studied the map till it was committed to memory. The choke point would be A56, the autostrade. It skirted the airport, and they needed to get over or under it without detection to get to the parking structure so Foltz, Marcella, and he could make their way to the private terminal. He knew the most dangerous task would be parking the car in the lot. Cameras were everywhere. It was in the early hours studying the map that a better plan came to him.

Zach drove within a block of the hotel he'd seen on the map. Marcella, Foltz, and he got out, Turner sliding into the driver's seat. Turner's weapon was at the ready. He swung the car around and drove three blocks to the Millennium Gold Hotel, where he parked the car and walked with Vargas through the hotel side door into the lobby with a clear view of the front door and passenger drop-off.

Zach walked up to the black Mercedes Viano, a six-passenger limo common to Europe that resembled an oversized, luxurious minivan. Zach tapped against the driver's tinted window. Surprised, the driver rolled down his window. "Senore Haper?"

"Yes, I'm Will Haper," Zach replied.

The driver jumped out of the car flustered, surprised. "I was in the terminal, and they said no planes were due in until eight, and they didn't have your name. I am Carlo. There are four passengers, no?"

"I'm sorry, we flew in very late last night, arrived at nearly two in the morning. We stayed at a hotel and had a taxi drop us off here to meet you. We didn't know how to reach you to let you know we changed our schedule, or you could have met us at our hotel. It's the three of us and two others. I thought when I made the reservation I told them four not including myself," Zach said, smiling. Foltz and Marcella were already in the limo.

"And the other two person, they are coming? Your luggage?" the driver asked in broken English.

"We need to pick the others up at the Millennium Gold Hotel, just down the road. We had our luggage transferred ahead to our hotel so we wouldn't have to bother with most of it today," Zach said.

"Yes, yes, I know the hotel, please get in," the driver said, opening the sliding side door for Zach, who slid into the Mercedes but not before staring at the light pole in the lot, with its security camera. Not good, Zach thought to himself.

The inside of the Mercedes was plush black leather, three forward-facing individual bucket seats, with two swivel seats facing the rear. The driver offered bottles of water to each as they drove to the hotel to pick up Turner and Vargas.

The limo pulled up to the front of the hotel and the door slid open. Zach didn't get out but showed his face line of sight into the lobby. Turner and Vargas walked out of the front door, Turner pulling his small wheeled bag behind him and pushing the bag into the open door. "Nice. Everything go smoothly?" he asked.

"Yes, and you?" Zach asked so the driver could hear, before saying under his breath, "Security camera in the lot. It might have caught my face."

"Was it facing the airport or the car lot?" Vargas whispered.

"The lot, not the terminal," Zach responded.

"Then it probably wasn't an airport security camera. They are usually manned. It likely is a lot security camera on a loop. They aren't linked; there has to be a reason someone would look at those, like a car theft or something. I think we're okay," Vargas said.

The driver turned at the light and asked, "You wish to see Vesuvius, Pompeii?"

"Actually, Carlo, we'd like to see the coastline from here to Rome. My business is tourism and we are scouting sites," Zack said.

"Rome? That is too far; I am not allowed to drive that far. I will have to check in with my company," Carlo said, his eyes darting in the rear view mirror at his passengers, seeking answers, looking at the fat man's face glistening with sweat.

"Carlo, I have a proposition for you. The quote for the day with your company was seven hundred euros. I'll pay you that and an additional thousand euros for your time if we keep it between ourselves," Zach said, looking into the rearview mirror at Carlo's eyes, which opened wide with the proposal.

"This is all legal, no? You aren't criminals?" Carlo asked.

"My heavens, no. As it turns out, my friends here were going to Rome and so we figured that since we would be going as far as Mondragone, we could just extend the trip and take them," Zach said.

That made some sense to Carlo, and it eased the decision he had already made to take the fare. Traveling along the coast would take longer, perhaps four hours, but even with lunch in Rome, they would still be back in Napoli before dinner and the time he was expected back.

"Okay, andiamo a Roma!" Carlo announced with a broad smile.

High above them, circling at twenty-two thousand feet was a Scan Eagle drone, one of the smallest drones in the CIA's arsenal. At just over five feet in length and ten feet in wing span, this one was painted with a nonreflective, radar-absorbing material. It could operate in daylight against a gray or blue sky without reflecting sunlight or radar signals. While it lacked offensive capacity, its high-resolution surveillance capabilities were unmatched, capable of reading a newspaper headline from twenty thousand feet. It had already locked onto the Mercedes Viano and the encoded signal emitter Vargas had taped to the sunroof. It would give eyes to Langley within a two-kilometer radius of the van.

The stress was beginning to bleed away, replaced with exhaustion. Vargas and Foltz were sound asleep. Marcella gazed blankly out her side window while Turner and Zach scanned the road ahead for threats.

After nearly two hours, they passed the seaside town of Formia. They were more than halfway there when the sat phone rang in Turner's ear bud. "Action One, Virginia One. Keep alert, Eagle has identified two helos closing from the south your location. Don't know if they are a problem for you or not. The special action team has launched and is eight minutes out just in case."

"Roger, Virginia One. How many minutes do we have before closure?" Turner asked.

"Three, maybe four," came the answer.

Zach looked at the map in the backseat before speaking. "Carlo, my grandfather landed at Anzio. I know it is a little out of the way, but would you take the next turn on the coast highway and go through Sperlonga?"

Carlo frowned—he knew it would add another thirty minutes—but replied, "Yes, sir; the turn is ahead."

Another ninety seconds passed before they were on the coast highway, with a steep drop on one side and sheer hillside on the other. Zach hoped they had enough time.

"Heads up, Action One, helos turned course when you did," the voice on the sat phone said, blaring in Turner's ear bud. Turner leaned forward and unzipped his bag, pulling out a folding assault rifle. He tapped his earpiece twice to let the others know they were about to be engaged.

Just then the hillside in front of the van erupted. Carlo swerved, yelling something that sounded like an Italian expletive. The black H160 Airbus chopper arched over to make another pass. A second chopper, smaller, flew alongside the cliff over the water parallel to the van.

Zach yelled to Carlo. "Don't stop! Faster, there's a tunnel up ahead. Open the back sunroof!"

Carlo floored the van and looked back, first at Zach in the mirror and then at the menacingly close chopper that matched their pace outside his window. The sunroof slid open, and Turner stepped up in the back of the van shouldering the Heckler & Koch MP5 special-operations weapon. He stayed low and waited for the chopper to make another pass. As the chopper came in for another run, this time it was more on target: three rounds ripped through the passenger-side front seat roof, the only place in the van that was unoccupied. Turner squeezed the trigger; the chopper was in his sights. Thirteen rounds a second erupted from the weapon. The sound was deafening and caused Carlo to lurch, throwing Turner off his feet. But the first dozen rounds shattered the chopper's front window, causing it to peel away.

"In bound, Action One; thirty seconds out," came the welcome sound of the quick reaction team in his ear bud. Turner yelled, "Cavalry thirty seconds out!" Carlo raced toward the tunnel entrance. Turner yelled, "Stop just inside the tunnel!"

The van skidded to a stop inside the tunnel. Turner and Zach ran back to the tunnel opening when the distinct burp sound of a minigun erupted. The second chopper fell straight down into the sea in flames. The chopper

Turner shot up opened fire on the special action team's gray Seahawk. This time the minigun was useless, facing ninety degrees to the attacking chopper. Small-arms fire burst out of the Seahawk's open door. The H160 began to smoke and sputter, banking sharply away and inland.

Zach and Turner ran back inside the dark tunnel with its jagged rock sides weeping water. Jumping in the van, Zach spoke to Carlo, who was shaking uncontrollably. "Carlo, look at me. You're all right. The bad guys are gone. Drive up to the end of the tunnel where a chopper can land."

Carlo shook, unable to speak. Zach reached out and held his hand firmly. "Carlo, do as I say. We're the good guys. I can't say too much, but we'll pay you as agreed, and we'll be on that chopper in a few minutes. You can say whatever you need to say to your employer. Tell them we forced you to take us here."

Carlo took a deep breath, swiveled forward, and started the van. At the other end of the tunnel, there was another tunnel up ahead. They drove through that one and a small beach appeared, with a Seahawk sitting, its blades revolving slowly. Two men dressed in civilian clothes each crouched on one knee, scanning for threats. Zach handed Carlo all the money they had and shook Carlo's hand. "Thank you, Carlo. You were very brave. Go home."

Sixty seconds later, the gray Seahawk lifted off, swiveling on its axis and accelerating out to sea and the safety of an amphibious carrier. They were safe. A wave of decompression swept over them.

Turner looked at Zach nodded, and gave a thumbs up. Zach began to piece the events together, searching for mistakes, for anything that would reveal how they had been tracked. He looked out the window of the Seahawk, the navy's answer to the Blackhawk. They approached the Wasp-class amphibious carrier's starboard side. The letters LHD-5 were emblazoned in white on its superstructure. The chopper rotated and landed.

A young seaman approached and opened the door. "Welcome aboard the USS *Nassau*, sir; follow me." Zach stepped down from the chopper and extended a hand to Marcella, who looked out at the vessel's large flight deck. Over a dozen choppers were lined up on either side of the super-structure. The place was alive with activity. They proceeded in single file to an open hatch with two marines lining the doorway. Zach felt overwhelmingly safe for the first time in days.

CHAPTER 24

THE MEDITERRANEAN

The yacht was built for it. Designed with a deep-V hull and its massive engines, it knifed through the eight-foot swells. It was making a break for the Eastern Mediterranean through the Strait of Sicily, the narrow passage between Tunisia and Italy. The yacht had run away from its tender, which was beating in the seas at a third the speed. The disappearance of Foltz could only mean he had turned or been captured. It made no difference. He couldn't be allowed to live. He knew far too much. But the news was not good. Berlin reported that he was with the Americans.

Inside, Hecox sat on the large white sofa, the young Ukrainian girl leaning against him. He ignored her, concentrating on his laptop, and every once in a while taking a sip of a gin and soda that rocked on the side table. He was growing weary of the engine noise and surging movement as the yacht surfed ahead on the downside of each swell.

On the bridge, the captain looked starboard at the lights of Malta sliding by. Radar showed three vessels in a tight grouping ninety kilometers ahead. Naval vessels. He swung twenty degrees to port, toward the Ionian Sea. The course adjustment would telegraph that the vessel was just another pleasure yacht bound for the Greek Islands, or so he hoped it would appear. The captain had learned the sea in these waters, knew there was no safety in the open sea against a naval vessel intent on stopping them. His orders were clear. Avoid all contact and transit the Suez if possible. Twelve hundred nautical miles; at this speed another forty-eight hours plus another four to take on fuel and water in Crete. That was if they didn't need to have any more evasive course adjustments like the one he had just committed to.

CHAPTER 25

LANGLEY

"What do you mean you can't locate Ratani's yacht?" Shaw asked incredulously.

"Capri was cloud covered for the past day. We have no assets on the island. We're searching satellite imagery, but there are quite a few boats of that size, and examining each of them takes time. The yacht never travels without its tender, so we are confident we can locate two boats of that size traveling together," Sarah said.

"What about the surveillance package, the locator beacon that Turner planted?" Shaw asked.

"It functions only if the boat is at a near standstill. When underway, much over ten knots, there is too much interference from the water on the hull and the magnetic effect of the spinning props. It broadcasts a subtle signal designed to avoid detection from the yacht itself," Sarah replied, staring at three screens over her head.

"So we have to wait until he reaches his destination. Hmmm." Shaw's comment wasn't a question.

"Maybe not. We've asked the Sixth Fleet command to search and listen. Their sonars will pick up the locator beacon underwater well before it can be detected by satellite," Sarah said. Shaw didn't quite understand how something that emitted a signature under the water could be detected by a satellite...but there was a lot of new technology that never ceased to amaze him. Sarah then continued. "The navy has sent two destroyers out, assigned to Destroyer Squadron Six Zero—one to the eastern Med from Gaeta and the other to the southwestern Med, off Egypt. They are working this into normally scheduled patrols and have two attack subs operating with them. It's likely their sonars will pick the yacht up long before it makes whatever port it is going to."

"Excuse me sir, we have a secure line coming in from the USS *Nassau*. It's Zach Greer," Sarah said.

"Zach, glad your team is okay. Talk to me," Shaw said.

Zach's familiar voice came across the line, filling the room. "We're fine; thanks for the extract. I don't know how, but they knew every turn we made, *every* move. They knew I made them in the harbor, the location of the safe house, our route out of Napoli. We were very careful. But we have Foltz. Now that he's safe, he wants full immunity, his bank accounts, his family, and protection; in return, he says he knows when the next major attack is coming and why."

"I'll call the attorney general and start the process. Right now, being on that vessel is the safest place he can be. He'll be surrounded by nearly a full marine expeditionary unit, over eighteen hundred marines. Get him talking. Start with asking where Ratani's yacht is headed," Shaw instructed.

Zach left the command center and went two decks down to where Foltz and the others were being housed. The ship was a maze; he wondered how personnel knew which way things were. The seaman showed him to a cabin, and he walked in to see Turner and Vargas sitting at a small desk playing cards. "Bored already?" Zach asked.

"We were killing time till you got back. Marcella went topside to get some air...that was a while ago; check her cabin first if you're looking for her. Foltz is under guard in a double cabin across the hall. What did Shaw have to say?" Turner asked, never once looking up from his hand.

"He wants us to interrogate Foltz here. He's getting the attorney general to start immunity documents." Zach paused before continuing. "Did

Marcella have clearance to go up on deck? They are pretty tight on security and safety here."

"Yeah, I assume so. Why the interest? You her big brother?" Vargas replied with a grin.

"No. No. She's not used to all this; she looks at the end of her rope. I'll be right back; I need to talk to Shaw again." Zach walked out into the hall where two young marines stood. "Corporal, can you take me to comms? I need to call the states."

"Yes, sir; follow me." The young marine turned and walked briskly down the hall with Zach following. Zach swore he'd make mental note of each turn so he didn't have to ask directions again. After two stairwells, they were at a door marked COMMUNICATIONS, directly next door to one marked COMMAND CENTER. "Sir, I'll wait for you here."

Zach turned and walked into the communications room. It was separated from the command center by a full-length glass wall with tinted glass. "I need to make a call to Shaw Ellis at the CIA; this is the secure number," Zach said, writing the number down for the communication specialist who was seated.

A siren blared. The lights went red and flashing. He could see people in the adjacent command center on high alert. Just then the intercom blared. "Battle stations! Battle stations! This is not a drill!" Then a burst of gunfire or missile launches—he couldn't tell—was perceptible from below decks. The glass panel separating the rooms swiftly parted like a sliding door, and he could hear people giving orders.

"Brahmos, two, on the horizon, twenty-seconds to contact. Missiles nine-five-two feet per second. Range, twenty kilometers. Bearing one-zero-three degrees," a female voice reported.

A calm directive came from the captain. "Launch SeeRam starboard batteries one and two—enable Phalanx. Get a helo up to increase the radar horizon. I want to know who's shooting at us. If they're shooting from over the horizon, we have less than...twenty-eight seconds to target the inbounds. We need to increase the horizon. Launch the ready Harriers."

"SeeRam closure at Mach four point eight, four seconds...detonation. One missile destroyed. Confirmed second missile still inbound. Contact in eleven seconds. Phalanx engaged," came a calm voice. Even deep within the interior of the ship, the sound of the Phalanx system could be heard, the ship's last line of defense. With a self-directed radar-guidance system, each Phalanx gun spewed out a wall of 20 mm tungsten sabot armor-piercing rounds at over seventy-five rounds a second.

Then a more excited voice came from the same radar officer. "Two new missile inbounds detected. Range, thirty-four kilometers, bearing one twelve degrees! *Hopper* moving into picket position and engaging." The USS *Hopper* was an *Arleigh Burke*–class destroyer; named after Rear Admiral "Amazing" Grace Hopper, it was only the second warship named after a woman from the navy's ranks. The *Hopper* had positioned itself between the threat and the carrier and was hurling a wall of metal toward the incoming missiles. At closure rates exceeding Mach five, the battle would be decided in seconds.

"Launch came from two Fencer SU-24s. Location of launch over Terni, Italy; they've turned and now are over the Adriatic on a flight path over Montenegro; looks like they are headed to the Black Sea," the E2D Hawkeye, call sign Angels View, announced.

"Russian?" Zach asked.

The commanding officer glanced at Zach, wondering why a civilian was in his command center, before answering. "Maybe; could also be Ukrainian, Algerian, or even Libyan or Syrian. It's a nineteen-eighties platform the Russians sold throughout the region. But the flight path suggests Russian or Ukrainian."

"Two F-22 Raptors from Bezmer closing on afterburners. They are three hundred kilometers and will be in range, roughly a hundred and fifty kilometers, to launch their missiles in...four minutes," the commander said.

"No! Shoot one but not the second. We need to know where they're heading, where he lands. And we need a team on him when he lands!" Zach blurted out.

The commander stared at this civilian barking orders and issued the order to his command officer. "Advise interceptors to take one down and follow the other. If he goes into Russian airspace, let him go. Get special operations command on the line." Just then the ship shook, knocking sailors nearly off their feet.

"The *Hopper*'s hit, sir! One got through. The other three were stopped," a voice sounded out.

"Provide all assistance. Get me Joint Command," the commanding officer said. A screen showed the USS *Hopper*, now no more than two hundred yards from the ship, listing badly; most of the ship was enveloped in fire and smoke. They stared as minutes later the ship rolled onto its side. A crew of nearly three hundred; everyone wondered how many had, or could, escape.

"Raptors have engaged. One Fencer down. Raptors disengaged, dropping low and are following. The remaining Fencer looks like it is on approach to Melitopol, seventy-five kilometers north of Crimea. It's in separatist Ukraine; Russian controlled—nothing flies in or out of that territory without Moscow knowing about it." The calm voice from the E2D Hawkeye belied the tensions that enveloped everyone listening. Russia had attacked, or condoned an attack against, an American warship.

Silence pervaded the room. Zach spoke first. "Is there satellite coverage? We have to know more. We need confirmation if the Russians were behind this."

"Avenger just launched an X47 from its location near Turkey. It will be on station in twenty minutes. That's the best we can do. By the way, who the hell are you and how did you get in here?" the commander said.

"Zach Greer, sir. I'm CIA. Your helos rescued my team a few hours ago," Zach replied. "What is Avenger?"

"Avenger is the *George H.W. Bush*, the newest carrier in the fleet. She carries the new X47, an unmanned stealth reconnaissance aircraft. Oh, and she's called the Avenger because that's the type of aircraft President Bush was shot down in during WW Two," the commander said before turning to Zach and sternly whispering, "Come topside with me."

Zach followed him up one level to the flight deck and walked out the heavy door held open by a seaman. He couldn't believe the scene in front of him. A dozen fire hoses blew water on the *Hopper*, which was burning on its side not more than a hundred yards to starboard. Scores of boats were in the water engaged in rescue operations. It was pandemonium. Choppers were landing and unloading scores of burned, injured sailors who were streaming into the carrier's superstructure.

The commander—his name tag read, "Quincy"—screamed to be heard over the roar of the flight deck. "You'll do well to consult with me from now on before ordering my crew around, particularly when we are at battle stations. Did your mission have anything to do with these attacks? Our Seahawks engage in a firefight with a couple of heavily armed choppers on the Italian coast and less than two hours later, two Russian-made fighters launch *Indian* antiship missiles against us. Start talking Mr. Greer."

Zach nodded, motioning back to the door where they could talk without yelling. The commander had taken him to see the results of the attack. It had worked. Zach knew the commander needed—no, *deserved*—to know.

"The agency has been investigating links that we believe show that Iran was not behind the May Day attacks. Judging by the fact that someone's tried to kill me three times in as many days, we may be close to them. Two CIA teams have been killed in the last two days...hunted and eliminated. My team escaped three attacks in less than three days, in large part by sheer luck. It's just a theory, but I believe the man we brought out of Italy was likely the target of the attack on your carrier group. He may hold the key and they want him, and anyone who he has spoken to, dead," Zach said.

Commander Quincy stared, without showing any reaction, before speaking. "Are you going to tell me who *they* are?"

Zach knew he needed to explain it, needed himself to hear it aloud. "Sir, I'm probably repeating what you already know but bear with me. The May Day attacks were orchestrated by two terrorist cells that entered the United States. They met up with three sleeper cells. Miami, LA, New York, and the grid in California were hit. Then they tried to set off two nukes, one on New York's water supply and one at Glen Canyon Dam on the Colorado River. I was at Glen Canyon, and we barely stopped it. A shallow victory. The collective opinion is that a group backed by Hezbollah and Iran was behind it. The president, Joint Chiefs, and NSA are compelled to retaliate. But a few, myself included, believe *we* are being manipulated...that we are being made to believe Iran is behind it, while a far more dangerous enemy is in the shadows pulling the strings. The task force I'm a part of at the agency has been following the money behind the attacks, and it led us to a group that may have been functioning for a generation or more—a group that has been systematically hunting down and killing anyone who has gotten too close to them, including me, and now, it would seem, your squadron."

"That's a hell of a story. How do you factor in the fact that the attacking plane was Russian built and landed in Russian-occupied Ukraine? If the attacks are related and if the same antagonist that attacked the states eighteen months ago were behind today's attack, how does it tie into Iran? It looks like it leads to Moscow," the commander said.

"That's how this group functions. They *manipulate*. They make things appear to be what they aren't. They direct others to achieve their goals— I don't even think Russia or Iran even know they are being controlled. Whatever they may be, they are manipulating us by *showing us* what we want to believe. Vast sums of money were made by them in the markets following the attacks eighteen months ago. My bet is they stand to make far more by us attacking Iran," Zach said.

"This is about money?" the commander said incredulously.

"I don't know. Money is one part of it. Maybe it finances something far larger," Zach replied.

The commander reached for his pocket and listened to the intercom phone. "Commander, the X47 is coming on station. We're also getting casualty reports from the *Hopper*."

"I'll be right there," the commander said, turning to Zach. "Come with me, Mr. Greer."

"Commander, is it possible to patch this in to Langley?" Zach asked as they entered the operations room. "The agency is running ops against this group as we speak. They need to know what the X47 turns up."

The commander walked to the communication's chief. "This is Mr. Greer; see that he gets your full cooperation and mirror what we are seeing to the folks he works with at the CIA."

A screen flickered, and the face of Shaw Ellis appeared. "Shaw, I assume you're up to speed on the attack against the *Hopper*. The navy has launched an X47 drone over eastern Ukraine and we have eyes on the air base where the plane that attacked the *Hopper* landed. Have you located Ratani's yacht yet?" Zach asked.

"Negative, Zach. We have drones and satellites looking but so far nothing. NSA is picking up a large amount of activity along the Ukrainian-Russian border, and two Udaloy-class destroyers left Sebastopol in the last fifteen minutes. They're at full speed headed to Istanbul, presumably headed to the Med. About a half hour ago, one of our satellites picked up significant activity at Kirovsky, one of their air bases on Crimea. And something that may or may not be related is that the Iranians just put the *Younis*, their only Kilo-class sub, to sea...also in the last hour. It's getting dicey, particularly with the knowledge that the attacking plane returned to a base within the Russian sphere of influence." Shaw paused, letting that sink in before dropping the next information. "Zach, they tried to hit Elle and one of our operatives in Milan *again*. This time we got them. Four bad guys down, two in intensive care, no ID, no clothing labels. Fingerprint and

DNA results just came back on three of them. Two former Recces—South African special ops—and one former Russian Spetsnaz. All mercenaries—private operators."

Zach let out a long, audible breath before speaking. "So we aren't talking Iranians or a Shi'a religious group, are we? Who would have access to Russian planes, Indian missiles, frontline mercenaries, and this level of logistical support?"

"Get Foltz talking, Zach. Commander, the Pentagon has tasked two of the Sixth Fleet's attack subs to find Ratani's yacht. Greer can explain that. I'm sorry about your men, but we need to contain this before it gets any larger. There are those here who believe there was direct Russian involvement. From what I see, I think both the Russians and us are being played against each other," Shaw said.

The commander was staring down at the digital display coming in. He read it twice before responding to Shaw. "Mr. Ellis, I take my orders from the Sixth Fleet Command, and my new orders are to mobilize my squadron to contain the Russian fleet that's moving to break out of the Aegean. I can spare one LCS, the *Fort Worth*. The two subs that were assigned to find your missing yacht have been reassigned to hunt for Russian subs. Sorry, gentlemen."

Zach thought for a moment and then asked, "What is an LCS? Whatever the ship is, I'd like to be transferred to it with our prisoner and my team."

"I'll have a chopper to take you to the *Fort Worth*; she's off the coast of Lebanon now. An LCS is a new type of ship for the navy—small, fast, versatile. LCS stands for Littoral Combat Ship. She's state of the art. Designed for close-in, fast, asymmetrical warfare. About four hundred feet long, shallow draft, and the fastest thing the navy has," the commander said before turning around and commanding the operations center to move away from the *Hopper* and head for the Aegean.

CHAPTER 26

MELITOPOL, UKRAINE

Two FSB (Russian Security Service) agents approached the hangar where the plane had landed less than an hour ago. The Russian satellite that constantly monitored eastern Ukraine showed the plane had taxied into the hangar. The cockpit canopy was open, and a ladder used to exit the fighter was in place next to the canopy. One of the agents scaled the ladder and looked in. The pilot was slumped in the cockpit, one bullet through his flight helmet visor and another in the chest.

Meanwhile, the X47 filmed the scene from high above. Its infrared sensors showed three images. Two moving...these would be the "hot," living, beings the plane had filmed entering the hangar. The other image was the plane, its turbofans still warm. The X47 began picking up several other inbound images. Two vehicles and a helicopter were converging on the airfield. The scene was getting too active for the X47 to remain on station.

Shaw, the Pentagon, and the command center inside the USS *Nassau* watched the same live feed from the unmanned X47. It circled Melitopol air base overflying the Molochna River, its milky color giving its name. The air base looked largely deserted. "Pull up satellite imagery from an hour ago," Shaw instructed. After several seconds, an image appeared: two trucks and a handful of men around the hangar. Two helicopters, Bell light tactical 407GT helicopters, sat near the trucks. Shaw spoke. "Well, well...you wouldn't expect to see two American-made helos in occupied Ukraine." They watched the feed fast forward. The next satellite feed showed both the choppers and the trucks gone.

CHAPTER 27

EASTERN MEDITERRANEAN

Zach and his team ran from the Seahawk helicopter to the open hatch. He stopped and looked around. He'd never seen a ship like this: gray, tilted surfaces; no portholes; all smooth surfaces. The helicopter rotated and took off; almost at once he felt the ship accelerate. It seemed one part warship and one part speedboat. He could feel the speed.

"Welcome aboard, Mr. Greer. I'm Commander Hall. Seaman Witter here will show your team to their quarters. I'll meet you in the mission control center in five minutes. I understand this ship is at your direction. The sooner I know what that is, the better we'll all be," the commander said. Zach sensed the commander was not pleased being assigned to a civilian when the rest of the fleet was moving to counter the Russian fleet.

Zach put his bag in one of the cabins and walked with the seaman to the control center. Inside, the room had no windows; a soft red light lit the space, contrasted with the hue of blue screens that were everywhere. A dozen technicians and warfare officers were in front of a myriad of monitors and computer screens.

Zach approached the commander. "Sir, the attack on the *Nassau* was meant to kill my team and our captive. I know it sounds implausible someone would try to sink a United States naval vessel just to do that, but there is good reason to believe that the attacks on the United States homeland last year and the *Nassau* were related. And the attackers were not Russian or Iranian. In the last seventy-two hours, this group has been systematically hunting down and killing our agents throughout Europe. They are well armed and directed. The attack on the *Nassau* was from two SU-24s carrying Indian-made antiship missiles. Russian aircraft do not carry Indian armament, and they don't fly back conspicuously into Russian-occupied eastern Ukraine. This group *wants* us to believe the Russians are behind the attack. This group is composed of business and political leaders based in Berlin and the Gulf states; they may even have members in our own country. What I do know is that one of those men is on a thirty-five-meter Ferretti-Pershing yacht, named *Gulf Vision*, which left Capri fifteen hours ago headed to the eastern Mediterranean, perhaps the Suez or Istanbul. I want you to find that boat and capture him alive."

The commander looked at Zach without showing any emotion. "That's quite a story, Mr. Greer...and I don't mind reminding you that the Suez and Istanbul are on the opposite sides of a very large sea."

"Yes, sir, but one of my team, ex-SEAL, installed a tracking device on the bottom of the yacht. When it stops, it should be audible for seventy-five to a hundred miles, depending upon thermals. If we can drop sonobouys in some key choke points, it might narrow our search. The navy assigned us two attack submarines to search for that signal until the fleet was scrambled to contain the Russian fleet." Zach knew that was not a coincidence in timing, and by the look of the commander, he likely did now too.

"Our helo will drop sonobouys at the chokepoints that are in range and listen for your vessel. I'll request a Poseidon aircraft to join the search. We can position ourselves midway, but that means we can't intercept. We have to make an election on where you want this ship to patrol if you want to intercept...off Egypt or in the Aegean," the commander said.

Zach knew there were hundreds of islands in the Greek archipelago and thousands of boats. It would be hard to find the vessel there. The eastern Med was a different story. Ever since the United States had made the blunder of supporting the overthrow of Gaddafi, that country had become a failed state, home to warring militants, Al Qaeda, ISIL, LIFG, and others. Syria and Libya were out of the question. Ratani would avoid those hostile regions at all cost. That left only Beirut, a handful of ports on the Turkish coast, Cyprus, Israel, or the Suez. Security at the Suez and Israel would be too great to come in undetected. Zach made the decision. "Position your boat in the Sea of Crete in the shipping lanes. Those are international waters aren't they?"

"Yes, to a point. From there we can launch drones to recon the major sea lanes. A vessel like the one you describe is fast, but a fast boat uses a lot of fuel. He'll need to take on fuel someplace. My guess he is will be averaging twenty to twenty-five knots max in these seas. If he is headed there and we know the time and his position when he passed Sicily, we can get to our staging point just about the time he gets there...*if* that's where he's going. A performance yacht is fast, but not as fast as this ship. We're four times longer and fifteen to twenty knots faster, even faster in heavy seas." He turned to the young helmsman. "All ahead flank, bring us to thirty-five knots, bearing three-three-zero."

Once again, Zach could feel the ship accelerate. "Sir, I need an interrogation room for our prisoner with an audio-visual feed to Langley." The commander nodded to the young seaman next to Zach to handle it.

Zach walked into the stateroom with the young seaman, whose eyes nearly popped out of his head. Turner had Foltz tied up, bare-assed naked, sitting in a chair facing the corner of the room, with the temperature in the room turned way down. Turner sat bundled on the other chair with his feet up on the cot, headphones in, reading a magazine. Turner put his magazine down and began with a slight smirk. "Thought I might get started. You know, time's a-wasting."

Zach stifled a laugh and turned to the young seaman. "It's okay; he's a professional. He's done this a lot."

"Uh, yes, sir. The quarter mess at the end of this hallway has a room with a video monitor; I'll set it up for you," the young seaman said, shaking his head in a way that seemed to say that he'd seen everything now.

Turner knocked on Vargas's cabin door. "Zach and I are down the hall three cabins on the right, interrogating Foltz if you're interested." Vargas shook his head no, going back to a book he'd picked up. He didn't get much down time and was enjoying every second of it.

"Can I have some clothes? I've already told you enough to ensure they will kill me. Give me full immunity as I asked and I'll tell you everything. These people killed an awful lot of people while trying to kill me today. I want them caught now as much as you. It sickens me," Foltz said.

"Give him his clothes back. He has a point. If we don't think he's cooperating, we can always take the cattle prod approach later," Zach said, shooting Turner a wink only he was in a position to see.

The screen came up and the audio crackled. "Shaw, this is Turner. We have Foltz in the room on audio and video, and he's prepared to talk."

"Good to see you're safe. Things are ramping up here, so Mr. Foltz, this is the DOJ document granting your immunity terms. It is signed by the attorney general, as you can see," Shaw said, placing the document in front of the screen for Foltz to read.

After a few minutes, Foltz looked into the camera on the monitor, took a sip of water, and began to speak. "Seven, maybe eight years ago, I was approached by a high-ranking diplomat in the Italian government, who told me my country needed me to perform a task. That diplomat was Sergio Marody; he is now a member of the cabinet...the current minister for foreign affairs. I was to transact business with a German businessman, Ritter, who controlled several consortiums that did business within Italy. I did and perhaps a year later, Ritter introduced me to Amir Ratani, a businessman with operations in the Gulf states and Indonesia. Ratani impressed me. He was refined and gracious. We did several successful small joint ventures, primarily pharmaceutical offerings and some oil refinery trades. Then, about three years ago, Ritter and Ratani met me in London for dinner with a man by the name of William Hecox. They told me that an opening on their board had come up and wanted to know if I was interested. I explained that my businesses kept me very busy and I was already on a number of boards and didn't really have time. They then told me the board was not a volunteer board, that it paid one hundred million euros a year, but I was required to attend every meeting, that the business of the board came first among my companies or my personal life, and that once on the board, one could not resign. You could only ask to leave or retire at the age of seventy-eight. I had just gone through a divorce, my two grown sons have little to do with me, and, frankly, I was bored with my businesses. They are profitable, making me several hundred million euros a year. It sounded intriguing and for the first time in a while offered me a unique opportunity, or so I thought, that I would be engaged in important questions, issues, and discussions among my peers, people of similar accomplishments. I viewed it as exciting and perhaps one last learning experience."

Foltz stopped to take another drink of water and continued. "The board meetings were all electronic. None were in person. The only people I knew were on the board were Ratani and Ritter. When the meetings were conducted, everyone's faces were in shadows; only their voices identified them, and we were only allowed to use the name of our country to identify ourselves. I was 'Italia.' It became apparent that the group controlled the decisions of many of the world's countries and economic houses. We would be told twice a year what investments we would have an opportunity of making. These were broad sector investments, not individual companies—you know, utilities, energy, food...that sort of thing. It was about finance and using funds to effect social change for good, or that was what I was told. Then investments would be made and world events would just seem to fall in place to make those investments wildly lucrative. All investments were made by the board's financial house. Each board member would decide what amount they wished to invest, and profits and losses were pro-portionately allocated. No individual trades were allowed. In hindsight, as you say, that should have caused alarm. But once in, there was no turning back, no resignation. That became apparent when the attacks on America occurred. Anyone who questioned...just...disappeared. Their seat became vacant."

Foltz looked down at the floor, his eyes glassy, swallowed hard, and continued. "We were told that the next investments would be currency trades against the dollar, and the purchase of gold. I invested fifteen mil-lion euros. It seemed risky. The American economy was rebounding, and gold was at an all-time low. When the attacks on your country occurred, I earned one hundred and ten million euros on my investment, and it sick-ened me. I knew there had to be a link. One board member, from Argentina, spoke up at the next board meeting, calling for answers to questions on what insight the board had as to the events. Argentina was replaced by Brazil at the next board meeting. I learned later that he was found murdered in Buenos Aires. The news reported he was a victim of a robbery, but we all knew better."

Zach interrupted. "The only names you know are Hecox, Ritter, and Ratani?"

"Yes. Hecox isn't on the board, though. He places the money for the board. Ritter later passed his seat on to another of his countrymen. He had a terminal illness; I understand he passed away recently. I don't know the name of his replacement," Foltz said.

"What countries are on the board?" Shaw asked.

"France, Germany, Switzerland, Brazil, China, Russia, Qatar, USA, Japan, United Arab Emirates, South Africa, and of course Italia," Foltz recited.

"The US," Turner said, saying what everyone was thinking.

"When is the next board meeting?" Shaw asked.

"It is set for April twenty-first. But investments were made at a meeting two weeks ago," Foltz said, silencing everyone.

Zach asked, "What industries were the investments made in?"

"Oil futures, gold, and drilling equipment," Foltz said.

"Just the investments you'd want to have if someone started a war in the Middle East," Shaw observed, before asking Foltz a last question. "How much did you invest, Mr. Foltz?"

"The minimum, ten million euros. I think that was why Ratani invited me on his yacht: he wanted to feel me out, determine where my loyalties were...maybe even kill me," Foltz said, beginning to sob.

"Turner, would you take Mr. Foltz back to his quarters and keep an eye on him?" Zach asked.

As soon as Foltz left the room, Zach turned to the monitor. "Ratani's the key. We need more assets on him. That's why the attack on the *Nassau* occurred, not to kill Foltz but focus our attention on Russia, away from him. Without Hecox or him, we'll never have time to avert this."

"They've made investments assuming the US will attack Iran. That can be controlled. I'll see what I can do with the Pentagon and the White House. Zach, be careful," Shaw added as the line was disconnected.

CHAPTER 28

WASHINGTON, DC

Within the hour, Shaw had managed to make it from Langley to the Oval Office. The president shook his hand as he walked in. "Shaw, good to see you again. You know Director Tankersfell from the FBI, Admiral Weams of the Joint Chiefs, and, of course, Director Harrence. At Director Harrence's suggestion, we've kept this group small. What do you have for us?"

Shaw walked to the monitor on the wall, inserting a thumb drive of the Foltz interview. "Sir, may I? You all need to see this. It is an interview of Giovanni Antonio Foltz, an Italian industrialist we captured and have on board the USS *Fort Worth* sailing toward Crete. You will recall my team and Foltz were rescued from attacking helicopters on the Italian coast by the USS *Nassau* right before it was attacked and the *Hopper* was sunk."

They sat transfixed listening to Foltz's interview. It was Tankersfell who asked the first question. "Can his story be verified?"

Shaw stood for a moment, carefully choosing his words. "A money trail led us to Ratani, Foltz, and Hecox. It's verifiable that large sums, nearly two billion euros, were reaped by accounts controlled by Ratani and Hecox immediately after the May Day attacks. Foltz was taken from Ratani's yacht, where both Ratani and Hecox were present. The money that funded the purchase of the nukes that attacked our country originated in Berlin and were sent through accounts Hecox controlled to a bank in the Caymans. Finally, the sole captured attacker mentioned the 'Twelfth Gulf Service'—this board has twelve members from twelve countries."

Admiral Weams spoke next. "The two Russian-made fighters that attacked the USS *Nassau* fired *Indian*-made antiship missiles and retreated to Russian-occupied Ukraine. Russia doesn't purchase those weapons, although they are available on the open market. They are a weapon of deniability, but if Russia was trying to distance themselves from an attack, they wouldn't have flown right back to an airbase they know that we know they control. What's more, the Russians look panicked; they didn't know this was going to occur and are scrambling their fleet."

"And if we invade Iran, we drive up oil futures and gold and set the stage for increased purchases of oil equipment for domestic oil production. Too convenient," the president added, walking away toward the window. "Admiral Weams, tell the fleet to take no provocative actions toward the Russian fleet, and find that yacht. For now we stand down on Iran but no public comments, we need to make sure these people don't believe we've changed our strategy. Get me President Putin on the line. Everyone stay here."

While they waited, Shaw felt compelled to add one last point. "Mr. President, Putin wants us to attack Iran so he can divert attention away from Ukraine and isolate us in the Middle East. We need to keep him off his game plan. I suggest not telling him anything about this group."

"I wasn't going to, but your comments are appreciated. I'll keep it short with 'his excellency,'" the president quipped.

The operator announced the line was active, and a familiar voice came on the line. "Mr. President, the Russian Federation is deeply saddened at the loss of life today by the cowardly attack on your carrier group in the Mediterranean. We know that the fighter plane that was used in the attack landed in the Ukraine. Of course, we have limited access there, but understand that the pilot was found still in the cockpit, shot dead when he opened his plane's canopy. Russia had nothing to do with this attack."

The president looked at those in the room before responding. "We know Russia was not behind the attack. That is why I am calling you. Your fleet is breaking out of the Black Sea, presumably in response to that attack.

Our forces have orders to take no provocative actions toward the Russian fleet. I'm calling you to ask you to issue those same orders to your fleet."

Putin was dumbstruck, pushing himself away from the desk. "Yes, of course. That is a wise suggestion. Ah, Mr. President, if I may ask, who *was* behind this senseless attack?"

"As I'm sure you can appreciate, an operation is underway and we cannot give that information out at this time," the president responded.

"Yes, of course. The Russian Federation stands ready to lend assistance in any way. Good-bye, Mr. President," President Putin said, hanging up and looking into eyes of the man in front of him. "Well, Aleski Tuperof, what are the Americans doing? Who attacked the Americans? If Russians had anything to do with the attack, I want to know!"

Snapping to attention, Aleski Tuperof responded, "Sir, I am as much in the dark about these events as you are...I will make inquiries and have answers!"

President Putin picked up the phone and ordered to be connected to Fleet Admiral Ivanovitch, commander of Russian Naval forces. "Admiral Ivanovitch, I have just spoken with the American president. He informed me that he knows we had nothing to do with the attack on the American carrier. You are to issue orders to stay clear of the American fleet and engage in no provocations. The Americans will be on a defensive war footing, but it is not aimed at our forces. Avoid any escalations."

"Yes, sir. I will recall several ships to Sebastopol as a gesture but keep the others on patrol in the Mediterranean," Admiral Ivanovitch stated.

"Proceed, Admiral, but instruct our submarines and intelligence ships to watch the Americans. I want hourly reports on the operations of the American fleet."

CHAPTER 29

BISSONE, ITALY

Elle had finally begun to relax. After several hours in the SUV, they had stopped at a safe house. Not just any safe house. She found herself sitting on a stone veranda on the second floor of a four-story villa built on the edge of the most beautiful lake she had ever seen, Lake Lugano. The lush mountains seemed to rise vertically out of the lake on the opposite shore. She drank sparkling water and sat bundled in a wool throw staring, trying to fit the pieces of the last two days into order.

Her phone vibrated, and she looked down at it. "Hello, Shaw."

"Elle, how are you doing?" Shaw asked.

"I'm fine. Safe. One part of me is trying to piece it together and another is trying to clear it from my mind, push it out," Elle said.

"I know you've been through a lot, but I'm going to ask you to do more. Your team is off grid. No one at the agency knows where you are or what your team is doing. I want to keep it that way. That's an advantage. Zach's team escaped three attacks, the last one by fighters that almost sank a carrier and did sink its destroyer escort. Nearly a hundred sailors and marines lost their lives. Foltz is talking, and he described one hell of a story. The Sixth Fleet is searching for Ratani and Hecox. They'll find him. We think we are getting close with tracing the Berlin player, or at least his accounts. I need your team in position in Berlin as fast as you can get there. You'll have all the backup you need once you're there. We underestimated these people before. This time we are going in strong," Shaw said, hoping the last comments would give Elle a feeling of safety.

Elle closed her eyes and took a deep breath, the serene beauty disappearing before her. "We'll do what you need us to do."

"Thank you, Elle. The past two days haven't been good for us, but that's all about to change. The president and Joint Chiefs are all on board. Get to Lucerne. I'll have air transport at Buoch Airport to take you to Leipzig just outside of Berlin. I'll call back in two hours after I arrange it. All of this is off the books: nothing goes through operations and nothing over agency servers," Shaw said before hanging up.

CHAPTER 30

USS *MOUNT WHITNEY*, EASTERN MEDITERRANEAN SEA

The command-and-control flagship of the Sixth Fleet doesn't have the physical stature of an Aegis-class cruiser or a *Nimitz*-class aircraft carrier. But the *Blue Ridge*–class command ship's plain support ship appearance belies its ability to transmit and receive secure data from any point on earth through HF, UHF, VHF, and SHT channels. The computing and communication abilities of the vessel are unparalleled. Every asset of the command ship was now focused on finding the *Gulf Vision*...and keeping a cautious eye on the Russian fleet flooding out of the Black Sea.

Two attack submarines and countless surface ships scoured the ocean. Overhead, three P-8 Poseidon aircraft roamed the eastern Mediterranean and Aegean, operating in tandem with the new Northrop Grumman MQ-4C Triton unmanned aerial vehicles, the navy's newest drone reconnaissance aircraft. Inside the Poseidons, a row of five operating stations monitored all surface and subsurface craft below them within a five-hundred-mile radius of each plane. At any given time, hundreds of ships were within each plane's orbit. Each needed to be ruled out, or in the case of the Russian naval vessels, monitored.

"*Fort Worth*, this is *VP Tangier*. We have a vessel matching target description two hundred and twenty nautical miles due east of Crete, bearing ninety-five degrees your position, speed twenty-eight knots."

"Get Mr. Greer here," the commanding officer in the combat center ordered. "And set a course to intercept."

Greer ran through the bulkheads behind the young sailor and was out of breath when he entered the command center.

"Mr. Greer, we have eyes on your vessel. It is two hundred and twenty nautical miles away from us. We aren't the closest vessel to intercept, but since this appears to be your hunt, you be the one to make the call on who intercepts. On its present course, the vessel looks bound for Turkey, perhaps Cyprus, or the coast of Syria. It's in international waters, but if it changes course to the north, it could enter Turkish waters before we can get there. If that happens, CVN-75—that's the carrier *Truman*—can launch a SEAL team to intercept within two hours. It'll take us five, maybe six hours to intercept. What's your call?" the commander asked.

Zach pondered the options and risks. He wanted to get his hands on Ratani, badly. But he knew Ratani would do the unexpected if he had the time. "This ship has a helicopter; can we deploy it to go in with the SEALs from the carrier if necessary? Ratani undoubtedly has satellite information and would detect us. A helicopter assault might preserve the element of surprise."

The commander relayed Zach's request and listened intently on the phone as orders were passed to him. Perhaps Zach imagined it, but he was sure he detected a slight smile on the commander's face. "Seems as though the decision has already been made. You're going to love this," the commander said, walking around the operations table and bringing up a large touch screen. A map of the northeastern Mediterranean appeared and with it a blinking orange boat icon and several other icons; each icon had a small flag denoting the navy to which each vessel belonged. There were three Russian vessels, two Israeli vessels off the Lebanon-Syrian border, one French vessel near Cyprus, three Turkish vessels near its shores, and four US vessels.

Zach pointed to the blinking orange icon. "Is that the *Gulf Vision?*"

"Yes. And here is our ship," the commander said, pointing to the US icon that had a blinking circle around it next to the *Gulf Vision*. "And over here is the USS *Truman*," he said, pointing to a large icon that was off the Libyan-Egyptian border.

"What's the US vessel closest to Ratani's yacht?" Zach asked, pointing to a cylindrical icon very close to the target.

The commander grinned. "That's the *Colorado*, a Virginia-class attack sub. The drone launched from the Poseidon aircraft and the *Colorado* will shadow the yacht while the *Truman* gets in position and we close. We want to know what port the vessel is headed to and who is supporting them. If it looks like it is shifting course toward a territorial water, the *Colorado* will stop it while the *Truman*'s SEALS and our helo launch. If not, we can intercept just outside the territorial waters of wherever they are headed. They won't get away. They're ours."

CHAPTER 31

BUOCH AIRPORT
OUTSIDE LUCERNE, SWITZERLAND

A single plane sat at the end of the runway, its engines silent and its navigation lights off. It was a large jet, perhaps eighty feet long. The silhouette of a man, perhaps the pilot, was visible in the faint light of the doorway as they drove slowly toward the plane. They stopped about a hundred feet from the plane. Jay stepped out of the SUV slowly, looking around as best he could for any sign of a threat. "You waiting on someone?" Jay yelled.

"Shaw sent us to pick up some homeless people. Hope you didn't bring along any followers." The reply came in a crisp British accent.

"No one but us homeless folk," Jay said, relieved and smiling.

The pilot then picked up a radio and spoke into it. "Hold positions until we get them loaded. When the plane's lights come on, break positions and get back to the plane."

Jay motioned for the three SUVs to park at the end of the runway and all to get aboard. Seven, including Elle, Jay, and Murph's team, scrambled onto the plane. Once in, Elle looked around. The plane was massive: two sofas sprawled nearly the length of the port side while a dozen broad leather seats were across an aisle. "Take any seat. Wheels up in two minutes," the pilot said before turning around and walking into the open cockpit door. The other pilot had already begun prechecks and spooling the engines up. It was deafening with the cabin door open.

Two men in black tactical suits appeared in the cabin door carrying black sniper rifles. One handed his weapon to the other and closed the cabin door as the plane began to taxi. The large man, an African American nearly six feet four, looked at the people in the cabin and pointed to Jay. "If I had a dollar for every time I have had to get that guy's ass out of a jam, I wouldn't be doing this!"

"Hey, Samuel. Good to see you," Jay replied, half laughing. The brevity broke the tension for a moment as the plane taxied to the end of the runway. Seconds later the big jet began to roll down the runway.

Samuel took his jacket off and sat his rifle in the forward closet, which was packed with various weapons. "It's a short flight; I need to go over things with your team," Samuel said to Jay.

They sat down at a table with four swiveling leather chairs around it: Elle, Jay, Samuel, and Ed, a slight man with piercing green eyes. Samuel spoke first. "Here's what we know. Right now the navy and a few of our folks are closing in on one of the leaders of the target group in the Mediterranean. Money for the nukes that were used against us came from a Berlin bank account. The German BND, codename CASCOPE, is assisting with domestic wiretaps and banking warrants. They will meet us in Berlin. The Berlin airports will be monitored, so we'll land in Leipzig; it's less likely anyone will be watching there. With any luck, the BND will have a name and a face matched to the account by the time we land. The German banking system is, as you can imagine, pretty organized and a lot less secretive than the Swiss."

CHAPTER 32

ABOARD THE USS *FORT WORTH*

"You look worried, Mr. Greer. Don't be. The *Colorado* and Poseidon are watching the yacht. It can't outrun or escape us," the commander said.

Zach tapped the map before responding. "I wouldn't be too sure. The sinking of the USS *Hopper* is proof these people think outside the box. They went after a carrier for God's sake. I'm not worried about the yacht; I'm worried about what *other* assets and allies they have...they know we are searching for them and must know we'll find them. So what's their game? Why stay with a vessel?"

The commander squinted at the map. His gut told him Zach was right. They were overlooking something. Why *would* they stay with the yacht? he asked himself before responding. "Time, that's why."

"Time? What do you mean?" Zach asked.

"There's only three reasons they'd stay with the yacht. One, they aren't aware the whole US Navy is searching for them and believe it's a safe means of travel...it's a big sea. Two, they need to access someplace or someone that they can do more easily by traveling by sea. Or third, they are buying time, stringing us out, diverting our attention from something else...everything takes more time on the sea," the commander said.

It had to be option three. They'd already spent twenty-four hours searching for the yacht, trailing it, and now it looked like it would be another five hours just to get within range of it. That's a very long time to give someone a head start on a plan, thought Zach.

"How long until we are within range? And how long till they reach territorial waters on their present course?" Zach asked.

"Four and a half hours until we intercept, perhaps eight until they reach Syria's or Lebanon's territorial waters on their present course. Of course, if they change course to the north, they could be within Turkish waters in less than three hours. But they haven't changed course in four hours," the commander said.

"I need to talk with my team. Thank you, commander," Zach said, turning and walking out of the command center. By now he knew his way back below to his quarters. As he walked, he kept asking himself what Ratani's plan was. Entering the large cabin, he was met by Marcella and Vargas. "Where's Turner?" Zach asked.

"Next cabin, sleeping. What's the plan?" Vargas replied.

"Still shadowing Ratani's yacht. A sub is under it, and a plane is just over the horizon. The boat won't get away, but maybe they want to be located," Zach said to blank faces. Zach then repeated his discussion with the commander. Vargas looked intrigued, pensive. Zach continued. "Langley wants to follow it, see where it's going, try to get a better understanding of who is behind this. The boat is on a course for the Syrian-Lebanon border. We'll know in four to five hours. I suggest everyone get some rest. This might be a long day."

That advice was heeded until an hour later when a high-pitched whistle sounded, followed by ominous words: "*GENERAL QUARTERS. GENERAL QUARTERS. ALL HANDS, MAN YOUR BATTLE STATIONS. MAN YOUR BATTLE STATIONS.*" Then the blaring of a claxon sounded throughout the ship.

Zach jumped off his bunk and opened the cabin door. Sailors were running down the hallway donning helmets. He remembered the briefing by the young seaman who had shown them their quarters and withdrew a thin life vest and helmet from beneath his bunk. "Get your helmets and vests on and get to our muster station. I'm going to the command center."

Turner burst through the cabin door, helmet and vest on. "Everyone follow me. Our duty station is on the helo deck. Now!" Everyone scrambled to retrieve their helmets and vests and follow Turner. Zach shot out the door for the command center.

When Zach got to the command center, the operational tempo was fast and at the same time ordered and professional. The commander saw Zach enter and waved him over. The commander was giving orders with his executive officer at a dizzying pace. "Launch ASW helo and UAVs, fifty-mile radius. Give me an ETA on the *Colorado*. Give me a time to intercept the low flyers from the *Truman*." The commander then turned to Zach. "Five minutes ago the *Colorado* was fired on by an unknown submarine. It sustained damage but has surfaced and is fighting to stay afloat. The Poseidon launched ASW measures and sank a submarine that looks like it had been waiting silently in the path of the *Colorado*. Three aircraft then engaged the Poseidon from a distance of nearly seventy miles. It's down and feared lost. The Poseidon's UAV confirmed the missiles were Fakour class...Iranian. The aircraft came in low out of Syria, popping up once they got over the Med."

"The *Colorado* never detected the other submarine?" Zach asked.

"Not until it was too late. The *Los Angeles*-class attack sub is completely silent. Only one or two other countries even have the capacity to detect one underway. But if one is on a steady course and an electric boat is sitting...not underway...the only sound the *Colorado* could have detected would be the flooding of its torpedo tubes. That sub was sitting with its tubes already flooded. It was an ambush orchestrated by the yacht; the yacht led the *Colorado* right to a trap. It's why their course never varied. Defensive measures defeated two of the three torpedoes, but the third detonated within range. Initial signatures on the torpedo indicate it was a Shyena...Indian," the commander said, continuing. "I'm going to be a little busy here. You're welcome to stay, but let my men do their jobs. Stay out of the way."

Zach walked out of the command center and up on deck, where he dialed Shaw on his satellite phone. "Shaw, Zach. One of our attack submarines following Ratani's yacht was just fired on by a submarine using Indian-made torpedoes. The attacking sub was sunk by the Poseidon, which was itself shot down by three fighters coming out of Syria. They fired Iranian missiles."

Ratani needed to make the United States believe that Iran was behind the attacks. He needed the US to retaliate against Tehran. Shaw could see the pattern. "Okay, that's two squadrons of fighters Ratani's group have that have launched Iranian and Indian weapons. Both can be purchased. But the submarine, that's a different story. Not too many subs on the black market. Any indication of the nationality of the sub?" Shaw asked.

"Not yet; things are pretty tense here. We have to make sure the president doesn't fall for the bait. There can't be retaliation against Iran. We need to get Ratani. We need to retrace when was the last time we observed him. Ratani's too smart to be on a cruise," Zach said.

"The president has given permission for a SEAL mission to take the yacht. How far are you from an intercept?" Shaw asked.

"I don't know. My guess is two...maybe three hours from what the commander here told me a few hours ago," Zach replied.

Shaw looked on his screen before replying. "I'm seeing that the ETA on SEAL team to target is evidently two hours five minutes, so you won't be far behind. I'll make sure they know Ratani and Hecox have to be taken alive. Gotta go...be safe, Zach." Shaw disconnected the line.

Zach stared out at the sea as he stood on the helicopter pad. He could see the plume of spray behind the ship. It was going as fast as any speedboat he had ever been on. This was a race he feared they had already lost.

He walked into the ship, to an area just ahead of the enclosed helicopter bay that was teeming with activity. There, he saw his team sitting on a metal bench under a metal staircase. Turner stood when he saw Zach approach. "What's going on?"

Zach relayed what the commander and Shaw had said. Turner spoke first, confirming what they all were thinking. "It's a ruse. Ratani's not on the boat. The boat was bait, part three of a tragic comedy."

Vargas added. "Langley has to back the timeline up. Where and how did Ratani get off the yacht? For Christ sake, he could still be in Capri sipping a lemoncello."

"Agreed. Langley's already on it. We'll know for sure in a couple of hours when they take the yacht. I'm going back to the command center," Zach stated.

Entering the command center, Zach saw the projected screen and observed multiple new icons that he couldn't make out. The commander walked over to him. "Things just keep getting better. Israel launched to intercept the squadron that attacked the Poseidon. One of the three jets was destroyed over northern Syria. The other two evaded radar somewhere over Syria. The Israelis reported the jets had Iranian markings. Right now units from Russia, Turkey, Iran, Israel, and the US are swarming the area, without any coordination. One wrong step and it could trigger something worse. Naval intelligence back in San Diego analyzed the sonar signature of the sub once it launched and began its retreat. They are pretty sure it was a US *Tench*-class sub...Turkish navy had two, both decommissioned fifteen years ago. They were built at the end of WW-Two. The yacht turned and is running north for Turkish waters."

"Can the *Truman*'s SEALs get them before they enter Turkish waters?" Zach asked.

"The SEALs are being assigned to us; they'll be here before we close on the yacht. The *Truman* is two hundred miles away from the rally point. Our orders are to intercept that boat *wherever* it is. We'll let the State Department apologize later. We've increased our speed close to fifty knots. We'll intercept in under two hours, before it can make it inside the twelve-mile zone," the commander said.

Fifty knots, Zach thought. It was well beyond the top speed of the smaller performance yacht, which was one of the fastest pleasure yachts made.

The crew of the *Gulf Vision* knew what they had to do to survive. The captain, a South African who had put to sea when he was seventeen nearly thirty years ago, knew the waters where they were headed wouldn't allow submarines. They were shallow and poorly mapped. The Americans wouldn't attack if he was within the twelve-mile territorial sea of Turkey...or so he hoped. He assumed the Americans would concentrate their efforts on the submarine and jets that had been the attacking force. In the meantime, they would dock and blend into the local population.

He scoured the charts for a small, shallow harbor no warship could possibly get into; the six-foot draft on his boat might very well be the difference of survival. There: Marmaris, a bustling harbor almost exclusively for small pleasure yachts. There was a cruise-ship dock, but it was shallow, only permitting small cruise ships. It had a narrow inlet between a small island and a peninsula where the Marmaris Yacht Club lay. Far too shallow and narrow for an American warship. The American *Arleigh Burke*–class destroyer was over five hundred feet long and drafted over thirty feet. Marmaris would be perfect, he thought, and as a resort town, there would be hundreds of yachts...they might blend in.

"Tell the crew we will dock in three hours. No more than one small bag each. Paco and his brother will remain on board to watch the vessel. *Everyone* else disembarks the moment we dock. Have a detail begin wiping the boat for fingerprints," the captain ordered.

Less than a hundred miles to the southwest, the USS *Fort Worth* slowed to twenty-five knots to permit the Seahawk to land on its stern. As soon as the Seahawk touched down, eight SEALs exited with gear, and the Seahawk lifted off. The ship accelerated again to its maximum speed. The transfer took less than four minutes.

The SEAL chief walked into the command center and walking to where Zach and the commander stood before a screen. On the monitor the sleek gray yacht was plowing eight-foot seas and had slowed in the heavier seas... the monitor showed twenty-two knots. "The Fire Scout, our UAV, is a mile behind the vessel and at about five thousand feet. The UAV's radar signature is so low they won't be able to tell they are being followed. They've slowed in the seas; we haven't. Looks like they are headed to Nimos, Bozburun, or maybe Marmaris, all small ports frequented by pleasure yachts. Chief, unless you have a plan to assault the yacht by helicopter, my plan is catch it and disable it with the fifty-seven before it can make port. The waters are shallow, so they probably feel they are safe," the commander said.

"Given their speed and how close the coastline is, if you can catch them, I concur. But aren't these shoals only twenty-five feet deep?" the SEAL chief said, pointing to the chart.

"Yes, they are as shallow as twenty feet in places, and it looks like he is heading for them for that reason, but it won't affect us...we draft less than fifteen feet. This boat was made to fight close into shore...in the littoral zone," the commander said.

"If we are that close to shore, won't the yacht, or Turkish navy spot us?" Zach asked.

"We're less than four hundred feet in length and stealthy...our radar signature resembles a seventy- to one-hundred-foot boat, and our speed denotes a fast pleasure yacht. Of course, if we are within eight miles or so from shore, we will be spotted for what we are, but we will close on them just before sunrise. With luck we will hit them and get back to international waters before sunrise," the commander said.

CHAPTER 33

LEIPZIG, GERMANY

The plane taxied into the open hangar just feet from two idling black Mercedes vans. They filed into the vans and drove out of the airport gate onto the E51 headed north, to Berlin. Elle's satellite phone rang and a thick German accent spoke. "Ms. Hardwick, my name is Frederick Ganz, BND. I am to liaison with your team. We shall have a judge's signature on a search warrant within the hour, but the bank must be served in a particular fashion, and the bank will not open until eight. That should give your people enough time to arrive in Berlin and meet us."

"I understand, Herr Ganz. I appreciate your cooperation and assistance," Elle responded.

"An additional point, Ms. Hardwick. Your team is not to have any weapons or take any activities that are not under our direction. You are guests of the Federal Republic of Deutschland and subject to its laws," Herr Ganz stated in a stern tone.

"I understand fully, Herr Ganz. You shall have our cooperation," Elle responded and hung up.

Elle rolled her eyes before speaking. "We have two hours until we get to Berlin. Jay, I need your team to split up. Take one van with all the weapons and two men and shadow us. I'll proceed in the other van with a four-man team to meet with the BND. He's expecting a CIA team without weapons, and he will have *one*...but if things go south, and I suspect they will, I want your team ready," Elle said.

CHAPTER 34

LANGLEY, VA

Shaw stared at the screen. A CNN reporter in Bagdad reported "sources" inside Iran were claiming an air attack against targets outside Tehran. The Iranian defense minister reported mass casualties as a result of "the unprovoked and illegal use of force by the United States and its proxy Israel."

"Get me General Taylor at the Pentagon!" Shaw barked.

A few long seconds later, General Taylor came on the line. "Mr. Ellis, we don't know what the hell is happening. It wasn't us. But it's big. We've stationed a satellite over where we believe Iran has been developing a large underground military installation northeast of Tehran. The images show that installation wiped out—literally, washed out. Iran has a large reservoir just upstream, Lars Dam. The dam is gone. The reservoir behind that dam was large. My folks are telling me twenty billion gallons. They sited the military installation just below it a few miles using the hydroelectricity it produced. The only reason you'd need that amount of electric capacity would be for nuclear centrifuges."

"If we didn't hit them, who did? Israel? The Saudis?" Shaw asked.

Sarah Tashkent interrupted, reciting what her screen said to everyone in the room. "The Lars Dam is the primary source of drinking water to over eight million people in Tehran, and the water that dam held provided the bulk of electricity to Tehran."

"Get me the president and get me Colonel Naif at the Iranian embassy in London!" Shaw ordered.

The call to the Iran's embassy in London was taken by a staffer. The colonel would return Mr. Ellis's call "when he could." The president had just returned from a dinner at the French embassy and answered the phone call in his limo. "Shaw, what is it?"

"Sir, a few minutes ago a hydroelectric dam was attacked outside Tehran. A suspected nuclear installation downstream from the dam was obliterated. The reservoir was Tehran's water supply. There will be mass casualties. The similarities to the attack on New York are overwhelming: a city of eight million without water. Of course, we didn't have anything to do with it. The Israelis are denying involvement as well. Iran will think it is us," Shaw added.

"Arrange a call with Rouhani. I want to speak with him directly. I'll be in the Oval Office in five minutes," the president ordered.

The president walked briskly by the quickly summoned staff and into the Oval Office. "Line One, Mr. President," came the familiar voice of his chief of staff, who seemed to appear out of nowhere in a tux. "Excuse the attire, Mr. President. I was at a function when I heard the CNN report."

The president picked up the phone. "President Rouhani, let me extend my country's sympathies and assure you my country had no involvement in this horrible attack."

A silence and then President Rouhani spoke through an interpreter. "Mr. President, your country has been on a path to attack Iran for several months. Are we to assume now that America wasn't involved? And if not America, then it's puppet, Israel?"

"President Rouhani, I know that the rhetoric has been high, but you are no doubt aware that one of our carriers was attacked in the Mediterranean earlier today. What you may not know is that it was attacked by antiship missiles made in India, launched from Russian jets, which landed in eastern Ukraine. Hours ago one of our subs was also attacked in the Mediterranean, this time by a submarine off the coast of Turkey and jets that came from Syrian airspace...jets with Iranian markings...all designed to make it appear

Iranian orchestrated. You may also recall that the attack over a year ago on New York City was one aimed at *its* water supply. I understand the dam outside of Tehran serves the water supply for Tehran. Acute similarities I would say." The president paused for effect before continuing. "President Rouhani, we know Iran was not behind the attacks on our country or the attacks in the last twenty-four hours. We *know* who is."

Much commotion and yelling could be heard in the background. It was obvious Rouhani was dealing with many who were convinced of America's involvement. But one voice could be heard in the background. The president's interpreter whispered on the secure feed. "A man in the background is calling for calm. They want to know who *is* behind the attacks on the US and Iran."

"President Rouhani, an operation is underway at this time to eliminate the threat against both of our countries. In the meantime, neither of our countries should play into the hands of the perpetrators, who want our countries at war," the president stated.

"Mr. President, we will watch what America does in the next few hours. We will initiate no retaliation...for now." President Rouhani's interpreter let the final threat fall.

The president hung up and turned to his chief of staff. "I'm going to the Pentagon."

Across the Potomac in the wooded hills of Langley, Shaw's thoughts were interrupted by Sarah. "Shaw, Colonel Naif is on the line."

Colonel Firouz Naif was the military liaison in Europe for the Quds Force, Iran's extraterritorial special forces arm of the Iranian Guard. He was educated in England and now based in London, and Shaw had reached out to him to open dialogue several times over the years in the hopes of someday averting a crisis like the one before them. "Firouz, thank you for calling me back. Our presidents have talked, and I wanted to share some intelligence with you about the attacks that have happened to both our countries," Shaw said.

"I am aware that there have been high-level communications, as I am aware there are many in the force who believe America is behind the attack on the Lars Dam," Colonel Naif stated solemnly.

"Firouz, we know Iran had nothing to do with the attacks on America, or the attack on the US fleet yesterday. And we know who attacked both our countries and are at this moment closing in on them," Shaw said forcefully.

Colonel Naif was silent for a few moments before speaking. "You say who as if a group and not a nation is behind the attacks. But we understand your fleet was attacked by fighters and a submarine."

The Quds Force's intelligence was to be commended. The details of the attack on the USS *Colorado* had not been made public. "That's correct. The attacks are not the work of a nation-state, but a group that engages in terrorist attacks to manipulate markets and behavior. It is a multinational group. That's all I can say at this point...but rest assured, we are taking action against them as we speak," Shaw stated.

"And what is it you wish me to do? Why have you reached out to me in particular?" Colonel Naif said wearily.

"Our countries have limited relations. It may be up to a few to contain this crisis. There will be calls in both our countries for retaliation...but that would be to give this group what they seek...war," Shaw said.

"I'll do what I can here. I assume I am at liberty to discuss this intelligence with General Soleimani?" Colonel Naif asked.

"Yes of course; I was hoping you would. I will be in touch with any further developments," Shaw replied.

CHAPTER 35

ABOARD THE USS *FORT WORTH*

"Target will cross the radar horizon in thirty seconds, sir," the young seaman reported, never looking away from his screen. The crew in the command center was tense but professional. They'd been at general quarters for nearly two hours waiting for this moment.

Commander Hall looked calmly over to Zach. "They know we are here, but they can't do anything about it. They'll run to the coast, but we'll catch them. My real concern right now is what we don't know. They've surprised us with the unexpected. Jets from Ukraine, jets from Syria, a World War Two-era electric sub. We've taken all the precautions. Our antisub helo is up, and we have an AWACs on station...but something tells me this won't go smoothly."

Zach nodded. The feeling of being out of control consumed him. The commander's apprehension fueled Zach's nerves. Zach watched the action board of the coastline of Turkey, a handful of cargo and merchant ships within the horizon and the yacht. Nautical dawn was still an hour away. Dawn would bring exposure and answers.

Zach walked out onto the fantail. Pitch black, only a sliver of moon—just enough to cast a shimmer on the rolling sea and the massive rooster tail that the water jets churned up behind the vessel. It was exhilarating. A warship nearly four hundred feet long moving at a speed only an offshore racing boat could match. The four Rolls-Royce engines fueled water jets kicking up spray ten meters in the air behind the boat. Despite the almost deafening roar, the drone of the engines and sea calmed him. He'd never been at sea like this. He'd taken several day cruises and once spent four days in the British Virgin Islands on a thirty-six-foot sailboat. This was different. Nothing but the stars above, slicing through indigo waves in an endless sea. His thoughts turned to Sandy. He hadn't talked with her in twenty-four hours, and only twice since her ordeal.

Zach opened the hatch, closing the sound off behind him. He went to the communications lounge and scanned in his card. Sandy's groggy soft voice soothed his ear. "Hello? Is that you, Zach?"

"Yes, honey. Sorry to wake you, but I might not get another chance soon to call," Zach said.

"I'm okay; where are you...or can't I ask?" Sandy replied.

"It's an hour later than you; that's all I can say. Still too early to call but I wanted to hear your voice. I am so sorry you had to go through that... because of me," Zach said, feeling a guilt so strong.

"I'm okay. It was short, the rescue team was on top of it, and now I have a permanent security team watching me. I feel rather like being in a fishbowl. I'd be more comfortable having my old service revolver instead. I think I fired it all of twenty times my entire career in the Park Service, but I always felt safe whenever I was out on the lake patrolling with it. Guns laws in London are so strict, only the terrorists have them," Sandy said.

Zach smiled to himself. "Your Wyoming roots are talking, girl. Anyway, I will be out of touch for another day or two, so I just wanted you to know I love you. When this is over, I promise we'll take some time off, maybe in Italy. I got a glimpse of Capri—I know you'd like it."

"Sounds good, baby. Take care of yourself. I'm safe here, don't worry," Sandy said, feeling a heart pang and touch of apprehension for Zach.

"Okay, gotta go. Love ya." Zach disconnected as a seaman approached.

"Mr. Greer? I'm Petty Officer Second Class Riley, sir. You're tasked to our team. I need to get you outfitted. Please come with me."

Zach didn't like the sound of that. The young petty officer had a trident SEAL insignia patch. Being "outfitted" and "tasked" to a SEAL team wasn't something he'd envisioned himself doing today.

As he approached the ship's armory, Petty Officer Riley stopped and handed Zach a stack of clothes: dark blue and black camouflaged pants and a padded jacket. "The jacket's buoyant and warm in case."

"In case of what?" Zach asked, knowing the response wouldn't be good.

"In case you pull a Jonah, sir." Laughs came from the three team members sitting around.

Oh shit, Zach thought. Then Riley handed him a holster with a Sig Sauer P226. This he knew how to use. "We'll go in first with the heavy weapons; you will come in second, but things might not be settled so...just in case."

The chief bellowed from the door. "Ten minutes."

Five team members went on board the Seahawk chopper as the doors of the hangar slid open. Three more went on board the Mark V fast boat, which was slung in the wet bay. "Greer! You're with me on the chopper. Two minutes to get into your gear. Let's go!" the chief added.

The night was still black as the hangar doors opened. All light was extinguished in the hangar as the Seahawk was backed out onto the stern. With not a glimmer of dawn, the stars enveloped them in a canopy of light. In the lee of the ship, the wind was gently swirling even though the boat was making near fifty knots. Zach wondered what was happening onboard the *Gulf Vision*. By now, they knew a warship was bearing down on them at a speed they couldn't outrun. Would they be calling for help, and how would that play out? A torpedo? Antiship missile? As he boarded the helo, Zach almost felt relieved he was going airborne...almost.

The helo copilot talked into his headset to all onboard. "E-3 reports no other surface contacts. No inbound aircraft. CAP on station. Poseidon reports no sonar contacts. Looks clear. Time to contact ten minutes once airborne. Please restore your seat backs to the *uptight* condition and fasten your seat belts low and snug in case we encounter any unexpected turbulence and gunfire." Always a clown in the crowd, Zach thought.

The blades began to rotate, and in a matter of seconds the chopper began to lift off and away from the ship. "Target twelve nautical miles bearing zero-eight-one degrees. Vessel will close in ten minutes. Standby." The copilot had set aside his sense of humor and was all business now. The helo would offload the team by fast rope when the vessel was disabled. The teams from the *Fort Worth* and helo would raid the boat at the same time, while the chopper with a sniper stayed airborne. After securing the boat, Zach was to be winched down to the *Gulf Vision*.

The yacht was now thirty miles from Turkish shore. They had done it. They would seize the ship at least five miles outside the territorial limit. Once airborne there was a faint orange glow to the east; the sun would be up in less than an hour.

Back aboard the *Fort Worth*, the crew was at battle stations. It would be up to the 57 mm gun to take out the rudder of the *Gulf Vision* if it chose to run. The Exec was on the bridge. "Announce our intentions, ensign."

The ensign picked up the microphone. "Vessel *Gulf Vision*. Vessel *Gulf Vision*. This is the United States naval warship *Fort Worth*. Cut engines and prepare to be boarded. Over." It was repeated three times without answer.

Then a Scandinavian accent came over the intercom. "United States warship, this is the captain of the *Gulf Vision*. We are a Bahraini registered vessel in international waters. We are proceeding to port."

"Negative, *Gulf Vision*. You will cut engines and be boarded or be fired upon. Over" The reply came. He knew the captain was buying time, running for Turkish waters. "*Gulf Vision*, we will fire to disable your vessel if you do not cut engines. This is your last warning. Over."

The young seaman announced, "Vessel has just accelerated from thirty-two knots to forty knots. They're running."

The Exec spoke into the intercom. "Fifty-seven, take out their propulsion. Fire when ready."

In the faint moonlight of the subtle dawn, Zach could see both the *Fort Worth* and its prey below, then the flash of the forward gun on the *Fort Worth*. Two quick bursts of light, no more than a second apart, and the aft section of the *Gulf Vision*, with its ornate gold inlay and lighting, was blown apart. The vessel came off plane immediately, diving nose first into the dark swells as it slowed from forty knots to a dead drift. A flash of mist visible from the fire enveloped the rear of the *Gulf Vision*. That would be the automatic Halon fire suppression system. Almost at once, the *Fort Worth* slowed, and the fast boat launched from the aft bay of the warship.

"Thirty seconds on station." The co-pilot's voice resounded. The team members now readied their gear and the thick black ropes that they would kick out in front of them. The chopper's doors opened on both sides to a hurricane of rotor wash. The fast boat was mere feet from the vessel when the ropes were kicked out and the first four team members were out. The ropes were electrically disconnected, falling almost the minute the attackers touched down on the ship's top deck. The port door to the chopper remained open, the sniper having taken position.

On deck, the attack was swift and violent. Three crewmembers, likely the security detail, were down almost immediately. One, two minutes passed. "Ship secure, captain and crew detained, three tangos down. Send the package down," the headset sounded. Zach knew he must be "the package."

Zach slipped into the hoist collar, making sure that it didn't cover his access to the Sig Sauer. He stepped into the doorway and was swung out by the crewman, down toward the *Gulf Vision*. He swiveled slowly as he descended to the rocking yacht below. The smell of the diesel spill at the vessel's stern was strong. Light was just beginning to break over the horizon, and he could see islands and land far off to the north. One of the

SEALs grabbed his waist and firmly planted him on the deck, pulling the harness off him. "Come this way," he commanded.

The three dead security detail members lay sprawled on the deck where they fell. As soon as Zach was inside the main deck parlor, the chief described the status. "The captain and eight crew are all on the forward deck. Five dead below, looks like they've been dead for a while. Four female and one male."

Zach walked below to where the bodies were. One look at the man sent a wave of disappointment through him. The women were in the wrong place at the wrong time. They were all young, all beautiful...were. "Where's the crew and captain?" Zach asked.

Zach walked to the forward deck and inspected each crew member. Ratani wasn't there. "Search again, every space," Zach commanded. As the team searched, Zach dialed the satellite phone. "Shaw, he's not here; Ratani got away. He's not on board. Hecox is dead. Looks like Ratani had him killed and got off the boat somewhere."

"The captain is Scandinavian. My guess is he has no allegiances. Lean on him...and the other crew members. *Find* Ratani," Shaw said, his exasperation audible.

Zach walked over to the captain. "Captain, come with me."

When the captain was separated, Zach got in his face. "This has two ways of ending. One, you tell me what I need to know and we take the bodies and most of your crew off the boat and you proceed a free man...or two, you visit a CIA site in a country in the middle east that has no legal protections and from which you likely will never leave."

The captain looked at him with solemn eyes before speaking. "I'm a dead man either way. If I accept your offer, my family and I will all be dead."

"We can make it look like you were killed...like you did your duty. You'll have a new identity. Ratani won't know," Zach stated.

"Ratani has people everywhere, in every country, every government... including yours. You don't know these people," the captain said with resignation.

"I'll get it out of your crew. You might as well be the one that tells me. Where did Ratani get off? Where did he go?" Zach asked.

The captain sat, weighing his options. "I'll talk, but on three conditions. First, you let my crew go...all except Anton and Yusef; they are Ratani's men, very brutal. They are the ones who did the killing. Second, no one, not even my crew must know I lived; you have to make it look like I'm dead. And lastly, you have to get my wife and my sister out of Oslo and to me when the time is safe."

Zach didn't hesitate. "I can do that."

"How do I trust you? I want it in writing," the captain said.

Zach walked to the back of the boat where two sailors were inspecting the engine and rudder of the boat to make sure the *Gulf Vision* was seaworthy and dialed his sat phone. "Shaw, the captain's willing to talk, but he wants conditions in writing." Shaw listened to Zach explain the details of the seizure and the captain's demands.

"I'll have a document sent to you in five minutes. Locate Ratani. With Hecox dead, this group's identity might slip away," Shaw stated. The two discussed how best to comply with the captain's wishes.

The document arrived and Zach went back to the captain, showing the document on a tablet. Zach explained what he had come up with to convince the crew that the captain was dead. Standing next to the captain, he summoned a young sailor who was on the mechanical detail looking at the damage to the *Gulf Vision*. "Sailor, give me your firearm please," Zach requested.

"Sir?" The sailor responded.

"Sailor, I work for the Central Intelligence Agency, and I need your help with a bit of deception. You suppose you could help me out?" Zach asked smiling at the astonished sailor. The sailor unbuckled his holster and handed his sidearm over. Zach removed the clip, ejected all shells, and removed the shell already in the chamber, handing the weapon back. "Put the gun in your holster but don't snap the holster safety strap. Then, when I nod you are to walk by the captain who will be standing between the railing and me. The captain will grab your weapon. Let him and when you hear the first gunshot hit the deck. You are not to interfere. We are going to make it appear the good captain was killed trying to escape. In reality, the captain will be safe, only his crew will be deceived. Understood?"

The young sailor straightened to attention. "Yes, sir; I understand."

Zach then walked over to the SEAL chief and explained his plan. The chief smiled and walked over.

Everything was ready. The stage was set within view of several members of the *Gulf Vision*'s crew. Zach staged the captain next to the railing as if he were interrogating the captain and nodded to the seaman.

What happened next was a blur to the *Gulf Vision*'s crew and a slow ballet to the actors involved. The young sailor walked between the railing and the captain, his weapon holstered on the side nearest the captain. The captain reached for the weapon, removing it from the sailor's control, and swung the pistol up toward Zach. Three quick shots rang out from the chief's Sig Sauer, all well placed inches away from the captain and out harmlessly to sea. The captain spun and went down, clutching his abdomen. Zach yelled so that all could hear. "Prisoner's down. Get a medic!"

The chief rushed over to the captain to conceal his body from the eyes of his crew. The SEAL medic ran to his side, checked the captain's pulse and shook his head. "He's dead."

One of the seals unfurled a body bag and they lifted the captain's body into the bag, zipping the bag and carting it off to the rear of the vessel, where they unzipped the bag and replaced the very live captain with one of the very dead security detail. One of the SEALs then took a blood-soaked rag and dropped it where the captain had fallen, moving it around on the deck under his boot before kicking the rag off into the water.

The chief spoke to Zach in a hushed tone. "We need to exit; AWACs reports two Turkish naval vessels approaching. Eleven miles out; they are definitely on a course to intercept us." The chief then gave the order for the *Fort Worth* to come alongside the *Gulf Vision* and transfer the captive crew. Several sailors came off the *Fort Worth* with a forensics suite of bags. They would scour the boat for any computer files or other evidence while the *Fort Worth* towed the vessel as far as possible from Turkish waters.

The crew walked over the blood-soaked deck where they had seen their captain shot minutes earlier. Eyes stared down at the bloodstained deck and then over to the body bag lying several feet away.

Once on board the *Fort Worth*, Zach walked past the young marine guarding the captain. "Okay, the crew has seen your blood on the deck and your body bag. You have the other terms in writing. Where's Ratani?"

The captain looked at the paper and set it down. "Ratani spoke with a woman. I think one placed inside your government. She seemed to know much about the search for him. Ratani called her Marco, I think. I remembered it because it was a man's name. We were met off the coast of Crete two days ago. Ratani was taking a plane from there to London. That's where he is, or at least that's where he was going."

"That's not enough. Who killed Hecox and the girls?" Zach pressed.

"Yusef. I learned of it when one of my crew went to make up the berths, the hour after Ratani left. I told Yusef such things could not occur on my boat and that the bodies needed a burial at sea. Yousef told me to shut up, that the bodies would stay and if I didn't like it I could join them. He is a psychopath," the captain said.

Zach's earbud sounded. "The medical ensign looking at the bodies found something. Hecox's eyes were closed with superglue. Something I guess funeral parlors do. Anyway, he opened Hecox's eye lids. He's missing his right eye. Doctor says it was surgically removed within minutes of his death."

Ratani had nearly a day's head start. Zach ran back to his cabin to get the secure sat phone and then ran back on deck. "Shaw, he's headed to London. He killed Hecox and ripped his right eye out. He obviously needed it for retina recognition to access files or accounts—Hecox's or the group's that Hecox manages. We need to shutdown Hecox's residence and his office if we can get to that also. I need a team to interrogate the crew, particularly two: Yusef and Anton; they work for Ratani. It was Yusef the captain says killed Hecox right after Ratani disembarked. I'm taking my team to London."

CHAPTER 36

BERLIN

The new Bundesnachrichtendienst offices were impressive. BND had just moved to its new location on just over fifty acres outside Berlin. The monolithic, nine-story building—actually a series of interconnected buildings—was reported to cost over a billion euros. Elle's van approached the first security gate and was ushered in after dogs inspected the van and sensors combed the undercarriage.

"Ms. Hardwick, I am Heinrich Statler, BND. I have been assigned to liaison with your team. I believe you spoke with my associate Frederick Ganz earlier. I have been assigned to assist you in any way I can. I understand that you have a request to investigate certain accounts that may have been used in terrorism activities. Any request must be made through a judicial magistrate. We have means to accelerate this process if certain emergency factors are present."

"Please, it's Agent Hardwick, or Elle. Here is a digital file that will explain our request, with supporting documents your judicial officer may need. Very simply, we have traced account transactions to funding for the terrorists that attacked the United States last year, resulting in mass fatalities and trillions of dollars' damage to the world's economy, including Germany's. We need access to these accounts and the people who are registered to them *today*. Additional harm is imminent."

Agent Statler opened the file and began reviewing the summary documents. In what seemed like an eternity, ten minutes, he looked up from his screen and dialed a number, speaking briskly in German. Hanging up, he addressed Elle. "We should have the necessary approvals and authorizations within the hour. Select one of your men. The other two must stay. The two of you can come with my men."

"Herr Statler, all of my men will be coming with me. My men are specially trained to review and understand the files and accounts in question. This isn't about nationalism or appearances, this is about a common threat to and goal of both our intelligence agencies. I am here under the direct orders of the director of the Central Intelligence Agency *and* the president of the United States. I do not wish to report that I did not receive your country's complete cooperation on a matter so important to my country."

She knew from Statler's eyes and his quickened breath that she had prevailed. He dialed a number and spoke in staccato German sentences, hung up, and replied. "My country wishes to cooperate to the maximum extent. If you need your men, you may have them. Now, if you will excuse me, I need to facilitate the warrants." Statler turned, jaw clenched, and walked out the door.

Elle sat looking around at the cold concrete-and-glass surroundings. Even more austere in appointments than most government buildings, it was an intimidating structure, made particularly so by the cold, gray, overcast European weather. She reached for her cell phone. No signal. Blocked, she assumed. She realized she'd been up for over twenty-four hours. She didn't think she would get the opportunity to sleep or see sunshine anytime soon.

CHAPTER 37

MILDENHALL, SUFFOLK, ENGLAND

The four-hour flight from Incirlik Air Base had given Zach a couple of hours of sleep. He was lucky to have been only a few miles off the coast of Turkey near where the United States maintained its largest air base in that country. Less than six hours after the takedown of the *Gulf Vision*, he was on English soil. Still, Ratani had a sizeable head start. The dossier gave him the address of Hecox's office and the account number of the account traced to the one in Berlin. The address was on King Street, near St. Paul's cathedral. It was only a few kilometers from where Sandy was. The idea of finding Ratani and being home with Sandy tonight crossed his mind—a fantasy he needed to stifle.

After nearly a half hour of silence, Marcella asked, "What does the dossier say about Ratani's whereabouts?"

Zach turned around to the backseat of the SUV where Marcella, Turner, and Vargas sat. "We have the address of Hecox's office. It has been under surveillance for the past week. No one has gone in or come out. Ratani hasn't been seen."

"So what's the plan?" Vargas asked.

"Our friends at MI5 are meeting us at Hecox's office. We'll seize his computer and records and see what we find. Ratani didn't extract his eyeball for nothing. I would have thought he would have acted by now. He had nearly twenty-four hours on us. At this point accessing the data outweighs sitting around any longer hoping Ratani shows," Zach said, knowing they were playing catch-up and that Ratani was too smart to think Hecox's office would not be watched.

Traffic on Old Broad Street was light as they entered the financial district. They turned on Throgmorton Street. It never ceased to amaze Zach how Londoners knew their way around. A block later Throgmorton became Lothbury Street and in another couple of blocks the street's name changed to Gresham. The SUV with Zach's team pulled over at the corner of King Street and Gresham Street. The second SUV, containing two MI5 men, pulled over a few meters ahead. Hecox's office was in the block; at one end sat the Bank of India, at the other the Bank of Italy. There was no way anyone could approach any office building on the street undetected. The road was narrow with four- to five-story financial buildings lining it; hundreds of windows looked down on the street. Few pedestrians were on the street. If anyone was looking, they'd be easy to spot.

They split into two groups walking on opposite sides of the street halfway down the block and converged on the building, ringing an intercom button. A security guard came to the door as one of the MI5 men flashed his identification. The guard opened the door. "Yes, sir, what may I do for you?"

"I'm Agent Friport and these gentlemen and miss are with me. We are here to inspect the offices of a Mr. William Hecox, deceased. I have here a Magistrate's Search Warrant and Writ of Assistance. Would you be kind enough to show the way to Mr. Hecox's office and let us in?"

"Uh, yes, suppose so. I mean you have a warrant, right?" the nervous guard asked, turning and waving for them to follow him into the lift.

The door to the lift opened on the fourth floor. "The office is right here." The security guard fumbled for the master key, unlocked it, and stepped aside.

The office was immaculate. A fine outer office with two chairs aligned on a Persian rug around a broad coffee table. A week-old issue of the *London Economic Times* and a tabloid lay on the table. Zach walked in and stood, studying the office, the placement of papers, and any sign of recent entry. "How often is the office cleaned and when was it cleaned last?" Zach asked.

The guard was surprised. "You're a yank?" Zach nodded. "It is cleaned once a week, on Thursdays I believe. Nancy cleans it; she has been the cleaning lady for nearly twenty years," the guard continued.

They walked from the reception office through a set of closed dark oak double doors into the private office. A massive partner's desk was against one wall with three computer monitors, two computers, and two sets of keyboards on it. On another wall was a long credenza laden with manila files.

Vargas approached one keyboard and began typing. "Password protected of course; it will take me a second or two...yes, I'm in." Vargas scanned through the file names with one of the MI5 agents and Zach looking over his shoulder, while Turner looked through the manila folders. Marcella stood in the middle of the room watching both efforts.

Ten, then twenty minutes passed. "Here, this is interesting. There is a program running in the background. It looks like it is an offsite remote access. What's strange though is it is one way. Yes...the other computer can access this computer remotely, but only as to certain files. The other computer is located here in London. The IP address shows it is in Kensington, near Hyde Park Gate. MI5 should be able to come up with an exact address. But...the bad news is that this computer has a camera that was activated the moment I logged in. It's likely whoever is on the other end knows what we are doing, and perhaps what we are saying," Vargas said soberly.

The other MI5 agent was on the phone relaying the information and looked around before whispering, "We'll have an address in ten to fifteen minutes. It'll take longer than that to get there. Let's go."

"I want the computer files cloned and sent to MI5 and Langley if that can be arranged," Zach whispered.

"Yes, I'll have a forensics team here within the hour. Steven, you stay here until they arrive, then meet us at the address in Kensington," the senior MI5 agent said to his partner in a hushed voice.

Zach's team took the SUV along with the senior MI5 agent. As they neared the Hyde Park Gate, the MI5 agent's phone rang. He listened before speaking to the driver. "Park at sixty Hyde Park Gate. It's the Baglioni Hotel. The address we want is three buildings down on DeVere Gardens. If we park at the hotel, we should attract less attention."

The SUV pulled up and a doorman walked out to meet the car. "Are you checking in?"

The MI5 agent showed his credentials and handed the man a twenty-pound note. "We are here on official business. May we park here discretely without drawing attention?"

"Yes, sir, of course. I will park it out front and no one but me will know. What is it? A Russian spy? Terrorist?" the young man said, clearly excited at the intrigue.

"Just a routine inspection. Thank you, son," the agent said.

"Here is the address. Mr. Greer, you come with me; we will walk around the block and approach the address from the south. Everyone else, walk around this corner here; you come in from the north. We have the address but we don't know which flat, or which floor, so we will need to clear a floor at a time as silently as we can, starting with the basement," the MI5 agent said.

The block was long and narrow. They walked briskly but not at a pace that would draw attention. Once they got to the end of the block, they made a right onto Canning Place and a quick right onto DeVere Gardens. When they were halfway through the block, Zach texted Turner to start his approach. They walked to the steps of the five-story white building and walked in the front door. There were twelve names on the mailboxes. None elicited recognition.

The basement contained two apartments, one a family from Nigeria, the other two college students. Neither fit the profile, and those from Nigeria didn't have a computer. They moved to the first floor and then the second. When they approached the top of the steps at the third floor, Zach saw it. A small camera, mounted opposite the east flat's door near the ceiling—an added security feature none of the other flats had. "Go past this floor; don't stop. I see something."

The MI5 agent nodded and they continued around the corner and up a few steps in the stairwell and stopped. Zach whispered, "The east flat has a camera monitoring the hall. That's likely our unit. Turner, take Marcella up and check out the final two floors. Vargas, you stay with us."

"How do we approach the unit with it having a camera?" Vargas asked.

"I saw a fire escape on the west side of the building. We go up to the fourth floor and go down the fire escape to the apartment on the west. The front door of that unit is directly across the hall from the door of the unit on the east. It looks like the angle of the camera will allow us to open that apartment's door without the camera seeing us. If we have that door open, we can storm the apartment across the hall so quickly they may not be able to react," Zach said.

"You do understand we have a warrant that extends only to apartments reasonably believed to be owned or controlled by Mr. Hecox, right? I am uncomfortable breaking into the neighboring apartment," the MI5 agent said.

"Hecox was fabulously wealthy and obsessed with security. It makes sense that he would own or control the other apartment on his floor," Zach said. This brought a faint grunt from Vargas.

"Hmm. That has a ring of logic but not a very loud one. On the other hand we will lose the advantage if we wait for another warrant," the MI5 agent said with a smile.

They went upstairs one flight and knocked on the door of the west apartment. A stately woman in her seventies opened the door. "May I help you?" She asked.

The MI5 agent showed his credentials and asked for her support. "Ma'am, we are conducting an investigation. Would you permit us to access the fire escape from your apartment?"

"Yes, of course. How exciting. Would you like some tea first?" the woman replied.

"No, thank you ma'am; perhaps later," the agent replied.

Zach slid the window up and looked up and then down the fire escape. He could see no cameras, no surveillance. He parted the drapes and stepped over the windowsill and onto the fire escape. The MI5 agent followed, with Vargas close behind. They walked down as softly as possible to the apartment below and peered in the window. A cat stared back just inside the window, hissing. No apparent alarms. Zach tried the window. Locked. He took out a knife and slid it across the window lock, turning the manual lock...the window slid open. Zach stepped in first, gun drawn. The apartment was empty. Fate was smiling on them.

They opened the front door, careful to stand back to avoid the hall camera. Zach peered closer to where he could see the edge of the camera. His memory was right. It was angled toward the door of the apartment across the hall and down the hall toward the stairwell. Someone standing in the doorway of the apartment across the hall would not be visible. Both Zach and the MI5 agent stared at the lock on the door across the hall. The door hardware in the building was all uniform and dated, perhaps from the 1950s. The door across the hall had a new dead bolt above the older door hardware. Double cylinder. They would have two, maybe up to four seconds to get in the apartment before someone in the apartment could react. "Best to use a large-bore slug to take that section of the door out. It doesn't look reinforced," Vargas said.

They only had standard-issue 9 mm weapons. Not enough, Zach thought. He texted Turner. The text came back: *Hate 9mm, happy to use my S&W40 w/10mm.* That a boy, Zach thought. The Smith and Wesson 40 had a larger bore, and the reduced-velocity shell gave vastly greater punch.

Turner, Zach, and the MI5 agent stood inside the open doorway of the apartment across the hall. Turner leveled his silenced weapon and took aim at the deadbolt. "Three, two..." The blast took out a foot of the door-jamb next to the hole in the door where the deadbolt had been. They flew into the room, guns drawn.

The room was empty. A large CPU sat on a table on one side of the room surrounded by four monitors. A screen lay face up on the table, with a withered human eye. The eye's vitreous body had begun to collapse and was drying now on the screen. Ratani had been here and was gone. The computer was still logged on. That was something.

"Cup of tea. It's still warm," the MI5 agent said.

Turner burst out the door and down the stairs. Vargas began accessing the files on the computer when Marcella yelled out. "Zach, come quick!"

Zach ran out the door and up the staircase, seeing Marcella lean over the other MI5 agent, who lay dead, shot in the back of the head. "It must have been silenced. I didn't hear anything. I was on the fifth floor and just came down."

"Cover the other stairwell!" Zach ordered. He radioed Turner and Vargas. "MI5 down, KIA, silenced weapon. Hostile is in the building; check exits, fire escape. Lock it down!"

The other MI5 agent who had just arrived heard that and drew his weapon again, moving up the stairs, while Vargas worked his fingers over the keyboard. Zach moved back into the apartment, his weapon trained on the door. The hard drive was key—that was to be protected. Turner came back up the steps. "Nothing on the street. Marcella, come with me; we'll go upstairs; the only place we haven't covered is the roof."

Vargas reviewed the screen. "We need to get this to Langley. I am finding deleted folders. Deleted within the hour. One folder has an identifier on it of *GS-accounts*. Here's another one. It contains a list of folders: 60518/DE/gpxcer; 60518/RU/gpxcer; 60518/AE/gpxcer; 60518/IT/gpxcer. It looks like another eight folders with the same suffix address have been erased."

"Wait, the file path extensions are two letters. They're country codes. DE for Germany, RU for Russia, IT Italy, and so on. Four files with eight deleted—twelve! Protect those files! Can the other eight that have been deleted be restored?" Zach asked.

"Maybe; forensics perform wonders. No such thing as a deleted file unless you really know what you are doing. Remember, that's what got a few political candidates in trouble over the years," Vargas said.

"Open the one with DE," Zach said, observing the MI5 man who had come back in shaking his head.

Three documents or folders were in the file. The first was an excel spreadsheet showing a capital account balance. The deposits showed 26 million euros over eighteen months. The value column showed 132 million euros. The second document contained only the phrase: *Heinrich Eteelman 1909-1978*. The third folder contained a series of line numbers. They had to be account numbers. He looked for anything that resembled an IBAN, an international bank account number. He typed in one of the numbers on his iPhone. Love Google, he thought, as a series of results appeared. The first three all were DBB—Deutsche Bayern Bank. "Bingo," Zach said, continuing. "Copy all to a thumb drive and take the hard drive and keyboard."

Marcella radioed. "Shots fired; shots fired! Turner's hit! On the roof!"

"Stay with Vargas here! Protect the computer!" Zach yelled to the MI5 agent. Zach raced out and up, rolling out of the door onto the roof, canvasing for any threats. He saw Turner on his side on the gray roof, his eyes fixed, a large pool of blood enveloping him. Marcella was crouched behind a ventilation duct motioning to the west.

"Next building over. I didn't hear a shot. I'm pinned down; go forward and I'll cover," Marcella yelled.

Zach looked for a target. He started to run forward and stopped. Where Turner lay was in a shadow of the building's elevator shaft. He would have been obscured from the other roof. He swung around as silenced shots hit near his head. There was fury in her eyes with shots barely missing him as he flung himself behind the elevator shaft. It had all been so obvious. Marcella...Marco...Marwa. It fit. He thought back to their escape from Capri and how easily Ratani's men located them on the Amalfi, and again along their journey from Napoli. He radioed...just in case. "Vargas, Turner's dead. *Marcella is Marco*. Repeat Marcella belongs to Ratani! Stay with the hard drive!"

It was a standoff. She was well placed, as he was behind roof obstructions. It would take a mistake for one of them. But time was on his side. She needed the hard drive destroyed before it could be taken offsite or remotely accessed and cloned. He waited. In the distance he could hear a helicopter. If it was for her, he was too exposed. He hoped it was MI5 coming to the rescue. The sound grew louder. On the horizon came a black and yellow helicopter with bold letters: *POLICE*—a welcome sight.

Just then a barrage of fire came at his position, he crouched and realized it was her; she was making a run for the roof door. Zach spun and lay prone on the roof, his weapon drawn, trying to control his breathing, leading the target. He fired twice. Marcella stumbled through the open door and fell down the first flight of stairs. He waved a thumbs-up sign to the helicopter and ran through the door. She looked up at him, placed her weapon under her chin, and fired.

CHAPTER 38

BERLIN

A young woman with a thick Bavarian accent walked in, pointing to a phone in the corner of the room. "Ms. Hardwick, you have a phone call. You can take it over there. It is the blinking line."

The excited voice of Jay came over the line. "Elle, where have you been! I've been trying your cell for nearly thirty minutes!"

"Sorry; they block cell transmissions in the building. I've been sitting waiting on paperwork. What's going on?" Elle asked.

"Shaw called. Greer's group have Hecox's hard drive and it contains a folder on the German accounts. Account numbers, multiple accounts, not just the one we had," Jay said.

"Stay on the line. I need to find someone to receive the account information," Elle snapped. She turned and walked back to the door and opened it to the surprised woman who had summoned her. "I need you to locate Herr Statler immediately. I have information he needs." Elle tried her best to sound abrupt and forceful. She'd learned a long time ago that being soft spoken in the German culture was often taken as a sign of a lack of authority, particularly for a woman.

The woman dialed a number. "Herr Statler, bitte kommen sie ins büro. Der gast hat informationen." Setting the phone down, she turned to Elle. "He will be right back."

"I need an email address to send information from my agency to Herr Statler, please," Elle replied.

The lady wrote down an address and handed it to Elle. "Jay, I have an email address here." Elle recited the address to Jay. "Jay, one more thing, have the other team stand by. I'll call you from a secure line when I am out of the building." Elle hung up as Herr Statler entered the office.

"We have uncovered a computer used to transmit funds to the bank here in Berlin; there are multiple account numbers. I'm having those account numbers emailed to you," Elle said.

Heinrich Statler was more relaxed and open now. He looked on his computer screen. "Very good. These are bank location and account numbers. Our warrants are being sent down now. I requested general access warrants based on the one account number you gave me—but the warrants should be broad enough to search these accounts as well. I do know that the account number you gave me is registered to a company, Lipzil, based in Zurich. The signature cards and records of who established the account, and these for that matter, will all be at the bank. Come, we'll go now; the warrants can be sent to us."

Elle and Jay followed the black Mercedes sedan carrying Statler and his two men into the banking center of Berlin. Elle looked out at the Spree, a calm river that winds its way through the city. At the Spreebogenpark the sedan turned on Wilhelmstrasse for the financial district. The sedan pulled over in front of an imposing new glass-and-concrete building with the bank's name inset in bold stainless-steel letters.

A security guard came to the door. Statler showed the guard his credentials and the guard directed them to follow him to the vice-president's office. There, the warrants were shown to a man with wire-rimmed circular glasses. The man looked the part of a banker: perfect tie, pinstripe shirt, and not a hair out of place. He nervously looked at Statler and then at Elle, then back to the warrant.

The vice-president sat, typed at a computer, and handed Statler a printout. Statler read it to Elle and Jay. "Arthur F. Brecht III is the name that appears on each of the accounts. He is an industrialist and one of Berlin's social elite. A large collector of art...and politicians. Before we accuse a man of this importance, I will need more information as to why you suspect his involvement."

"Please ask the banker if we can have a private office," Elle said.

The banker led them to a room with floor-to-ceiling glass walls. Elle turned so that her lips were only visible to Statler. "When the May Day terrorists struck the United States, they attempted to set off two nuclear devices. The nuclear weapons were sold on the Russian black market, and the money used was traced from an account in Zurich to the Grand Caymans. From there we traced an account from Zurich to this bank. This morning, we seized a hard drive from a London financial broker who was transferring funds for the terrorists, until they killed him. The Zurich account was registered to an industrialist from the United Arab Emirates. We have reason to believe the people that were behind the attacks on America were not Islamic terrorists but *economic* terrorists, which fits precisely the profile of your industrialist."

Statler didn't move. The information was indeed disturbing. A German industrialist...it would be embarrassing for his country. Elle knew what he was thinking and continued on. "I suspect you are contemplating the repercussions of a German elite being involved in this. Don't. If we are right, there are industrialists from a number of countries, including mine, involved."

Statler turned and looked at Elle, nodding his assent. He straightened his suit coat before commenting. "Brecht lives in a penthouse a few miles southwest from here." He opened the glass door and walked out to the waiting banker. "Thank you for your time. We are done here."

The ride to Brecht's penthouse was quiet. Elle was excited they were getting closer. With Brecht they could possibly break the organization wide-open. Statler, for his part, feared the inevitable fallout of arresting one of Berlin's wealthiest citizens on the suspicions of the Americans, but that conflicted with his feelings as an intelligence officer—he wanted this man as bad as anyone.

They drove down a narrow street with beautiful turn-of-the-century street lights and abundant gardens. The street was lined with Mercedes, BMWs, and an occasional Ferrari. The two vehicles pulled up to a five-story white building. A doorman and a valet walked out to meet them. Statler talked with them as Elle and Jay stepped out of the car.

Statler turned to Elle. "He says Mr. Brecht is in the residence as his driver is here. He has the top two floors of the building. He will announce we are here, but only use my name and no titles. Just that I am from BND."

Jay radioed the other team members to watch the rear of the building, as the building manager greeted them. Again, Statler spoke in German to the man who seemed less than impressed. Statler motioned for Elle and Jay to come over. "There was no answer to the page; the manager will take us to the apartment and see if we can talk with Brecht."

Walking out of the elevator, they encountered a strong smell that permeated the floor. It smelled of a cleaning solvent. The manager held his nose, clearly disturbed. After several rings and knocks, the manager used his key, opening the front door and announcing himself loudly. "Herr Brecht, bitte. Mr. Hedder hier. Sie haben die Besucher." He repeated the same introduction, again to no answer.

Statler pushed into the home. The circular foyer had a black walnut floor with a white Tibetan rug and a chrome circular table. Expensive artwork adorned every wall. The smell was worse in the apartment. They searched the floor and ascended an elaborate glass staircase to the upper floor. Elle looked inside the first bedroom. "In here," Statler said in a loud voice from down the hall.

Elle saw the body slumped over a writing desk, a pool of partially dried blood had dripped from the desk onto another white rug. "Herr Brecht!" the manager yelled, running over to the body.

"Halt! Do not touch the body or disturb anything," Statler yelled in German.

"You need to come take a look at this," Jay yelled from inside the bedroom's bathroom.

The bathroom was huge, maybe eight hundred square feet. White marble floors and walls with a dark wood ceiling. In the shower sat a galvanized bucket, perhaps a meter in diameter and half a meter deep. In it was the source of the smell.

Jay pulled the shower door open and wrenched back from the smell. "Geeze." He looked down into the bucket and saw what looked like metal shards. There was a glass jar of perhaps four liters in size next to the bucket.

"Don't touch that! Nitric and hydrochloric acid," Statler said seeing the label on the jar.

Jay commented. "Hard drives and backup tapes are missing from the next room. My bet is that's what is in the bucket. I was able to access the monitor. What is frozen on the screen is the first few lines of a text. It reads, 'You are to assume directorship. Auf wiedersehen.' It was sent to a number in the States. Area code 707."

"That's California, north of the bay area," Elle said. "Get the number to Shaw, now!"

CHAPTER 39

SEVASTOPOL, CRIMEA

Aleski Tuperof's plane landed at Kacha, Sevastopol, the Russian Federation's naval base at the tip of the newly annexed Crimea peninsula. From the air, Aleski could see the geographic importance of Sevastopol. It had been a strategic naval asset since the sixth century, first used by the Greeks. Subsequently sacked by the Mongol Horde and abandoned, Russia established its naval presence there as early as 1783. It's mild weather and access to the Mediterranean meant it was impossible for Russia to allow a NATO presence in Ukraine that included Crimea.

A peninsula blessed with an abundance of deep-water ports and airstrips, it was home to the Russian Federation's Black Sea Fleet. Aleski walked out onto the tarmac to meet Admiral Victor Arkadi Fedosovitch. He thrust a hand out that the admiral shook firmly. "The president said you are to oversee the operation in the Ukraine," the admiral said.

"The operation is a military one. I will not interfere with strategic operations. My role is to understand how two Russian fighters were used in the attack against an American carrier and then landed in Ukraine. And how a group of Russian SU-24s could take off from Syrian airbases to stage a second attack," Aleski Tuperof yelled over the deafening roar of two Mig-31s that were taking off.

"I can say with absolute certainty that no active-duty aircraft from the Russian air force were involved. The two fighters we recovered in the Ukraine were delivered to the Syrian regime in 2012. Assad assures us Syria had no role in this. Which means someone appropriated four line aircraft from the Syrian regime...or Assad is lying. Syria is in chaos, so it is conceivable, even likely, Assad had no knowledge," the admiral replied, as they walked into the operations building.

Inside, a large map of the Eastern region, from the Caspian Sea to eastern Ukraine, was on a monitor that stretched nearly two meters in length. On the monitor, the location of each ship in the navy's Black Sea fleet was in red. Aleski could see seven ships in the Mediterranean and many more in the Black Sea. In white were US vessels and in black were other NATO warships. Four white dots were in the Black Sea; scores of white dots were in the Mediterranean. "How is it the Americans are in the Black Sea, this close to Russia?" Aleski asked.

The admiral looked at the map and smiled. "The Black Sea doesn't belong to Russia. It is bordered by six countries. That makes it an international waterway. The Americans often operate in the Black Sea, although the depth of the Bosporus and Dardanelles straits make it impractical for submarines to transit submerged."

Changing the subject, Aleski wanted to know what the admiralty had learned. "What have your men discovered at the airbase in the Ukraine?"

The admiral sat down and began to describe his findings. "Two SU-24s. Both were delivered to Al-Dumayr in Damascus in February 2012. They were outfitted later with recessed aluminum pylons with impulse cartridges. There were three point launchers used to launch Indian-made air-to-ship and air-to-air missiles: Astra air-to-air Mach 4.5 and BrahMos air-to-ship missiles. All ordinance was expended. There were no fingerprints in the cockpit. Identification will take several days. We were able to lift several fingerprints from the engine cowlings, but they are not coming back with any known persons. The custodian in the hangar said he heard the ground crew speaking with two men in a truck. They were speaking Russian."

"The base they flew out of has not been active, I understand. The landing of the jets must have attracted attention. Have there been any reports of where these people went?" Aleski asked.

"No. The Americans have been operating drones in the vicinity and must be searching for the same information. I have requested back-satellite imagery from Moscow but have nothing yet. From that airstrip there are only three directions they could have gone: north to Belgorod Russia, west to Poltava, or east to Luhansk or Donetsk. We have checkpoints outside Begorod—they did not go into Russia. They wouldn't go to west to Ukraine; they would be detained. They had to go east into separatist-controlled Ukraine. As you know, we have units throughout this area, but they could have easily blended in if they are, indeed, Russian, or at least Russian speaking," the admiral said.

"What about the attacks on the American antisubmarine aircraft and Iran? Were these aircraft and pilots behind that too?" Aleski's head hurt there were so many factors and threats.

The admiral shook his head before responding. "They were different pilots and different planes. The plane that attacked the American carrier landed in the Ukraine before the attack on the American Poseidon aircraft and the Iranian dam. But our intelligence tells us they too were attacked by SU-24 aircraft, so there is every reason to believe the same group was behind the attacks."

Aleski chose his words carefully and deliberately, watching for the admiral's reaction. "Could this be a rogue element within the Russian armed forces?"

The admiral straightened. "Comrade Tuperof, the plane in Ukraine was Syrian. If the pilots were Russian, they are likely mercenaries and not members of active duty. *We both* would know if an active-duty Russian pilot fired upon the Americans."

It was the appropriate response, but the look in the admiral's eyes revealed concern—genuine worry. Russian planes were used for a reason: to assign blame. Russia, Iran, and America were being pushed into conflict. It was the "why" and the "what next" that worried him. He asked the obvious. "How are the Americans reacting?"

"That is the only positive thing. They know it is not Russia. There have been high-level talks between our countries. They believe these events are linked to the attacks on their country," Aleski stated.

Admiral Fedosovitch knew the Americans would be going ape right now. He had served in Washington, DC, as a naval attaché in the 1990s. He had great respect for America's military and its people. But there would be some within the military who would believe Russia was behind the events. The longer it took to solve this, the louder those voices would become.

The admiral thought it best to let Aleski know what intelligence he had received right before Aleski's plane landed. "A few minutes before you landed, we received intelligence from our people on the ground in Damascus. They believe the fighters that attacked the American Poseidon aircraft were refueled and refitted at a Syrian air base southeast of Damascus. They took off less than an hour after they landed and returned a little over three hours later. That is the time period within which the Iranian attack occurred. The reconstructed radar paths reflect they flew over ISIS and US-backed rebel elements, as if on an attack sortie, before disappearing low. There are reports the pilots were Russian. The planes are still on the ground."

"They must be taken alive. We need to learn who is directing these men. What assets do we have in Syria?" Aleski said.

"I have checked on this. The GRU forty-fifth Spetsnaz Regiment based here in Crimea has two teams that are in theater. One team is at a Syrian army training base north of Damascus and the other is off the coast of Syria on board an *Akula*-class submarine. They are on a routine training mission. I have alerted both units to be on standby awaiting your direction," the admiral reported.

Aleski snapped. "I want plans for these two teams to seize the airbase, planes and their crew...alive. This must be done immediately."

Turning to his executive officer, the admiral issued orders. "Inform the CO to develop a plan that can be implemented within the day." The executive officer rushed out the door.

Aleski knew he would need to report this to the president. But he could only imagine the risks of a rushed attack.

CHAPTER 40

OUTSIDE HAZM, SYRIA

"**V**lad, set the charges on the planes. Put all the flight suits and anything else that could contain DNA on it with them. I don't want any trace of us when we leave," Andrei said, watching the three pilots sitting in the cool shade of the bunker playing cards. Vlad Kalinin had been with him since Grozny, when they were both young officers. He'd seen what mother Russia was capable of doing and was sure they would scour heaven and earth to find whoever was behind the attacks. "When that's done, we should take care of all the loose ends," Andrei said glancing at the three pilots and their ground crew.

Andrei had contempt for the pilots and ground crew. They had been paid well and had either spent their money on vodka, hookers, and cigarettes or sent it home. They cared little whom they worked for and less of themselves. They had lost loyalty and purpose and were now for hire to anyone. Andrei hated what had happened to his Russia. Capitalism and freedom had destroyed it. He would be done with it all after today.

Andrei put a wide-brimmed Havana hat on and walked outside the hardened aircraft shelter. The hat would protect him from satellite and drone recognition should anyone be looking. He walked the fifty yards across the searing hot taxiway to the next aircraft shelter. He connected the towing sled to the front wheel of the new Sikorsky S76-D jet helicopter. It was configured with four beige, plush swivel leather seats in the back and the two cockpit seats—four seats more than would be needed. He checked the range and flight path. It would take two hours, but that was only because they wished to stay well clear of Jordan's and Israel's long-range radars. They would still make the 16:00 appointed meeting time in

Cairo with plenty of time to spare, he thought, walking back to the other shelter.

Vlad looked at him and whispered under his breath, "All set."

"Attention, you lazy bums. We have another mission. Flight crews and pilots report to your aircraft. This will be a short sortie. A no-risk one," Andrei said firmly.

Grumblings came from the card game; evidently someone thought they should have time to play their hand out. Two of the ground crew, who hadn't been in the card game, were woken. They all walked lazily over to the adjacent aircraft shelter. One of the pilots looked surprised. "Where's my flight suit? It was hanging over here!"

"It's in your cockpit," Vlad responded. The pilot shook his head, no doubt thinking how dumb that was.

Vlad walked around the back side of the mechanic's table and waited until the full ground crew and pilots were assembled together. He lifted the assault rifle and unleashed its thirty-round clip. All three pilots and three of the ground crew went down. The remaining member of the ground crew took off for the door as Andrei raised his Makarov pistol and brought him down with two rounds. Vlad reloaded and walked methodically to each victim, firing again. He dropped the weapon among the corpses and calmly walked toward the door of the shelter.

"Put your flight helmet on before going out and set the charges for ten minutes," Andrei said. That would give five minutes to get the chopper airborne and away from the base before anything alerted the local population less than a kilometer away.

CHAPTER 41

LONDON

"Elle, the hard drives are toast here. Shaw tells me you salvaged some data. We got a hit on facial recognition off a traffic cam in London. Ratani took a limo to a nearby private airport. The limo driver gave us a description that matches him. The plane filed a fight plan to Frankfurt, but I assume that's a fake. Since you're there, send part of your team to Frankfurt. I'll pick you up in Berlin; I'm already airborne. Once we track where the plane's going, I'll need all the help I can get. My team took quite a hit here," Zach said.

"I heard about Marcella...and Turner. Sorry, Zach," Elle replied.

Zach didn't respond. He was still trying to reconstruct how he missed so many signals—signals that could have prevented Turner's and a lot of other deaths. The transponder had been disabled on Ratani's plane, but military radars were searching for any craft without a transponder. Zach wanted to be there when they closed on him, wherever that would be. All Zach knew was that he'd be traveling at nearly four hundred miles an hour with no destination...just east.

"Mr. Greer, we'll be landing in Berlin shortly. We received instructions from German intelligence that they will meet us at a hangar on the south end of the runway. Do you want us to top off the fuel or get back in the air?" the pilot asked. "We'll have about four hours of fuel when we land in Berlin. It'll take us twenty minutes or so to refuel."

Zach pondered where Ratani was going. He knew they were after him, knew that the first place they'd look would be the Gulf countries. Ratani was too used to luxuries to ever hide in Syria or Iraq. No, Zach bet on Beirut or Europe. Suddenly, the world looked smaller for Ratani. "Does a Citation-4 have the range to Beirut from London nonstop?" Zach asked in reply.

"No way. Best they could do is eastern Europe, maybe Istanbul. If we don't refuel and with the weight of the additional passengers, we won't make Istanbul, but we will be able to get to anywhere else in eastern Europe," the captain replied. Zach wondered if he was making a mistake not taking the time to refuel.

The plane landed and taxied to a hangar with three black Mercedes sedans inside. Zach and Vargas looked at Elle out the window. She looked nothing like she did the time Zach saw her before. When he had seen her in London, she had seemed out of place in the agency. She resembled more a supermodel or statue: tall, striking, heels that revealed the calf line of a model, not a hair out of place. Standing there now, she looked vulnerable and tired in black jeans, a long sweater, and running shoes instead of her signature stilettos.

The door to the plane opened, and Zach walked down the steps, shaking Elle's hand. "Good to see you, Elle. Been quite a day or two. I was glad to hear you made it out of Milan. Ready for a little payback?"

Elle smiled. "Ready for payback, a bath, maybe a scotch, and fifteen hours of sleep." That was the confident Elle he recalled.

Elle turned to Herr Statler. "Heinrich, I hope by now I can call you by your first name. Thank you for everything. I am in your debt. My country thanks you."

Herr Statler nodded. "Safe travels, fraulein...and good hunting."

The plane had been given a priority clearance and was taxing toward the runway when the pilot came on the intercom. "Mr. Greer, your plane is on an approach to Budapest. They located a small business jet with no transponder. The plane reported an electrical problem to air traffic control over Prague." At once, they were accelerating down the runway. "Flight time: thirty minutes."

CHAPTER 42

HAMZ, SYRIA

Coming in broad daylight was against all the rules. Russian aircraft operations, mostly resupply cargo planes, regularly flew these days into Syria, but not small aircraft; not tactical aircraft. The two Antonov AN-12 tactical turboprops were dropping from 27,000 feet at their maximum dive angle toward the airport. The Spetsnaz major's straps dug into his shoulders as he stared between the pilots nearly straight down at two airfields within kilometers of each other, each with its distinctive cluster of eight reinforced airplane shelters at the end of each runway and three surface-to-air missile batteries. It was a familiar design, a trademark Soviet design, built to defend against Syria's nemesis, Israel, that lay less than fifty kilometers to the west.

"That smoke...coming from the end of the east-west runway. Land there!" the Spetsnaz captain ordered.

The plane's descent rate pushed the limits of the planes, audibly straining the airframes. At an elevation of five hundred meters, the planes pulled up, arced, and landed on the tarmac, reversing props and coming to a stop less than fifty meters from the aircraft shelter that was engulfed in flames, black smoke billowing out of it.

Two Tigr vehicles bolted out of one transport and raced to the other end of the tarmac to search the shelters there, while a few men tried to get into the burning shelter. The heat was too great—an inferno of burning jet fuel, planes, and bodies that could be seen at the edge of the flames. An accident? Or was it planned? Whatever it had been, they were too late.

The radio came to life. "Captain, Sargent Luvik here. There's a young Syrian boy here who says he heard gunfire *before* the explosion. He says he saw a helicopter leave."

"Bring the boy here," the captain replied.

The vehicle arrived at a shelter a hundred meters away from the burning shelter. The heat was apparent even at that distance. The captain took off his hat and pulled out an energy bar. The boy stared at it as if it was gold bullion. The captain framed his words carefully and spoke to him in Arabic. "Son...what did you see? Tell me and I will give you this."

The boy looked around nervously and replied. "This base has not been used in a long time. The airbase south ten kilometers is what the planes now use. A few days ago, three planes landed here. But not Syrian. I have never seen a marking like this. It was green and white with a red circle in the middle."

The captain moved closer to the boy so he could almost reach out and touch the bar. "Did you see the men? How many were they? And did you see a helicopter?"

"Yes, yes. I came to see if I could work for them. You know, make some money. It has been hard here. The men were taken away months ago; it is just my three sisters, mother, and me. They were Russian. They yelled at me to stay away...not come closer. One man yelled in Russian and the other yelled in Arabic. I know it was Russian because I sometimes deliver bread to the other base where Russians train men from my country," the boy confidently said.

"You said you saw a helicopter. What can you tell me about it?" the captain said breaking off a piece of the bar and handing it to the young boy.

The boy hungrily tore into the bar. It was so sweet, like nothing he had eaten. Talking with his mouth full, he began. "It was silver. Very fast. It left right before the explosion and fire." The boy pointed to the inferno.

"Did the helicopter have any markings? Letters, numbers?" the captain asked.

"Yes, I think. I remember it had numbers on it and a little blue statue on the tail. It looked like the pictures I saw in school of France—you know, the tower," the boy said.

"The Eiffel Tower?" the captain asked, puzzled.

"Yes, I think that was the name. We saw pictures in school. It was in a big city. It's been a long time. School has been closed since the war came." The boy looked down.

"The gunfire you heard. Was that before the explosion and fire?" the captain asked, prodding.

The boy thought before replying. "Yes. The shots were before the fire. Many shots. A machine gun I think."

The captain handed him the rest of the energy bar. "You have been a big help. Do you think you could recognize the helicopter if I showed you pictures?"

The boy nodded eating the bar. The captain took out a metal case and opened it. He began typing and pictures of helicopters appeared on the screen. The boy had never seen a computer. Everyone had a cell phone, but computers were only in the cities. He finished the bar and kept shaking his head every time he was finished looking at the pictures on the screen. "Stop. That one!" The boy pointed to the image of the sleek Sikorsky.

The captain got up, reached in his chest pocket and took out a stack of Syrian pounds. He peeled away ten one-hundred-pound notes and handed them to the boy. "Take these and give them to your mother. She can buy food with them," the captain said. He knew it was little more than five euros, but it should buy food for the family for a few days.

The boy quickly took the money and pocketed it. "Thank you. I maybe can do other work for you tomorrow?"

"Perhaps, if we are still here. Run along now," the captain said.

"Send the description of the blue Eiffel Tower and Sikorsky to Moscow. See if they can make sense of it," the captain ordered his communication specialist. The captain wasn't happy. They missed their target by less than an hour. Moscow wouldn't be pleased.

CHAPTER 43

BUDAPEST, HUNGARY

Their plane touched down at Liszt Ferenc International Airport and taxied to the private terminal. The Citation was sitting on the tarmac next to where they parked the plane. Two sedans pulled up to bring the new arrivals to the terminal. Zach nodded to Vargas, who ducked under the tail and ran to the Citation. He peered in the open door. The plane wasn't occupied. He put on gloves, climbed the ladder, and looked around.

The plane was empty. He checked the trash; nothing. Checked the onboard phone and looked in the cockpit. Nothing to reveal where Ratani was headed. He placed two trackers, one in the main cabin and the other in the cockpit. He then took a screwdriver out and unscrewed a panel in the cockpit marked AVIONICS. He pulled two wires loose from behind a computer board and reassembled the panel. That should delay any departure.

"The pilots had to leave a number. They are staying at the Marriott. It's near the Chain Bridge. The passenger arrival log says Carlos Anthony. Ratani's using an alias. He gave an address in London," Elle said.

"See if anyone knows who picked him up and where they left him off. We might get lucky. In the meantime, let's start with the pilots," Zach replied. The cars raced out of the airport for the short ride to the Danube.

Elle glanced down at her phone. "Looks like Vargas had some luck. He called seven five-star hotels and located a 'Mr. Anthony'...he checked in half an hour ago. At the Four Seasons of course."

She could see it in Zach's eyes. They both could feel it. If Ratani just checked in, he would probably be in his room. They had him. "It is the old Gresham Palace. Park the cars next to the hotel at the Academy of Sciences. We'll attract less attention walking into the hotel. With only five of us, we can't afford to let him get past us. Vargas, you stay in the lobby and watch the elevators and the lobby bar. Elle and I will go upstairs," Zach said.

They drove slowly around Széchenyi Square. In the middle of the square to the west was the famous Chain Bridge over the Danube, and to the east was the Gresham Palace, built by Thomas Gresham, founder of the London Exchange, which was now the Four Seasons. Half a century ago, it was a dilapidated barracks for the Red Army; today, it was an opulent hotel. They drove by the entrance to the end of the square and parked in front of the Academy of Sciences.

Elle stopped when she saw a reflection in a window. "My god!"

Zach pushed himself in front of her, reaching for his weapon. "What is it!"

She uttered a faint laugh. "I just saw my reflection in the window. I can't go into the Four Seasons looking like this!" Zach stared at her. He had been on the run for three days. He'd had a boat shot out from under him and been the target of a missile and countless threats. He couldn't recall the last time he shaved. He looked in the reflection.

Zach started laughing, which bewildered Vargas and the others following a few meters behind. Elle was right. They would actually *attract* attention looking like this. Zach stood there with Elle, straightening his hair and trying to straighten his clothes. He needed to look the part of a wealthy tourist, not a disheveled spy. Elle pulled a wet wipe out of her bag and handed it to him. They both laughed. The others stopped, attempting to look like tourists while watching the scene of Zach and Elle primp for their entry.

The wet wipe was of little help for Zach. He had lived in his clothes for two days and they were a wrinkled mess. As for Elle, she had transformed.

Makeup in place and her hair brushed back, she looked the part of the privileged wife. She slipped a ring off her right hand and onto her wedding finger and reached over to hold Zach's hand as they approached the opened door of the hotel.

Their arrival hadn't allowed coordination with the local authorities, so they would have to discern Ratani's room number the old fashion way. They stepped into an elevator and punched the third floor. "Stay here and keep an eye out," Elle said as she began walking down the hall from the service elevator, "I'm going to find the maids' supply room. It should have an arrival and departure room chart. We'll be able to narrow it down to the rooms that checked in today."

She stood staring at the paper. It was written in Hungarian. Thank god for apps, she thought. She pulled out her phone and set the translation app for Hungarian to English and scanned the paper. There were eight rooms that checked in today. The readout at the top told her the printout had a date and time stamp that showed it was less than twenty minutes old.

One of the rooms was on the third floor. Elle went to it and listened. She could hear voices, Russian voices. Elle shook her head and they went to the elevator. "Okay, seven more, all on the fourth and fifth floors," Zach said. They walked to the three rooms on the fourth floor. "There...the one with the 'do not disturb' light on," Zach said.

They listened at the door. There was no sound. Elle took a small case from her bag and slid two metal prongs, a "smoker," into the lock. The door released. Zach drew his weapon. He wished he had a suppressor on it. If he had to shoot, the whole hotel would hear it. Elle slowly opened the door— no safety chain. She opened it all the way and they stepped inside. The room was large, a suite. Zach motioned for her to check the bath while he looked in the bedroom.

It was empty: no luggage, no clothes. The bed had been sat upon, but other than that, it looked like a pristine empty room, waiting for a guest. A pad was next to the phone where the bed had been sat upon. Zach softly ran the pencil across the pad. He held it up to the light. "Vigado 1—is that a street, an address?" Zach asked.

"I don't know. The concierge will know," Elle replied.

"I don't like it. No bags, nothing disturbed. Ratani's not coming back and may never have been here," Zach said closing the door behind him.

Zach walked up to the concierge, a twentysomething girl with a perfect complexion, a girl not burdened by Budapest's Soviet past, who was multi-tasking: talking on her cell phone with an ear bud and working her fingers furiously over a keyboard. She took the ear bud out of her ear and smiled. "How may I help you, sir?"

"I am looking for directions to an address, Vigado 1. Do you know the address?" Zach asked.

"Yes, of course, sir. It is directly across the square just downstream of the Chain Bridge. It is a pier. Do you have a reservation with a tour? Can I assist you with a dinner cruise?" the girl asked.

"Thank you, no. You've been very helpful." Zach quickly turned and walked briskly across the lobby to where Elle and Vargas were standing at the door. "Let's go! He's gone. He's on the river!"

They ran across the square to the water's edge and looked down. No boat was at Viagado 1. The only person on the dock was a man in his sixties with a several-day-old stubble beard, coiling a dock line. Zach ran down the dock. "Excuse me, do you speak English?"

"Nyet. Nyet. Ya govoryu po-russki," the man replied, staring at Elle, not once looking at Zach.

"One of us needs to find someone who can translate Russian," Zach said to Elle.

"I'll go. Beats standing here alone being ogled by him!" Elle said, turning and jogging back toward the hotel.

In less than five minutes, the young concierge was being pulled down to the dock by Elle as fast as the girl's heels would allow. Elle had told the young girl she was the executive assistant for a movie producer. The girl had dropped everything at that.

Now the old man on the dock was leering intently at two beautiful women. "Was there a boat docked here within the last hour?" Zach asked.

The girl translated in Russian and the man looked up from her breasts long enough to reply. "One boat. I ran it off. It wasn't supposed to be here. This pier is reserved."

"Did a man get on the boat from this dock?" Zach asked while the girl translated his questions.

"An Arab," the old man said, spitting out the words disapprovingly.

"Tell me what the boat looked like," Zach asked.

"Ten, twelve meters. Powerboat. Gray cabin and a white hull," the old man replied.

"Did they go up river or down river?" Zach asked.

"Down river," the old man said after the girl translated.

Zach pulled out twenty euros, handing it to the man with a note attached. "Thank you. If you remember anything else, call me at the number on this piece of paper." The girl repeated this in Russian to the old man.

They started to leave when the old man added, "Bratislava."

The young girl stopped and turned. "Chto?"

"Bratislava. The boat was Slovakian. I could tell from the registration emblem. All boats must have a country code and hull number," the man replied in Russian.

The young girl translated and then asked the obvious question. "What is this about? You aren't movie producers, are you?"

Zach looked at Elle and nodded. Elle turned to the girl to explain. "No... we aren't. We are counterterrorism agents. To keep you safe, you must not speak of any of this, but you have been very, very helpful. Thank you."

The girl smiled and turned to walk back toward the hotel. "It was fun. I am here if you need me."

"We need a boat. He's running down river. We can still get him," Zach said, dialing Shaw back in Langley. When Shaw came on the line, Zach explained the situation.

Shaw paused a moment before responding. "The closest base to you that we launch drones from is Aviano, Italy. It's close; we can have a drone airborne in thirty minutes, but it'll take an hour or so flight time. In the meantime, find a boat! We have agents downstream in Romania. I'll have them make sure the boat doesn't get any further." Shaw hung up.

"I love Google! There are several luxury speedboat services in Budapest. This one has a twelve-passenger water limousine," Elle remarked, calling the number.

"Okay. Vargas, you take the rest of the team down river. Get to a place you can watch the river. He doesn't have more than an hour or two head start. Elle and I will get a boat," Zach said.

Why would Ratani allow himself to be so exposed, literally on a slow boat in the middle of an international watercourse? The answer was as obvious as Zach's question. He was more exposed by road, air, and train...

and he assumed no one would be on his tail so quickly. He had taken precautions. He would assume that within hours, they would know he had landed at Budapest. He would also assume it would take hours to track him to the Four Seasons and there the trail would go cold. Even at a lazy ten knots, he could make Belgrade in a day or two or get off at any number of small towns. He could even have a boat waiting for him in the Black Sea. Zack knew that if they hadn't come across the notepad in the hotel room or the old man on the dock, Ratani's plan would have worked. It still might.

CHAPTER 44

MOSCOW

Aleski took the call, listening intently. His face went ashen. "Keep this between us. No one but the president, you, and I should know this."

He went down the hall to the president's office and announced himself. "I need to speak to the president immediately."

The assistant rose, nodded without a word, and went in through set of double doors. A few seconds later, two men exited the doors. "The president will see you."

Aleski walked into the room. Putin sat behind a massive ornate desk that made his modest stature appear even smaller. Aleski stood before the desk and began his report. "President, our Spetsnaz team hit the airport in Syria where the planes that struck the Americans and Iranians launched from. It was an abandoned airbase. Reports are that they spoke Russian. Our team arrived minutes after the planes and at least six men were consumed in an explosion within one of the airplane bunkers. The bodies are charred beyond recognition. I have ordered a forensics team be dispatched. An eyewitness reported hearing gunfire *before* the explosion and a helicopter taking off from the base just before our team arrived."

"They spoke Russian?" the president asked.

"Yes, sir, but there's more. The witness reported that the helicopter had an emblem...of the Eiffel Tower, in blue." Aleski paused, gathering the words to say next.

Putin squinted and asked, "The Eiffel Tower?"

"Colonel Talin at FSB doesn't believe it was the Eiffel Tower. I don't either." Aleski spread out prints before the president before continuing. "At a distance, moving, the Eiffel Tower resembles an oil derrick. See?"

The president stood walking around the desk and staring at the images. One picture froze his gaze. Dapeneft. The Dapeneft logo. A single blue oil derrick set against a white background, with the name Dapeneft in small red letters below the derrick. It was the second-largest oil producer in Russia.

"Ivan Balandin?" the president said, his face beginning to redden.

"That is my conclusion. Note it is circumstantial; it is only a theory for now. I have told Colonel Talin to tell no one until we speak," Aleski said.

Ivan Balandin was one of the most powerful oligarchs in Russia, and one of Putin's closest supporters. He was a powerful ally and a formidable foe. At the age of fifty-one, he was reportedly worth six billion euros.

"Keep this between us. Make sure Talin is loyal to us. Have him pick two of his best and trusted agents who are to only report to him, and when they do, he is to report directly to you. You, in turn, will update me the moment anything happens. Get surveillance on Balandin but be careful. I know his head of security. He is former FSB," Putin cautioned.

Aleski knew Putin was insulating himself should things not be as they seem. Balandin must never be aware he was under any scrutiny unless it had first been confirmed he was involved. That was being made harder with time. What was clear is that whoever was behind these attacks were covering their tracks...eliminating all who were no longer necessary.

Putin sat, staring at the images Aleski left behind. He could see it. It made sense in some ways but not in others. Balandin's reserves would be worth vastly more if the United States went to war in the Middle East. And if Russia, no *he*, was seen to be behind the attacks as an ally of Iran, he would not survive the political fallout at home or abroad. Balandin had been one of the loudest voices pushing to annex Crimea. But that seemed to change when Putin moved into Ukraine, as sanctions had taken a toll on Balandin's bottom line. Still, Putin had his doubts. If Russia was seen as complicit, more, not fewer, economic sanctions would result. This weighed against Balandin's involvement.

CHAPTER 45

EAST OF BUDAPEST

The drone would be operating ahead of them. Zach felt like this time they were closing in. The water limousine sped down river at twenty-five knots. The service had been told that a valuable disk drive had been forgotten by a client who left on vacation without a cell phone. They were to search for the vessel and return the drive. They didn't know what the vessel name was, so they could not be hailed on a radio. It was a plausible story; the limousine service could care little if the people wasted money on such nonsense.

Zach sat near the front of the boat, which was enclosed with glass for viewing on three sides. Elle sat across the center aisle. The boat cut down the channel's smooth waters only occasionally disturbed by the wakes of cruise and cargo barges. The Danube was a fraction of its former self. Like all major river systems, it had been used, diverted, and rechanneled greatly in the last two centuries.

When Slovakia began diverting the full flow of the Danube for hydroelectric use in the nineties, the Danube dropped to levels preventing barge traffic, forcing the countries to settle their dispute before the World Court. While an integrated watershed approach was now being pursued by the ten countries through which the Danube and its tributaries flowed, its levels still made it a dangerous river to navigate. No one would proceed at night who was not intimately familiar with the river...particularly in a boat with a deep draft as the one described by the old man.

After four hours, they crossed into Serbia, traversing a wetlands preserve that made them glad their captain had thirty years of experience.

The drone covered the area four hundred river miles ahead, well into Bulgaria and Romania, finding nothing. The drone circled back having exceeded the target's maximum range. The agency asked and received overflight permission from Hungary, Romania, and Bulgaria, but Serbia and Croatia had both refused. They would have to be the ones to search for him along the more than five hundred kilometers the Danube flowed through Serbia.

The agency mobilized dozens of assets to scour marinas, ports, and piers along the Danube to find anyone had seen the boat or Ratani. British and German security services joined in the search with Interpol. Ratani was the most wanted man on the planet.

The captain turned to them. "We are an hour from Novi Sad. It's a large city. We can stop there for something to eat, if you wish."

Elle and Zach were feeling anxious. They should have caught the boat by now. Elle knew Novi Sad. It was Serbia's second largest city. Ratani could disappear there.

They passed Eagle Island, another wetlands preserve, rounding a small island. "There! Ahead. A gray boat! It fits the description," Zach yelled.

Elle stood up, taking the captain's binoculars. Sure enough, it was the vessel, just as the old man described. On the stern was a man looking back through a set of binoculars at them. "Time to come clean with our captain," Elle whispered to Zach.

Zach moved back to where the captain stood. "Captain, the boat we are looking for is ahead. We didn't tell you the full story. We work for a governmental antiterrorism agency. A known terrorist is on that boat. We need to catch him and we need your help. We will pay you three times what we are paying your company, in cash. No one needs to know. But I won't lie to you, it could be dangerous," Zach said.

The man looked at Jack, ahead at the boat, and down at a stack of euros Zach held out. "You are Interpol? FBI? CIA?" the man asked.

"American," Zach replied.

"Okay, I do this. I hate these people," the man replied, taking the money from Zach. He accelerated the throttle and the boat surged forward.

"We need you to look like you are passing him on the right, just like we are all tourists. Then when you are just past him swing aside him and I'll disable the boat," Zach told the captain. "They'll be watching us closely, so don't look nervous or directly at them," he added.

Zach bent down in the boat to avoid being seen. He wanted to duck out of sight and take one quick glance with the binoculars. He needed to know how many were on the boat and where they were. They would be assaulting a moving boat that was likely heavily armed.

Zach went down on his knees on the deck, grabbed the binoculars, and inched them up to the bottom of the window. Two men on the stern, one in the cockpit, and another one or two he could see were in the main part of the boat. Three on security detail outside. Three against two and Ratani's boat had height and defense. It was risky, but they were out of time—out of options. They wouldn't be able to launch an assault when the river became congested near Novi Sad.

Zach put the binoculars down and got up as if he had been searching for something. The time was now. "Okay, captain, bring us past them on the starboard side about twenty meters from them."

Elle chambered a round and stuck two spare clips in her front pockets. They began to close on the boat. One hundred meters, then seventy, fifty. Out of the corner of his eye, Zach could see the two men on the stern raise assault rifles. Forty meters. A white light and concussion roiled over them, then the sound, deafening. The glass windshield shattered, slamming into the captain, who lost control of the boat, which then glided to an idle. The other boat was gone, exploding in a ball of flame.

"What happened?" Elle yelled. Zach could barely hear her yell. His ears rang and his face felt sunburned, scorched.

Zach grabbed the steering wheel and looked at the captain's slumped body. He had taken the full impact of the windshield, which had hurled glass shards into his face and neck. He was bleeding, but the wounds looked superficial.

"Zach, I think I saw a missile streak over us before the explosion. I looked up because of a noise and light. Something hit the boat!" Elle said.

Zach found the binoculars on the floor and grabbed them. He looked carefully, scanning the sky on a grid pattern. He couldn't hear or see any aircraft. Nothing, then a shimmer...a glint of something high above. Not a plane, something slower and smaller. The agency's drone? Had it launched a Hellfire? Why? Zach wondered.

"What did you do!" the captain yelled to Zach.

"Nothing. A missile, I think. I caught a glimpse of something right before the flash," Zach yelled to Elle who was wiping water spray from her eyes.

The captain maneuvered the boat near the sinking, burning hull. The stench of diesel and death wafted through them. Two bodies were floating, burned and dismembered. "Get close to the bodies," Zach ordered the captain.

Zach took a pocket knife out. "Do you have any jars with lids or baggies?" he asked.

The captain stared at Zach in disbelief and horror, but handed him a box of small plastic garbage bags. Zach began cutting chunks the size of a golf ball from each of the bodies and body parts. "What are you doing!" the captain exclaimed.

"Identification; we need DNA samples," Zach replied. The boat sank under the water. All visible body parts had been sampled. There was nothing left except an oil slick and a few floating items of debris. Zach looked down; he had thirteen plastic bags, which he carefully tied and placed inside a larger bag. "Take us to Novi Sad; our work is done here," Zach told the captain, who brought the boat back on plane. They were glad they could breathe fresh air again as the wind hit them—air devoid of the smell of death.

Zach dialed the satellite phone. "Shaw, bad news. We caught up to the boat. It was heavily guarded and we were beginning an assault when it was blown out of the water."

"What do you mean? By who?" Shaw asked.

"No idea. We were beginning an assault, no more than fifty feet away, when I believe a missile struck the boat. Someone was watching, making sure we wouldn't get to Ratani. I collected as many samples as I could but I have no idea if the parts came from Ratani or if he was even on the boat," Zach said.

"Are Elle and you all right?" Shaw thought to ask.

"Yeah, we're fine. A little hard of hearing. We are getting off at Novi Sad. We need to be picked up. We have the samples with us," Zach said.

"I'll have a plane there in an hour. Get to the airport," Shaw said, hanging up. Shaw sat wondering. A missile. From a drone...a plane...from shore? All traces of the group were being eliminated.

CHAPTER 46

LANGLEY, VA

Shaw and Sarah Tashkent stood over the shoulder of the computer foren-sics chief in one of the windowless and most secure offices in the build-ing. The hard drive had been flown by the air force at nearly twice the speed of sound back from London. With each keystroke, deleted files began to be repopulated on the drive and screens around the room. There were few times in his multidecade career that Shaw found himself speechless. Before him was a tale no one would believe.

The group had manipulated currency markets and made billions when the country was attacked eighteen months ago. The proceeds were set forth on the capital account ledger marked DE. The participant from Germany had invested 50 million euros and been rewarded four months later with a deposit of 739 million euros. The same return percentage was shown for the investor from the UAE, which would have been Ratani; the same return percentage for the investors from Russia and Italy.

The most recent ledger balances showed balances for all twelve partic-ipants from twelve countries. The investment deposits ranged from 10 mil-lion euros to 700 million euros. The deposits had been made four months ago. Only one entry was shown after the deposits: a sizeable bulk deposit made six weeks ago.

They watched as additional deleted files were reconstructed. US, Iranian, and Nigerian oil production had been shorted. The group planned on a catastrophic fall in select oil markets, while leaving others intact. Looking at the date six weeks ago, it corresponded to the day the US oil producers suffered their single worst trading day, which followed three attacks on the oil and gas fields in Texas, Colorado, and North Dakota, that had captivated the news channels.

"Those three fields, the Bakken, Niobrara, and Eagle Ford fields, produce high levels of oil, not just shale gas," one of the analysts remarked. "Looks like those attacks out west weren't the result of a radical environmental group as we thought."

"So their goal was market manipulation in the US. Then framing Iran for an attack by the US would eliminate Iranian and Gulf oil production just as sanctions were fully lifted. What about Nigeria?" Shaw asked.

"We can only assume our pursuit of the group disrupted their plan in Africa. But if African, US, and Middle East oil shipments were constrained, it would spike oil prices and leave Russia as one of the few producers with secure supplies," Sarah remarked.

"Do the files have any account information to trace the twelve investors?" Shaw asked.

"Not yet. These files appear to have the balance sheets but not account and transfer information, but we aren't through. It will take us hours, perhaps several days, to complete our work," the forensics chief said.

Shaw patted him on the back. "Good work. Call me if anything that links these ledger accounts to people or places turns up. Anything, no matter how small," Shaw said, turning and walking with Sarah out of the office. As soon as they were in the elevator alone, Shaw spoke to Sarah. "Search for anything with Russian oil producers or pipeline companies. See if any of them in the last year began projects that would indicate they intended to start new shipments to Europe or abroad. Anything unusual: ports, pipelines, new refineries that otherwise wouldn't be justified."

Sarah's brow deepened. "There is one thing we picked up several months ago that looked out of the ordinary. We reported it in a memo, but it didn't seem like much." She started typing on her tablet. "Here, Dapeneft, one of the large Russian oil producers, began working on a refinery near

Volgograd. Oh God, they worked with Arabesco! At about the same time, Dapeneft took a majority interest in a pipeline corridor that runs from the Volgograd field to southern Russia, near Crimea. It's an unusual location for a refinery...it's inland, not next to a port. There's a limited market for refined oil in southern Russia."

"But with Crimea in Russian hands, they would have a seaport on the Black Sea and a pipeline corridor at the edge of eastern Europe. Who owns Dapeneft?" Shaw said.

Sarah's fingers flew across the tablet's keyboard. "Ivan Balandin, a billionaire oligarch," she said.

"We need to see his accounts eighteen months ago, when the currency manipulation profits were realized. If the Russian member is Balandin, we need him alive—we need him before they kill him," Shaw said.

CHAPTER 47

LAGO COMO, ITALY

The sun warmed the crisp air on the bougainvillea-filled veranda. The veranda was one of Ivan Balandin's favorite places in the world. It was his favorite place to start the day, with his customary double espresso and breakfast panino. He perused his emails and the news while overlooking the serene lake—a view that reminded him of a fairy tale. It was his refuge, the only place he felt secure and relaxed. Today, though, he felt anything but relaxed or secure. His security had doubled their detail. News of Foltz's disappearance and of the deaths of Hecox, Brecht, and Ratani shattered his illusions of security.

With Hecox dead, there was no way to alter his investment position. If he wasn't killed, he'd be killed in the market. With each day, it looked less and less likely America would go to war. Putin had performed as he had wished. Putin had annexed Crimea just as planned. His refinery and pipeline construction projects were on schedule. No doubt they would at least bring some measure of economic recovery to him should the group's investment plans be disrupted.

His estate was perched on a hill covering forty hectares, nearly one hundred acres, which had been in the same Italian family for nearly five hundred years before he purchased it a dozen years ago. A ten-thousand-square-foot main home with multiple guest houses, it was one of the largest and most private estates along the shores of Italy's coveted lake district. A single closely monitored driveway, high walls, and a constant manned presence at its private dock made it the safest place he could be. The verandas overlooking the lake were shrouded from any vantage point from the road and cliffs above by the massive stone walls of the main residence. He could run his worldwide operations from here, secure from the fate of others whom someone was clearly hunting.

The lake changed airflow. The cold water made the air sink over its surface. It was always dead calm in the mornings, but the valleys and heat always changed that by early afternoon. That needed to be accounted for, but it was otherwise a perfect environment. It took the 0.338 Lapua magnum shell just over three full seconds to reach its target, 1,600 meters across Lago Como. One moment, Ivan Balandin sat peering over the pristine beauty of the lake, the next he sat headless in the chair, the sound arriving seconds later. There wasn't anything his security detail could do; they had already failed. They should have known their employer was within range. There had been longer shots. Chris Kyle's 1,970-meter kill in Sadr City in 2008 and even British corporal Craig Harrison's double kill in Afghanistan at nearly 2,500 meters. Because of the lake effects, it was a shot only a handful of people could make, but certainly one a Spetsnaz sniper had trained for.

An embarrassment had been prevented, a betrayal resolved. To Aleski Tuperof, it closed a chapter. The seizure of Dapeneft by the authorities would demonstrate Putin's strength and increase his coffers, and if some spilled to Aleski, well, so much the better.

Across the Atlantic the news of Balandin's removal was a gut punch to Shaw. Their last known lead, eliminated—this time out of arrogance.

CHAPTER 48

WASHINGTON, DC

Shaw sat in the Oval Office with the president, FBI director Tankersfell, Admiral Weams, and Kate Helmsworth. It was a sobering report delivered by the agency's director Harrence. A multinational group that had existed for nearly two generations was responsible for nuclear terrorism in America and nearly global war, all to manipulate markets for gain. They had used institutions and religion to do their work for them. Twelve men, from twelve countries.

"As I understand it, four of the twelve are dead, assassinated before they could be captured. Their banker is dead. We know the countries of the other eight but not their identities. The account information is a dead end. Do we know if we've crippled this group, or is it a Lernean Hydra that will just regrow another four heads?" the president asked.

Shaw responded. "This group has lived in the shadows for sixty years. They aren't accustomed to running, or exposure. They know that we know they exist. Today, all communications, banking, and money transfers have a money trail. They have covered their tracks but at a loss of at least a third of their membership. They are businessmen, industrialists, not warriors. They're scared, wounded, maybe mortally. Our belief is that the organization is not operable. But we need to expose the remaining members...press to a kill."

"This can't become public knowledge. It would panic markets and destabilize regimes," Kate Helmsworth added.

"I agree, Mr. President. We know the leader—chairman as they called him—was Brecht, who died in Berlin. We know he communicated with a cell phone with a California area code right before he died. It seemed to convey his title to that person. The phone was registered to a truck mechanic who died over three years ago, so the number was cloned for one-time use. It leads us to believe the American on the group is active and now in charge. That will be our primary focus," Shaw added.

"We are going to need some very broad FISA warrants to go back and see if any industrialists in America had communications with those who were killed," Director Harrence said. He knew this president had wanted to shrink, not expand, such surveillance. He waited, uncertain of the response he would receive.

The president looked out over the south lawn, thinking how different things were now, how the world had become more, not less, dangerous. "Do it; whatever you need. If that isn't enough, I'll personally brief congressional intelligence committees," the president said.

CHAPTER 49

RUSSIAN RIVER VALLEY, CA

Fog brought coolness and moisture to the grapes...and a cloaked stillness to the valley. The culmination of two generations, gone—the organization was devastated. They would be hunting them, him. He knew that. But all networks had been eliminated. Search efforts for him would be futile. He employed the protocols that had been established half a century earlier. They'd stay silent, not appoint any new replacement members. Silence would shroud their activities until the right time.